Harte Broken
A Dose of Love, Book 1
By

Jill Boyce

ISBN: 978-1-952661-31-0

Acknowledgments

I praise God, who whispered these stories to my heart and placed the perfect people along my writing path at the perfect time.

I thank my husband, children, father, in-laws, stepmother, family, and friends for their love and support.

I am grateful to my mentor and friend, Carrie Turansky, for her generous spirit and wisdom, and my editor, Cynthia Hickey, for believing in my work.

I especially thank my mother, who passed away four years ago on the day of my daughter's birth. Her death inspired my first book, *Harte Broken*. She instilled in me the love of books and the desire to dream big. I love you, Mom.

My hope is my stories will provide comfort, laughter, and encouragement to my readers. May God bless you all.

Psalm 147:3 He heals the brokenhearted and binds up their wounds.

Chapter 1

July 2, 2017, Sunday

Amy Harte stared at the brass nameplate in front of her as she knelt on the cool green lawn. She ran her fingers over the letters, tracing the precious name. Her gaze shifted to the tilted vase attached to her mother's headstone, and she reached out to straighten it. A light breeze blew past, carrying the sharp scent of freshly cut grass.

"I'm sorry, Mom. I'm so sorry." Only silence answered. She drew in a shuddering breath. Today marked an anniversary she never wanted to celebrate. One year ago, Amy had graduated from residency and fulfilled a lifelong dream to become a physician—but on that same day, she lost her mother. How does one celebrate when the best day of life is also the worst?

Guilt washed over Amy as she reflected on how she'd let her mother down. She'd missed being with her when she passed and still carried the burden of failure to save her mom despite being a physician tasked with healing others.

The phone call Amy had received earlier that morning from her father rose in her thoughts. "Hello," she'd mumbled.

"Amy? Did I wake you?" Her father's low-timbered voice bellowed.

"Dad, are you okay?" Amy rubbed the sleep out of her eyes

and tried to gain her bearings.

"Yes," her dad's voice trailed off.

"What's going on?" The last year's events flashed through her mind, and she felt a rock developing in the pit of her stomach.

"It's about the house. I got a call Friday morning from the bank and met with the manager."

Amy ran a hand through her hair, relaxing a bit. "Dad, you haven't had a mortgage in years."

"Well, that's true. We did pay it off a few years ago."

"Okay, so then what's the problem?"

"The problem is that because of the cost of your mom's treatments and then the funeral, I had to take out a second mortgage on the house. I didn't know what else to do…"

She frowned. "So, what does this mean? Can't we ask the bank for an extension? I'm sure they'll understand."

"They understand, but that doesn't change the fact that the bill is due. The bank manager said that I have sixty days to come up with the rest of the loan, $50,232, or the house will go to foreclosure," his voice cracked.

She could tell he was close to tears. "Oh, Dad. Don't cry. We'll figure something out." Amy wracked her brain, calculating her student loan balance, which teetered over the six-figure mark, and considered her rent and car payment. She just started working at Metropolitan Hospital, so her savings account was anemic.

"They can't take your home." She'd had tea parties there with her mother. It was where she had learned to ride a bike and gotten ready for prom. "Where would you live?" Amy tried to conceal the rising panic in her voice.

"Don't worry about me. The money from my pension more than covers my monthly living expenses, and I'm sure I could find something reasonable to rent."

"No. Absolutely not. We lost mom. We can't lose the family home."

"Well, if you come up with a way to make fifty-grand in the next sixty days, let me know. Otherwise, I think it would be a good idea if you came over in the next few weeks to go through things."

"Don't start packing up yet, Dad. I love you." Amy hung up and made a silent vow to save her childhood home.

A butterfly landed on her hand, snapping Amy out of the

memory. Hot tears stung her eyes, and a single droplet rolled down her cheek. She wiped it away and shook her head. No time for tears today. She stood and brushed tiny blades of grass off her faded mint-green scrub pants.

A grey-haired older gentleman dressed in overalls stood a few feet away, raking mulch into a flowerbed. "You've got to receive God's forgiveness sometime, young lady." He continued his work as he spoke, not lifting his head.

Amy stood straighter and pressed her lips into a firm line. "Excuse me, what did you say?"

The stranger halted his task and rested his arm on the rake. His eyes found Amy's. "I said, you're going to have to accept God's forgiveness…only way to move forward. Guilt will eat you up inside and make it hard to love and live." The man shrugged and resumed his work as if never a word was spoken.

Her mouth fell open. *What does he know about God's forgiveness? He's probably crazy.* She started to refute his intrusion, but her pager beeped, reminding her to get moving. She walked to her car and hopped inside.

The muggy summer air, combined with choking grief, made breathing difficult. She cranked up the air conditioning and drove across town, arriving at the parking lot of Scottsburg, Virginia's community hospital. She stopped the car, stamped down the emergency brake, and paused. "Come on, Amy. Get it together. You're a professional." She slid out of the car and walked toward the hospital with hurried steps.

Straightening her shoulders, Amy stepped past the main glass doors of Metropolitan Hospital and entered the five-star, luxury-hotel-like foyer. Despite the crystal chandelier hanging overhead and a white marble floor below, the classic scent of bleach revealed it to be a well-endowed medical facility with an expansive, wealthy board of directors and donors.

Amy strode into the Emergency Department and sent a nod to her best friend and lead respiratory therapist. "Hey Beth, how's it looking today? Swamped already?"

Beth, petite with shoulder-length blond hair, leaned against the central nursing station, the main activity hub. She flicked her hand with a quick wave and grinned. "Hey, Amy!"

Glancing at the large whiteboard filled with patients' names and room assignments confirmed her assessment.

Blowing her bangs out of her eyes, Beth nodded her head. "Yeah, it's been a madhouse. I thought people slept in on Sundays."

"I suppose some people use Sundays to get things done. You know... laundry, dishes, late brunches, grocery store runs... or go to church, I guess."

Some people, but not Amy. Tears threatened to spill over again, but she turned her head away and forced them back down. She held her breath. A gentle hand settled on her arm, and Amy met Beth's sympathetic eyes.

"Hey, do you need to go home? I know this must be a hard day for you. If you want, I can tell them you didn't feel well."

She gulped in a fresh breath of air and exhaled. Amy shook her head. "No, I'm fine." As she reached for a chart, the overhead paging system announced an incoming emergency.

An ambulance siren blared, and two EMTs burst through the ED's double doors.

Amy rushed toward them.

The first medic rattled off statistics. "Victim is Brian Broadstone, driver in a two-car motor vehicle accident. He suffered a head trauma and suspected concussion, with a laceration to the right scalp. Vitals are stable."

She shifted her eyes from the patient to the medic. "Thanks, I'll take it from here." She grabbed her stethoscope from her neck and began her exam. After finding the patient in stable condition, she sent him to get a head CT.

The emergency department double doors parted again, and a tall, handsome man with dark brown hair burst through them. His eyes widened as he saw Brian's stretcher roll away. "Hey, where's my brother going?"

He wore a black short sleeve t-shirt stretched snugly across his broad chest and thick shoulders and flattered his fit physique. His chiseled jaw clenched, and concern clouded his chestnut eyes.

Amy's cheeks warmed, and she blinked hard. *Pay attention.* She shook her head, gathering her thoughts. "Hi, I'm Dr. Amy Harte. Your brother's stable, but I sent him off for imaging. A head injury warrants a thorough workup. Were you in the car with him?" She smiled, hoping to ease his worry.

"Yeah, sorry I'm late. I rode over in the ambulance but stepped outside for a minute to call my dad. I didn't want my parents to hear about the accident from someone else."

Nodding her head, Amy understood. She knew how Scottsburg's rumor mill operated.

The handsome man met Amy's gaze, and his serious expression relaxed as he took a few steps closer. "Is he going to be okay?"

"I think he'll be fine, but I don't want to miss anything. Are you okay? We can evaluate you, too."

"I'm fine. Not a scratch on me." He stretched his hand toward Amy. "I should introduce myself. My name is Seth."

She shook his hand, and a shiver traveled down her spine at his touch. Releasing his grip, she cleared her throat. "Nice to meet you. If your brother's tests are normal, then he may be able to go home tonight as long as someone stays with him." Amy attempted to keep her tone even and professional. "Where were you guys headed so early this morning?"

The good-looking stranger grinned and shifted his weight. "Well, this week is our mother's birthday, so we were headed to grab breakfast, then take in the early church service so we'd have time to get things together afterward for her big day."

She raised her brow. "Did you make it to breakfast?"

Seth shook his head. "No, we didn't. Come to think of it, I'm starving. Do you think I have time to run to the cafeteria and grab something before Brian gets back?"

Amy smiled and nodded. "Sure. That's fine. I'll let him know where you went. If you're like me, it's hard to function before coffee."

Seth nodded. "Same." Seth searched her face, his eyes warm with interest. "Would you like a cup? I'll bring you one back."

Amy's cheeks burned, and her palms grew damp. Her fingertips tingled. She longed to say yes, but she feared that the names on the whiteboard were multiplying by the minute.

Someone tapped her on the shoulder. She turned, and Dr. Mark Blakely stood with two foam cups in hand.

Mark wore a confident grin as he eyed Seth. "No worries. I've got it covered." He passed one of the cups to Amy.

She hesitated, then accepted it. "Thanks, Mark."

5

Disappointment flashed across Seth's face for a moment. "Okay. Thanks again for taking great care of my brother." He smiled and reached out to shake Amy's hand again. "I'll be right back." Seth turned and walked away.

Mark left Amy's side to attend to another incoming patient.

Amy wished she could have talked to Seth longer, but Mark had impeccable timing. Mark asked her out on a date weekly, despite her lack of encouragement. She suspected Dr. Blakely's dating record included most of the female population of Scottsburg.

Amy approached Beth standing at the nursing station and noticed an unmistakable smirk on her best friend's face. "So, I see you've met the new Chief Financial Officer."

Exhaling for the first time in a minute, Amy asked, "What do you mean?"

Beth's grin widened, and she crossed her arms in front of her chest. "Seth Broadstone. The charge nurse told me your patient's brother is the new CFO of the hospital. Apparently, he started a few weeks ago. So, this should be interesting. I saw the look between the two of you." She winked.

Amy rolled her eyes. "I don't know what you're talking about...there was no look. Besides, right now, I don't have time to date anybody. I have a lot on my mind." Her thoughts drifted to the conversation she'd had with her dad about her parent's house. "I'm channeling all my energy into work." She owed it to her mom.

Beth's face fell, and she grew serious. "Hey, I get it. Your work is your life...but don't forget to make time for some fun, too. I guess we hadn't met Seth yet because he's stationed on the fourth floor with the administrators."

Shrugging in nonchalance, Amy agreed, "You're probably right." She secretly hoped this wouldn't be the last time their paths crossed.

Chapter 2

July 2, 2017, Sunday

Seth stood outside of the Metropolitan Hospital parking lot with a cup of coffee in one hand. He ran the other hand through his hair and glanced at his watch for the third time in five minutes. His father should be here soon. Seth's thoughts wandered to the beautiful Dr. Harte.

How did he not know she existed? Probably, because he spent his time on the administrative floor trying to keep donors, board members, and shareholders happy. Seth stepped into the position of Chief Financial Officer for Metropolitan Hospital only a month ago.

He wished he could have talked with Dr. Harte longer and maybe asked her out for a real cup of coffee sometime, but he wondered if something existed between her and the guy who brought her the drink. Seth shook his head. It didn't matter. She stirred something inside him he had never experienced before, and it felt risky. Opening his heart to the possibility of love could only lead to heartbreak and loss. Besides, he had his hands full right now.

David Broadstone, Seth's father and CEO of the family's software business swung into the lot. He flung his door open, hopped out, and grabbed Seth in a fierce hug. "Seth, I'm so glad you're okay. How's your brother?" Worried lines furrowed in his father's forehead.

Seth squeezed his dad, happy to see him despite the circumstances. David wore his typical attire: a charcoal grey button-up dress shirt, a thin black satin tie, and starched khaki pants. The outfit sold the title of Chief Executive Officer of Health Tech Solutions. Only his shoulder-length white hair pulled back in a low ponytail—a relic from his days as a hippie—betrayed his corporate image.

Seth and his father remained close, despite his father's subtle and not-so-subtle requests that Seth join the family business. Brian, younger at twenty-eight years of age, held the company's second-in-command rank as Vice President of Finance and Contracts. Seth's parents frequently mentioned how "wonderful" it would be if Seth rejoined the fold. "It sounds like they might keep him for a few more hours."

"Well, let's go check on the boy. I've been worried sick." Mr. Broadstone looked up at his son. Deep-seated lines formed around his emerald green eyes, crinkling from years of laughter and family vacations at Cove Beach along the North Carolina coast.

"He's finishing up some tests and scans right now. I just spoke with his physician from the Emergency Department."

The Virginia summer sun beat down. Seth's dad wiped the sweat off his brow with the back of his hand. "Well, it's too hot to stand out here all day. Why don't we head inside to wait for him and cool off?"

He thought about seeing Dr. Harte again, and his pulse quickened. Seth tried to think of a reason to delay going inside but found none. Nodding his head, Seth conceded, "Yeah, okay, Dad, sounds good."

His father followed him into the welcoming embrace of the hospital's central air conditioning. Brian arrived in a wheelchair pushed by an older nurse with blond hair, his head wound obvious. Brian had a four-inch-thick gauze bandage encircling his head, a bandage over his right cheek, and a faint dusky purple bruise pooling below his right eye.

Seth caught his breath. Though the accident could have been worse, the thought of losing his brother tugged at his heart and rattled him. Seth tried to lighten the mood. "Hey, nice headgear.

You look a little like a mummy. Well, a mummy with a shiner." Seth lay a hand on his brother's shoulder.

Brian gave a chuckle. "Wow, thanks a lot for your empathy. I feel so loved." Seth's little brother clutched his chest soaking up the drama as the grandstander in the family. "I can still whip you in a tennis match any day." Brian challenged Seth with a grin.

"Ha, I'll believe that when I see it. I won't take advantage of you today. Wouldn't be fair." Brian became serious. "Hey, what happened? That guy that hit us came out of nowhere! Is he okay?"

"Yeah, I think so. The medics said the driver was texting, and he swerved into our lane at the last minute to avoid hitting a cat. The cat lived, by the way." Seth laughed. "He just has a few minor scrapes. The guy, not the cat. Hopefully, he learned a valuable lesson not to text and drive. And you, well... your head was never normal, so no harm done there." Seth ducked in time to avoid a retaliatory slug to the arm from his brother. "Kidding, kidding... mostly."

Brian looked up at his big brother. "Hey, did you meet the ER doctor? She's a looker."

Seth's face warmed. "I briefly spoke with her after they took you upstairs." He ignored his brother's statement and changed the subject. "Speaking of Dr. Harte, I thought you had to stay tonight for observation or something."

"Oh, she let me off the hook. Said all my lab tests and studies looked great and I'm the perfect specimen of a man."

Seth shot his brother a withering look.

Brian smiled, looking between his father and his brother as if they were about to win a prize in a game show. "Okay, okay, I may have added that part myself. She said I'm fine and that as long as I don't drive for a few days and stay with someone tonight, then I'm good to go... so, who gets the honor of my presence tonight?"

Seth stared at his father. "I'll flip you for it. Loser takes Brian home."

Brian's lips formed a frown, and he pretended to feign hurt. "Hey, that's no way to treat your favorite brother."

Seth snorted. "I'm kidding. You're welcome to stay with me tonight, and I'll drop you off at mom and dad's tomorrow on my way to work or maybe she can come to my house and sit with you. And you're sure it's okay with the doctor if you bail tonight?" Seth became serious once again. He didn't know what he would do if something happened to Brian.

Seth peered around the room, searching for Dr. Harte. He found her standing next to a petite blond woman next to the nursing station.

Amy met his gaze, picked up her clipboard, and walked toward him. She stopped by Brian's wheelchair and extended her hand to David Broadstone. "Hello, I'm Dr. Amy Harte." She turned to Brian and raised her eyebrows. "Brian, it looks like you're ready to go. Can someone stay with you tonight?"

Brian sent her a broad grin. "No problem. Seth generously offered to let me crash at his house." Brian winked at Seth.

She nodded. "Great." Her eyes skimmed her clipboard. "Oh, I almost forgot. On your abdominal scan, the radiologist noted that you only have a single kidney. He stated the right kidney was surgically absent." She paused, waiting for an explanation.

Seth stepped forward and placed a protective hand on Brian's shoulder. "He lost the right one a long time ago. Is the left one okay?"

Amy skimmed the report and lifted her eyes up, locking them with Seth's. "Hmm. Yes. He does have some mild bruising on the left kidney, so that, combined with his head injury, means he needs to rest. No heavy lifting, no physical activities for several weeks, and…" Amy set her gaze on Brian, "No driving."

Brian started to protest, "No driving? You can't be serious."

Seth cut off his brother's incredulous rant, "Thanks Dr. Harte, for all of your help. I promise we'll take good care of him. I'm sure you're busy." He took Amy's hand one last time, and his neck burned. Seth cast a quick glance at his brother, who now wore a knowing grin.

Seth's father leaned in and shook Dr. Harte's hand, too. "Yes, thank you for all you've done for my son."

Dr. Harte said her goodbyes and returned to the workstation.

Seth took over, pushing the wheelchair out the hospital doors with his father in tow. Once standing on the curb next to the parking lot, Seth turned to his dad. "Thanks for coming and bringing the car…and not telling mom. She would've had a fit."

Seth's father squeezed Brian's shoulder. "Of course. I'll call your mom and fill her in on the way home. She went to church early to practice with the choir. I didn't want to upset her if I didn't have to do it. You know how worked up she gets around hospitals."

Brian nodded in agreement. "Good call." Brian's grin spread, taking up most of the residence of his face.

Seth raised his eyebrows. "What?"

Shrugging, his brother sent him an even stare. "Oh, nothing…I was thinking about how red your face got when you were talking to Dr. Harte."

Seth clenched his jaw. His brother could act childish sometimes…actually a lot of the time.

"Oh, and she mentioned you," Brian teased his brother.

Seth stood straighter. "Oh, really? What did she say?"

"She said that she met you and spoke with you about my status, and you seemed like a nice guy."

Seth frowned. "Oh, okay. That's all?" Meeting Amy Harte sparked something within him, and his conversation with her came easy. Seth hoped for a better report than "a nice guy."

"Well, she blushed when I mentioned you to her. So, that might mean something… maybe you should call her, you know, to thank her for the excellent care she gave your intelligent, dashing younger brother." Brian wore a glint in his eye.

"You know, maybe you're right. I should call to thank her. Purely out of courtesy, of course."

"Of course." Brian grinned.

Seth sunk into deep thought about the sparkling blue eyes and sincere smile of Dr. Harte.

Chapter 3

July 3, 2017, Monday

Seth's phone rang on his way to Metropolitan Hospital Monday morning. He pulled it from his pant pocket and lifted it to ear while continuing to dodge cars as he walked across the parking lot. "Hello."

Seth's father's voice boomed from the other side of the phone. "Hey, son. I'm checking in on Brian. How did he do last night?"

"Huh," Seth uttered, distracted by fellow passer-byes as he neared the entrance, "Oh, great. Dad, he did great. I kept him awake for the recommended amount of time. We talked and watched a tennis match on tv."

"Good, good. Glad to hear it. I talked to your mother today, and she said she'd go over to your house while you're at work to see if Brian needed anything." His father went silent.

Seth paused and stepped aside out of the way of the early morning hospital congestion. "Yes? Something on your mind? I have a lot of work to do today to prep for the upcoming board meeting for Open Hearts." Seth smiled, thinking about the philanthropic organization he founded and managed for the hospital.

"Funny you should mention that…I understand why Open Hearts is important to you," Mr. Broadstone hesitated, "but… all your education… wouldn't you rather work with the family at

Tech? You spent all that time in college, and now you're working for the local hospital and running a one-man altruistic operation to cater to families battling cancer."

Seth's mouth opened in rebuttal. "Dad, I—"

His dad continued, "and it's admirable. The hospital serves the community well, and I know firsthand how Open Hearts helps families through a storm in life... but family... family matters. Health Tech grows daily, and we're getting busier. Not only could I use your expertise in finance, but I'd love to see you more. I know your brother misses you, too. And your mother and I hope to retire someday, maybe enjoy a grandkid or two..."

Man, his dad could pour it on thick. No pressure. "Dad, you know I love the family, but I only live twenty minutes away from you and mom, and Brian and I still squeeze in brotherly time such as trips to the local ED."

His father sighed in defeat, and Seth felt a wave of guilt wash over him. Seth stepped into the protective big brother role at the age of seven when Brian turned two and began his own battle with Wilms tumor, a cancer affecting the kidney. Brian faced removing his entire right kidney, chemotherapy, and radiation. Since then, Seth feared the possibility of losing someone he loved.

Seth didn't want to let his family down, but he cared about his job at Metropolitan and his work for Open Hearts. He found it rewarding. His parents admired his efforts, but Seth knew his dad hoped to relinquish the business to his eldest son one day...

Seth exhaled and looked at the time on his phone. "Dad, I have to go, or I'm going to be late. I'll call you tomorrow."

"Alright, son. Talk to you soon."

Seth put away his phone and sailed past familiar faces in the hospital foyer. He pressed the elevator button, distracted by the discussion with his father about the family business and the recent encounter with a particular female physician. Once Seth settled Brian in for the night, he lay in bed, awake, thinking about Amy's floral-scented hair when she leaned in to shake his hand. She seemed self-assured, smart, and confident, but still feminine and soft. He knew their hospital positions might complicate things, but he wouldn't mind seeing her warm smile once again. The door opened, and he entered, nearly plowing down his boss and the CEO of the hospital, Ed Baker.

"Woah, there son, you 'bout ran me over like a bull in a china shop." Ed slapped Seth on the back and chuckled with his son-of-a-gun manner.

"Sorry, Ed, I didn't see you there." Ed Baker had been the CEO of Metropolitan Hospital for several years when Seth joined the administrative team last month as the youngest member of the Board. Seth didn't carry as much decision-making power as Ed and some senior members of the group, but his educational record gained him the Board's respect.

Ed couldn't be more different from Seth. His cheeks and nose emanated a rosy glow from years of sun and his affinity for whisky. He golfed weekly and held a membership at the same club as Seth's parents.

While he appreciated Seth's input for the hospital's financial well-being, he only tolerated Seth's involvement with Open Hearts. Seth sold the philanthropic idea to Ed and several senior board members by emphasizing the tax credit it provided the hospital while improving its humanitarian image in the community.

His boss adjusted his tie, which appeared to be cutting off the circulation to his large neck thickened by years of steak and potatoes. "I'm glad I ran into you, my boy. I wanted to talk with you about filling the Chief of Emergency Medicine position. As you know, our top guy is heading out soon, and we need someone to helm the staff in the ED."

"Absolutely, sir. I saw a memo the other day on my desk about Dr. Bowers retiring." Seth smoothed his shirt and began making a mental list of tasks to complete.

"Yep, those are gonna be some big shoes to fill. I got one guy in mind already, but everything needs to be on the up-and-up. Have to post it and make it official and all. You know how it is." Ed grinned, and his bulbous nose reddened deeper to a shade of purple.

Seth wondered if the elevator slowed since last week, as the trip to his floor felt like an eternity. Not that he disliked Ed. He just didn't like the way he did business.

Ed maintained a tight-knit all-male circle of administrators and bosses. Officially he gave everyone a fair shake, but off the record, he took part in the local you-scratch-my-back-I'll-scratch-yours game. Seth suspected Ed cared more about the hospital's numbers on paper pleasing the Board of Directors and other shareholders and padding his own bottom line. Often, Ed insinuated that if Open Hearts didn't present such a positive image to the community, he would scrap the charitable program.

"I know how it is." Seth stepped off the elevator as the door opened, eager to get away from his boss and this conversation. "I'll draw up some numbers for the position. I know you mentioned a bonus in the memo. That's generous of you." *And unlike you.*

"Generous is my middle name." Ed Baker let out a deep belly laugh. "Ah, son, who am I kidding. I'm not trying to be generous if you want to know the truth. If we put in a sign-on bonus clause, the hospital lawyer told me that the applicant cannot leave the post for at least two years. Might make it four. Anyway, it's good business. We lock someone down, then if they leave early, they pay that money back. I don't think they'll leave, though." Ed flattened his rumpled suit jacket and turned to head toward his office.

Seth's face screwed up with genuine confusion. "What do you mean? The job hasn't even posted yet. How do you know this person won't leave?"

"Well, I don't know for sure, but Dr. Mark Blakely has been with the hospital for over a year, and he doesn't seem to be short of admirers. I think he'd be our top man to steer the ship. Plus, he's got a great golf swing and is buddies with several other board members. It'd make for an easy transition because the rest of the administration thinks he's a great guy." Ed started to walk away, signaling that the conversation was over.

Seth interrupted his boss's departure, "Ed, don't write off the rest of the team in the ED yet. I met one of your newer physicians, Dr. Harte, over the weekend. She seemed like a capable, compassionate, and quality candidate."

Ed Baker doubled over in laughter. "Dr. Harte? Isn't she that young gal that joined us about a year ago? You're a joker, son, quite a joker. She's got to be twenty-eight at most, and I don't know that she's up to the challenge of managing the entire ED."

Seth felt his jaw drop in disbelief at the blatant sexism and disregard for Dr. Harte's experience, regardless of her age or gender. "I wouldn't count anyone out of the running. Some people may surprise you. I bet she's tougher than she looks."

"Well, I'll give you this much, she sure is easier on the eyes than Dr. Blakely."

Appalled at his boss, Seth's mouth fell further toward the floor while his neck warmed, thinking about Dr. Harte's deep blue eyes. Seth took this as a signal to walk away before an argument ensued. "Mr. Baker, I've got to run. I'll get the position announcement typed up and sent to HR so they can post it today. I'll run some numbers, but we should have enough left in the general fund to float $50,000-60,000 for the bonus. I'll cc you and the other Board members once it's done."

Seth turned on his heel and headed toward his quiet office on the third floor, far away from the ED on the first floor, still thinking about Dr. Hart. His boss was wrong. He bet she had more strength in her than her 5'2" frame presented. Seth sensed she kept a wall up, but he hoped if he saw her again, she might let it down for him.

Chapter 4

July 5, 2017, Wednesday

Amy went to work on Wednesday distracted and distressed about the turn of events with her father's house. She leaned against the counter at the nursing station in the Emergency Department and sighed. Going over her father's financial plight in her mind more than a dozen times since speaking with him left her still with no feasible solutions.

Someone sidled up next to her, brushing her arm. Amy opened her mouth to greet the interloper and met the gaze of Dr. Mark Blakely. She clamped her mouth shut.

Dr. Blakely rested his arm on the counter next to Amy. "Well, aren't you chipper this morning? What did you do, forget your precious coffee?"

Amy met Mark's gaze with a furrowed brow. "Ha ha. You're hilarious. Just so you know, I'm dealing with a real problem here."

"What happened? They only had decaf at Joe's today? Ran out of regular? That is a hardship." Mark's mischievous twinkling indigo eyes settled into a serious expression for a second before giving Amy a subtle wink.

Warmth spread across Amy's cheeks and her stomach churned. No one could deny Mark's good looks. He was not boy-next-door gorgeous. No, Dr. Mark Blakely was drop-dead-stop-walking-in-your-tracks handsome. His curly, jet-black hair and wide grin weakened many women's knees, and although Amy hated to admit it, at the moment she might sink to the floor in a puddle. She chastised herself.

He had a reputation as both a capable physician and a ladies' man. Amy preferred staying predictable and safe, like sitting at home on her worn, yet comfortable, grey couch on a Friday night with buttered popcorn, chocolate, and plenty of streaming television to binge watch. Unfortunately, Mark seemed interested in her, and that made Amy nervous. Very nervous.

Amy suspected her face resembled a cherry tomato. She clutched the chart to her chest. "No, my problem stems from something much greater than a caffeine shortage…For your information, I found out yesterday that my dad's house is at risk of foreclosure. Or auction. Or something equally awful meaning he won't own it anymore." Amy's vision blurred with tears. She willed herself to hold them back. She would not let Mark see her cry.

Mark patted her shoulder, attempting sincerity. "Hey, hey. I'm sorry. I didn't mean to make you cry. I didn't know it was something serious. Listen, I'm sure it's not as bad as you think."

Amy sniffled. "No, actually, it's worse. Somehow, I have to help my dad raise over $50,000 in the next sixty days or my childhood home will cease to exist. The bank will swoop in and take it and that will be that." A single tear trailed down Amy's right cheek.

"Wow, I'm sorry, Amy. That is terrible. Hey, you know what?" Mark snapped his fingers. "What if you could make more money?"

Amy's eyes widened. "Well, Mark, thank you for that brilliant plan. I never thought of that. I'll just march myself upstairs to the CEO's office and demand more money. I'm sure he'll be so happy to oblige. Get real, Mark. I've only been working here for a year. Why would they hand me a raise?" Her voice dripped with sarcasm.

She closed her eyes and reflected on the comfort of her childhood home. Amy could almost still hear her mother's laugh sitting around the kitchen table. The scent of earl grey tea intermixed with baker's chocolate from homemade cookies filled the air as the two of them reviewed the events of the day. Her mother threw her head back and cackled as Amy told her about a boy she liked or how she nearly hit the wall in the garage because her driving skills bordered on dismal.

Amy opened her eyes and scanned the nursing station that provided the familiarity of a second home and exhaled. Alarm bells dinged, nurses shuttled patients in wheelchairs, and two people called for her attention at the same time.

"I have to get back to work. Thanks, Mark, for suggesting the imaginary raise, but until that happens, I really need to focus on keeping this job." She turned on her heel to address the next patient on the white board needing her expertise.

Mark grabbed her arm. "Wait a minute, you didn't let me finish."

Amy turned around and looked into his deep, blue eyes. She shook her head. "What?"

"I wanted to talk to you about the Chief of Emergency Medicine position." Mark's mouth settled into a serious line.

"What're you talking about? We already have a Chief, Dr. Rick Bowers. He's been in charge here for about a hundred years."

"Okay Miss Smarty Pants, I know, but he announced yesterday while you were off, that he's retiring. He's taking a three-month cruise around the world and hanging up his stethoscope." Mark smiled and his usual smugness returned. He reached for a patient chart, already mentally moving on to the next task.

"Seriously? I didn't see that coming. He loves his work. So, what does that mean for the rest of us? Who are they going to hire to replace him?" An idea began forming in Amy's mind.

"Well, that's the thing. They don't have anyone in line for the job. I heard from Ed Baker, the CEO, they hoped to hire within the department. You know...someone like you." Mark sent Amy a pointed stare. "I also heard the promotion includes a $60,000 sign-on bonus. Upfront. But keep that piece of information under your hat. Ed told me himself this morning on the way in, but it's not public knowledge yet. I think they'll post the job later today."

Amy stopped fiddling with the chart in her hands and raised her eyebrows, hopeful. "No joke?"

"No joke. I thought about the promotion and wanted to talk to you about it—"

The overhead paging system blared overhead, commanding

Amy's attention. "Dr. Harte, paging Dr. Harte. Please call extension 3401."

"Listen, Mark, I've got to take this, but thanks for telling me about the job. I'll definitely apply. I know it might be a long shot, but it's the best chance I have to save my dad's home. I'll talk to you later." She walked over to the three-foot tall desk housing endless rows of computers, screens, and monitors. They all dinged and beeped, beckoning her. She picked up the black house phone and impatiently punched in the number 3-4-0-1 and waited for the expected ringing.

A familiar voice surprised her, "Hey, Dr. Harte, it's Brian Broadstone's brother, Seth."

Amy's head shot up. "Y-yes," she stammered, "What can I do for you? How's your brother doing?"

Seth's voice filled with gratitude. "Brian seems fine, thank you. I'm sorry to bother you at work, but I didn't know how to reach you otherwise. I wanted to call and thank you for everything you did for him. You took great care of him and I appreciated it."

Amy twirled the coiled phone cord around her finger, recalling Seth's warm smile and kind eyes. "No problem. Just doing my job."

"Well, if you're ever near Joe's Coffee shop, I'd love to repay you—" another loud overhead announcement interrupted Seth, "CODE BLUE ED, bay three, CODE BLUE ED, bay three."

"Seth, I'm glad your brother's better, but I've got to go." Amy slammed down the phone, already running to the code. She reviewed her mental checklist, preparing to give CPR. It never got easier. Statistically, most patients didn't survive a Code Blue, but she strived to always do her best. Sometimes the young and healthy ones pulled through. Sometimes. Amy drew in a deep breath and muttered under breath, "Here we go."

Chapter 5

July 9, 2017, Sunday

Amy opened her eyes, forgetting the day for a moment. She sat up, stretched her arms, rubbed her crusted eyes, and yawned. She nearly hopped out of bed and to rush to the shower, but paused when she remembered it was Sunday, the day of rest. Yeah right, not working for the ED, but for Amy, today promised respite. She had pulled two double shifts, from Friday evening into Saturday night. Amy crashed on top of her grey down comforter, leaving her hair still in a ponytail last night. She hadn't even washed her face. Now her worn makeup smeared like a Picasso painting, and her light green scrubs displayed a million wrinkles from sleep.

As her first Sunday off in a month she wondered what to do. *Hmm.* She considered going for a run, then laughed. Amy loathed running. No, she only ran if chased by a possible murderer or a large, snarling animal. No running. She could go to the spa and get a massage. No, that wouldn't do either. Relaxing stressed her out. Coffee? Coffee would definitely happen.

Amy grabbed the remote lying next to her on the comforter and switched on the television in her room. Immediately, a short-haired woman came on the screen. She talked about how anger could steal Amy's joy and how she needed to learn to let go of it to keep her peace. *Church.* Amy could go to church. She hadn't been in over a year, not since her mother died. Amy grew up attending church every Sunday morning and evening, and sometimes Wednesday nights, too. She participated in the youth groups, Bible studies, accountability partners, all of it.

Although Amy still believed in God, a surge of anger arose inside her when she thought about her mom. She found it unfair that someone so young and healthy could be fine: laughing, shopping, telling stories, and then, months later, resemble a withered shell of their former self. And then, just be gone. Gone. Only a year ago Amy's life changed forever.

Amy had nearly finished her emergency medicine residency and couldn't wait to practice on her own, a dream of hers since age eight. So, when her mom told her the devastating news about her diagnosis one evening, Amy fell into hopelessness. She still easily recalled the conversation. She sat in her apartment, alone, on her couch after a long shift at the Carilion Clinic ED when the phone rang.

Her mom spoke with a shaky voice, "Amy, honey, the Dr. told me today that I have T-cell lymphoma, a rare type. It's…aggressive."

Amy's ears throbbed and her mom's voice became distant. She could not focus and thought she might faint. Her mother, her best friend in the world, her soft place to land, had cancer. Cancer. She despised that word.

She did everything possible to help her mom fight the relentless disease. Amy went to medical appointments with her and asked a million questions. She encouraged her mom, telling her the disease wouldn't win. Under no circumstance, could Amy lose such a precious person in her life. Before Amy's mom, Caren, fell ill, strangers mistook her for Amy's older sister, rather than her mom. Caren had bright blue eyes, short, dark brown hair, similar in color to Amy's, and a smile that lit up any room. Quieter than Amy, her mom seemed reserved to those who didn't know her well. To those close to her, Amy's mother exuded life and joy. Her mom loved to dance and spent Saturday night's spinning and whirling around a local club, The Hanger, that played Big Band and throwback swing music. That's how Amy wanted to remember her mom, cackling and twirling and smiling through those big blue eyes. Fresh, hot tears of grief and anger threatened to flow, and

Amy's throat tightened. Life seemed cruel sometimes.

In March, Amy found out about the cancer diagnosis. Three short months later, Amy stepped off the stage of an auditorium after accepting her certificate of completion of her residency when her dad called her out of the blue. Her parents wanted to attend the ceremony, but her mother had a follow up appointment at Drake Medical Cancer Center a few hours away from home that day. Her mom went there weekly for an experimental treatment.

The night before graduation, Amy's mom called her. "Honey, I'm so sorry your dad and I can't be there tomorrow for your big day. I know how hard you've worked for this dream since you were a little girl. We're both so proud of you." Amy's mother told her she felt short of breath and her doctor wanted to keep her overnight for observation. Her mom's voice sounded weaker, tired, almost defeated.

Amy swallowed hard, recalling the memory. "Mom, you know I love you right? Like, so much. You're the best mom in the whole world. I don't care if you aren't there tomorrow. I only want you to get better." Amy wanted to leap through the phone and squeeze her mother. She felt like a three-year-old again, getting ready to enter preschool on the first day, alone and unsure of what to expect next.

As always, Amy's mom reassured her. "I love you, too, baby. I love you, too. It'll be ok. Everything will be ok. I'll talk to you soon. I'm so, so happy for you. Take care of yourself."

Amy spoke to her dear, sweet mother for the last time that night. The next day her dad called her on the phone as she walked off the stage. "Amy, A-Amy, um, I don't know how to tell you this... something happened."

"What, dad? What's wrong?"

"Your mom went to sleep last night, and seemed fine, comfortable for the first time in a while. I must've fallen asleep in the chair, too, maybe for a few minutes, half an hour at most. When I woke up, I touched your mom's shoulder, and... I knew she was gone."

Amy felt like a truck hit her chest. She couldn't breathe.

Her dad continued through wracking sobs. "I called immediately for help, and they tried to save her. They ran a code for almost forty-five minutes. It felt like hours, but it was too late. We didn't want to upset you yesterday because of your graduation

23

today, but your mom's cancer quit responding to treatment. It spread... a lot. They sent someone in to talk to us yesterday evening about the possibility of hospice, and we cried together for hours. Neither of us wanted to quit fighting yet. We told them no. We wanted to try another experimental option. Your mom felt down until she talked to you, and then she perked up and seemed in better spirits. But... I think she knew. I think she knew that the good Lord was calling her home. So, she went to sleep and never woke up. For that, at least, I'm thankful. That she went peacefully."

"What're you telling me, dad? Mom's gone? That's it... she's just... gone. No! I just talked to her last night! She was fine!"

"I know, sweetie. I know it's hard to understand."

"It's not fair for God to call her home when I still need my mom here. Where is the goodness in that? Why would He do that? It seems selfish to me!" Amy screamed into the phone, in a state of shock.

He pulled in a breath and tried to comfort his daughter. "Amy, you can't blame God for this or get mad at Him. Blame the cancer. You know that sometimes bad things happen. There's brokenness and sin in the world. I don't like it any more than you do. I'm mad and lost, but I know that God only wants good things for us. You know Jeremiah 29:11 says 'For I know the plans I have for you declares the Lord, plans to prosper you and not to harm you, plans to give you hope and a future.' I'm thankful he didn't let her suffer longer. This isn't God's fault, and it's not yours either."

The phone slipped out of Amy's hand, falling to the grassy ground below with a soft thud. She looked around her, shaking in disbelief. Other families carried on in celebration, oblivious to the trauma she just endured. Tears streamed down her cheeks. *Not her fault. Not God's fault. Then, who's fault was it?* And that was the last time Amy considered going to church... until today.

Reflecting on those painful memories brought new, fresh waves of grief along with them. She scanned her vacant, rumpled room. Guilt over standing on a stage accepting a certificate instead of holding her mother's hand consumed her, and she threw herself across her bed and cried until she fell asleep.

Chapter 6

July 9, 2017, Sunday

Seth pulled into the parking lot of his church, LifeMakers, and thought about the events of the past week. He drove to his parent's house after work on Wednesday for his mother's birthday celebration, his head spinning from his talk first with Ed Baker, then Dr. Harte. Amy spoke with him briefly, but at least he had the chance to thank her. It surprised him how the short chat with her caused his pulse to quicken and his palms to sweat. He couldn't recall another woman making him feel that way.

His mother appreciated her gift of tickets to a local musical coming to town soon. She loved singing, the theatre, and Broadway. The brothers completed the gift by bringing dinner to the house from their mom's favorite Italian restaurant, Angelo's. Seth considered cooking the birthday dinner himself, but compared to his mom, nobody in the family could cook. She held the title of master chef.

Seth smiled at the look of surprise and joy on his mom's face when she opened her gift. Brian carried on in good spirits, other than finding out his car landed in the auto shop for at least a few days, if not a week. The happy evening came to a crashing halt when his father raised the topic again of Seth joining the family at Tech temporarily to lighten Brian's load while he "healed" from his injuries. Seth internally groaned. It's not that he didn't care about his brother, quite the opposite.

He never wanted to imagine what life looked like without his family. Next to God, they were the most important thing to him. However, Brian suffered more of a glorified bump on the head and, but as the baby of the family he milked the sympathy all week long. Plus, his parents capitalized on any excuse to get Seth to join the family business.

Seth yanked the emergency brake, ensuring he wouldn't return from the church service to find his car at the bottom of the steep hill on which the church now sat. Unusually late getting to church, he glanced at his watch realizing service began in two minutes. He hopped out of the car, slammed the door shut, and took purposeful, long strides to the front of the church.

He casually waved and smiled at people he recognized as regular attenders and reached out to grab the golden handle of the large, wooden front door of the church. As he readied to open the door, a hunched female form appeared at his feet, blocking his path. Ever a gentleman, Seth bent down, extending a hand to help the mystery woman. When the brown-haired figure lifted her head, he locked eyes with Dr. Amy Harte. Seth's heartbeat against his chest like a drum.

Chapter 7

July 9, 2017, Sunday

Amy readied herself for her first visit to church in over a year. She had grabbed her purse, took one final look in her rearview mirror, and scurried as quickly as possible in her three-inch wedge booties across the grey, graveled parking lot like a new fawn stumbling on its legs for the first time. She noticed a pleasant, smiling woman with short, slightly curled blond hair greeting people. Amy stretched out her arm and shook the greeter's hand.

The greeter shook Amy's hand with vigor. "Good morning! Welcome! If you head inside and go to the right, you'll find coffee and tea, and the main door to the auditorium is just past the coffee stand. You can't miss it!"

Amy returned a smile to the welcoming blond woman and nodded her head in understanding. She reached for the thick, golden door handle when her phone vibrated. Digging into her purse with shaking hands, Amy tried to catch the call. *Please don't be the hospital. Please let no one have called off today.* She glanced at the number, recognizing it as her hairdresser's, and sighed in relief. As she placed the phone into her purse, her toe entangled in a crack in the concrete sidewalk in front of the main door. Amy caught herself before face- planting on the cement, but her phone flew out of her hand and onto the ground, just in front of her now-stubbed toe.

Frustrated, Amy grumbled to herself and knelt down to retrieve it when another hand brushed hers causally, attempting to pick up the phone at the same time. She raised her head to see who belonged to the helpful hand and felt warmth spread from her chest up to her face. Fire filled her cheeks. Flames. Standing there, holding her phone, both handsome and helpful, was Seth Broadstone. He looked the same as he did in the hospital. *No, that's not true.* Somehow, he looked better, more relaxed and self-assured. His hair still swooped perfectly to the side, gelled, and well-maintained. His disarming smile revealed perfectly straight, white teeth. His kind, bright blue eyes twinkled.

Amy noticed butterflies swirling around inside her stomach. Her hands trembled. She took a mental inventory of her appearance. Her outfit was ok, not spectacular, but not tragic: cuffed jeans with purposeful distressing on the thighs, ridiculously tall wedge black booties, and a soft black blouson sleeve sweater that flattered her small waist, simple, not trying too hard, but respectable.

Thankfully, Amy threw on some makeup in her driveway earlier before taking off for church. Nothing fancy, just mascara, peachy-pink blush, minimal foundation, and a hint of rose lip gloss. She rubbed her lips together. At least her hair looked good. On a typical day, Amy piled her chest length, wavy, dark brown hair on top of her head in what she prayed looked like a planned, put-together top knot. It was often, in fact, not planned or put together, but again, perhaps appearances deceived.

On her days off, though, she relished fixing her hair. It became an event. Amy's naturally curly hair refused to decide whether to declare itself Botticelli or straight. Over the course of her life, she had tested every anti-frizz, pro-curl, pro-straighten treatment known to mankind. By now, she decided that her hair had a mind of its own and she could do nothing about it. On days when it cooperated, she washed it with Moroccan oil shampoo, covered it completely with a keratin conditioner, tortured it with a round brush and diffuser until her arm throbbed in pain, and then added a dab of smoothing serum. Finally, if all went well, she curled it with her trusty ten-year-old pink curling iron, taking care to rotate each curl away from her face. A quick finger combing, some hairspray, and voila—hair perfection. This did not occur often. But today, her hair hung down her back in beautiful, glossy soft waves, behaving itself. Thank goodness for that.

Seth's jaw dropped, and he looked as surprised to find Amy's face attached to the body reaching for the phone on the ground. He smiled at her. "Amy! It's great to see you! I didn't know you went to church here." He picked up the phone and returned it to her before standing.

Amy accepted the device responsible for the reunion and rose from the ground. She tucked a stray piece of hair behind her ear. "Well, I don't... not really." She stared at her feet for a second before meeting his gaze.

Seth's eyebrows raised, puzzled.

Amy fiddled with a frayed edge of her distressed jean. "I used to go to church all the time, but I haven't been for a while... it's a long story. A friend of mine at the hospital mentioned how great the pastor's sermons were here, so I took advantage of my day off."

Music swelled from inside the church building and the drums grew louder. The pleasant greeter ushered them both into the foyer and shut the front door with a thump. She gave them both pointed looks.

"Hey, it looks like the service is starting. What do you say we grab a quick coffee together after this? I'd love to hear your long story." Seth sent Amy an encouraging smile.

Amy paused, debating for a moment.

"It's just a coffee. Plus, I want to thank you for what you did for my brother."

Amy grinned back, while Seth held the sanctuary door open for her. She gave a quick nod and took a deep breath before entering her first church service since her mother left her a year ago. Today promised to hold new experiences.

Chapter 8

July 9, 2017, Sunday

The church service ended too soon for Amy. It seemed as soon as she sat down and began listening to the pastor speak, it was over. The pastor talked about anger and guilt and letting it go of it to keep one's "peace." She was so intent on retaining every morsel of information and did not realize how rapidly the hour passed. She looked up from taking notes in her old, dusty Bible, and met the warm gaze of Seth, who sat beside her during the service.

"So, why don't I just meet you at Joe's? Do you know how to get there?" Seth raised his eyebrows.

"I'm an ER doctor. If I know about anything other than medicine, it's caffeine in all its various forms. Especially coffee." Amy felt her heart rate rise, either from the expectation of a caffeine bolus, or because of how close Seth stood next to her.

Seth nodded his head and chuckled. "Ok. I'll meet you there. I just need to help put the extra chairs up after service, but that won't take long. I'll meet you over there in about fifteen or twenty minutes."

Amy smiled and gave a nod of understanding. She gathered her bag and Bible, stood, and raised one hand to wave goodbye to Seth. "Ok, see you there." She hesitated. Her nerves jittered and her stomach rolled. Even though Seth said he wanted to take her out to thank her, the outing felt like a date, which Amy hadn't had in a year or more. Ever since she lost her mom, she operated under the assumption that keeping people at arm's length prevented herself from getting hurt or hurting anyone else.

She walked to her car, slid in, and turned on the ignition. Her black SUV roared to life, and she tore off towards the coffee shop, thinking about this unexpected turn of events. She paused at one of the few traffic lights in her small town of eight thousand people, thinking about church. The music during worship impressed her. The auditorium filled with loud drums, flashing lights, and a lead singer wearing lots of leather and flannel with a long beard and a killer voice.

The packed sanctuary with at least four hundred people singing, clapping their hands, and waving their arms in praise boasted joy. Amy sang along but didn't raise her arms above chest height. She smiled to herself. When the pastor came on stage, everyone sat down, and the large hall fell quiet. The hairs on Amy's arms raised, and the experience felt pivotal. She wanted to change.

She listened to the entire sermon intently. The pastor preached about letting go of past hurt, guilt, and disappointment. He spoke about following peace and learning to let God remove the burden of old anger and pain. It was hard to comprehend, but he made it sound simple. "Let go. Just let go Amy," a still quiet voice whispered in her head. *Easy enough to say.* Amy shook her head as she pulled up to Joe's Coffee Shop. She parked the car, grabbed her bag, and hurried inside.

Amy went to the counter and ordered her usual, a tall French vanilla skinny latte. *Yum.* The mug held the perfect blend of warmth, sugar, caffeine, and frothy milk. *Perfection.* Not much in life topped it. The barista, a tall, lanky guy, wore a brown apron with the shop's logo blazoned across the front. He handed over her cup of happiness and smiled in recognition. Amy grinned back sheepishly. He knew her order, but this one consistency of life comforted Amy. At least some things didn't change.

She sat at one of the few open tables in the café and took a tentative sip of her steaming mug of coffee. Amy kept glancing at the door, trying to appear nonchalant. After Amy's sixth furtive glance, she noticed Seth.

He looked around the small cafe section of the coffee shop,

filled with about ten or twelve small tables. Seth caught Amy's gaze and he walked over to join her at the small two top table.

Seth pulled back his chair and smiled as he sat down. "Hey, thanks for saving us seats. It's always packed in here, but it's even worse on Sundays."

"No problem! I love this place. It almost feels like a second home." Amy grinned behind her cup at the truth of that.

"So," Seth paused, smiling at her "what did you think of the service?"

"It was good... great, really." Amy searched for the right words. "It's been a while since I've gone to church, but today felt as if I returned home, if that makes sense."

Joe brought over Seth's Cafe Americano and sat it down in front of him. Joe cast a glance between Amy and Seth before giving her a knowing look. Amy blushed. "Enjoy! Let me know if you need anything else."

Seth grinned. "Thanks." He took his first cautious sip of coffee as the barista walked away. "It does, for sure, but why the break from church? What about this long story you mentioned earlier?" He sent her an encouraging smile.

"Well, I've been through a tough time over the last year...I guess you could say I've struggled with my faith." Amy trailed off, looking away from Seth.

Seth looked unsure of what to say next. "Oh, wow. I'm sorry, that's rough...what happened? If you don't mind me asking?"

Amy took another sip of her drink, debating how much personal information to divulge. She glanced at Seth and despite only knowing him for a short time, his kind eyes put her at ease. "No, it's ok. I haven't talked to many people about it, that's all."

Seth sent her an understanding nod. "You don't have to talk about it, but I'd love to hear your story. I've been told I'm a good listener... unless you ask my brother."

Amy chuckled and drew in a breath. "Ok... well... about a year ago I graduated from residency. I'd looked forward to that day for most of my life. Unfortunately, that same day I lost my mom... to cancer."

Seth reached across the table and placed a gentle hand on top of hers. "Amy, I'm sorry. That's terrible."

Amy's eyes landed on her hand under Seth's and the rest of her story spilled out. "She got sick suddenly, and fought hard, but before I knew it, her fight ended. She had always been the picture of health. She exercised, ate healthy, never smoked, went to church, read her Bible. She lived well and was a good person. My mom—Caren was her name—she loved God, and everyone loved her. She was my best friend. Then one day she got diagnosed with lymphoma, and there weren't a lot of treatment options for it... so..."

Seth squeezed her hand.

Amy's voice cracked and tears flooded her eyes. She paused and pulled in another breath. "When she passed away, I wasn't there with her. She went to her doctor for a planned visit and my parents didn't want me to miss my graduation. Even though I knew she was sick, I didn't expect her to die then. Not that day. I should have been with her. I've wrestled with understanding why God takes away beautiful people from our lives. Basically, I've spent the last year sad, guilty, and angry. Angry at myself, angry at life, angry at cancer... angry at God. Isn't that terrible? To be angry at God?" Amy looked into Seth's eyes and wished she could take back all the emotional baggage she'd just unloaded onto him.

Seth squeezed her hand.

Her fingers tingled.

Seth offered her a kind smile. "I don't think that's terrible at all. It sounds like a terrible situation. You're normal and you reacted the way most people would to something tragic. It sounds like you've been trying to make sense of something hard to understand. Even if you're angry at God now, you won't always feel like this. God still loves you. Revelations 21:4 says, 'He will wipe every tear from their eyes. There will be no more death or mourning or crying or pain...'"

A single tear rolled down Amy's cheek. She quickly swiped it away with her finger and sighed. "Thanks for listening. My close friends and family know what happened, but I haven't really talked to them about how it affected me. I worried they would think I was a terrible person, or just tell me to get over it. Plus, I try to put on a brave face. Lately, I'm tired of looking one way on the outside and feeling the opposite on the inside. Like I'm a phony."

Joe brought over a second latte to Amy and another Cafe Americano for Seth. He winked at Amy. "It's on the house.

Thought you guys might need a refill."

Amy pulled her hand away from Seth's, accepting the cup from Joe. She smiled. "Thanks, you're the best." Joe bounded to his counter and the long line of customers already forming in his absence.

After another draw of caffeine for courage, Amy continued baring her soul. "I've thought about going to church for a few months now, and today was my first Sunday off in a while, so I thought, no time like the present. Like ripping off a bandage." Amy gestured the action of tearing off a bandage from an old wound.

She met Seth's gaze. His eyes were a striking turquoise, like the color of the Caribbean Sea. Her cheeks burned, and she opened her mouth to ask him how his brother was doing, when the bell over the coffee shop door jingled.

Amy glanced up and her mouth snapped shut. What was Mark Blakely doing here?

He stood at the doorway, wearing what she could only describe as a devilish grin along with a grey, short sleeve polo shirt and crisp, white Bermuda shorts. She squirmed in her seat. He walked toward her table. Amy looked down at her hands now clenched in her lap.

Mark sidled up to the table she was sharing with Seth. "Hey Amy! It's a little early to be up on your day off, don't you think?" Mark winked at Amy and folded his arms across his chest.

"Well... I uh... um... I woke up early and had the day off, so I thought I would go to church." Amy clamped her mouth shut and stared at her hands again, scrutinizing her fingernails.

"Church?" Mark chuckled. "Why in the world would you want to spend your morning off at church?"

Seth peered up at Mark. "What's wrong with church?" Seth sized up the interloper.

"Well, there's the getting dressed up, smiling at people you don't know, sitting for hours, and then listening to someone tell you how to live. Who needs that kind of energy in their life?"

Amy shifted in her chair. "Well, actually, I used to go to church all the time. I just hadn't gone in about a year, so I thought it was time. And this church wasn't like that at all. Most people wore jeans, there was a free coffee bar—"

Mark interrupted her. "Free coffee. Now you're speaking my language."

Amy rolled her eyes. "Everyone was nice, and they had a rock band that played music. Oh, and the sermon was about improving your life by doing what God says. It felt encouraging and uplifting... all that good energy stuff." Amy chuckled, trying to break the palpable tension between the two men.

Mark scrutinized Seth closer and a look of recognition spread across his face. "Hey man, I know you! You came in the ED last week with the guy in the car accident, right? Haven't I seen you around the hospital before, too?"

"Yeah, that was my brother in the ED. I started working at the hospital about a month ago in the finance department. I'm the Chief Financial Officer," Seth replied politely. He crossed his arms.

"Woah, impressive title. So, you're probably on the Board with my buddy Ed Baker. You know, the CEO of the hospital? Good thing my girl Amy was there to take such good care of your brother." Mark placed a hand on Amy's shoulder possessively and smirked. "She's the best. Gorgeous, funny, smart, but a little cranky before her morning jolt of caffeine. The whole package." Mark winked again at Amy.

Amy's stomach tensed and she pulled away from Mark's touch. At this rate Seth might think she put Mark up to this stunt as a personal advertisement or that Mark was her boyfriend. No, a normal person couldn't have orchestrated such a scheme. So, that only left the latter option. Mark looked like he was dating Amy, which he was not.

She cleared her throat. "Um, thanks Mark, for the infomercial on my life... but, really, it was nothing. I just did my job. Mark and I have worked together for about a year. He's a great friend." Amy tried to stress the importance of those two keywords. She glanced at Seth, and his shoulders relaxed.

Mark grinned. "For now." Mark stared at his watch. "Well, I've got to run some errands, but it was nice talking with you Seth. Glad your brother is doing better. And Amy, I'll see you soon." Mark sent her one final wink, then sauntered over to the counter where he flirted with the barista before leaving.

Amy shook her head. "Don't pay attention to him. He's like

that with everyone. He's even worse with me, because I keep turning down his invitations for a date. It's all a game for him."

Seth cleared his throat and rubbed his chin. "Well, he seems interested in you, but then I can totally see why." A slow, sincere smile spread across his face. "What's not to like?"

Now Amy knew her face resembled a tomato. "Uh, thanks." She looked away, embarrassed at all the unexpected male attention. "What about you? Mr. Chief Financial Officer. That's impressive, too."

Seth raised his steaming cup of coffee to his mouth and took a slow sip. "Well, I just started at Metro Hospital about a month ago, so I'm still getting settled. I spend most of my time on the fourth floor trapped in my office. I'm also on the Board of Directors, but that's not my main function. Mostly, I'm responsible for managing the hospital's budget and ensuring it operates with integrity." Seth took another drink and shrugged.

Amy's phone vibrated, and she peered down at a new text message.

"Excited to see you later, honey. I'll make dinner at the house. Don't be late! Love you, Dad."

Amy checked the time. "Oh! I didn't realize it was after 3:00! I'm supposed to meet my dad for an early dinner around 4:30, and I still need to run to the grocery store and stop back by my house. I hate to leave...I've really enjoyed talking with you." Amy grabbed her cardigan off the back of the chair.

Seth's face clouded. "Oh, I'm sorry! I didn't mean to keep you so long. Do you have to work tomorrow?"

"Yeah, bright and early. 6:00 a.m. shift. Twelve hours, at least." Amy scrunched her brow and stuck out her tongue in disgust. She was not a morning person.

Seth's expression turned hopeful. "Do you work Friday evening?"

Amy's hand trembled as she picked up her purse. Was Seth asking her out on a real date? *Could she say yes? After all, he worked with her... but she wanted to forget that for now. What if he broke her heart or it affected her job?* "No, I'm off Friday, so that evening is free. No plans, yet."

"Well," Seth drew out the word, "there's this awesome Christian band playing at church Friday night around 8:00 p.m.

Would you want to grab a bite to eat beforehand and then come with me to the concert?"

Amy's stomach flipped, and she released a soft sigh. "What about the fact that we work together?"

"I don't think the hospital policy says anything against it." Seth's eyes twinkled.

"Sure. That sounds fun. Where should I meet you?" Amy hoped he would come pick her up, but also dreaded the awkward first date car ride. Not that it was a date.

"No way! I'll come get you. What's your address?" Seth pulled out his phone, ready to type in the information.

"132 Fox Hill Road. You can't miss it. It's a little white and grey Cape Cod style townhouse with black shutters and a red door. Ignore the dying lilac bushes out front. I have a knack for saving human lives while killing agricultural ones." Amy prayed her joke would cover her nerves.

"Got it. Cape Cod house with dead plants." Seth grinned. "Ok, I'll pick you up at 6:00 p.m. and take you to this great Mexican restaurant that's new."

Amy slung her bag on her shoulder. "Awesome. That sounds great! Sorry, but I've got to run. If I'm late meeting my dad, I'll never hear the end of it."

"All right, see you Friday night." Seth stood first, waiting for Amy to follow suit.

She rose, debating whether she should hug him or shake hands. Amy waved good-bye at the same time Seth reached in to give her a hug, and her arm got trapped against Seth's chest. They both erupted in laughter.

"Ok, I'm leaving now, before I fall down or do something else to embarrass myself." Amy waved again, successfully this time, and gave Seth one last flirtatious smile before heading out the coffee shop door, with the bell jingling behind her.

Chapter 9

July 9, 2017, Sunday

Seth watched Amy walk out of the familiar coffee shop and stood with his feet planted, stunned for a minute. He ran a hand through his dark hair and exhaled for what felt like the first time since she arrived. She took his breath away. He dated a few women in college on and off, but nothing serious. Seth focused on school with the goal of achieving his Master of Finance and landing a gig where he could use his business skills while making a difference in his community. He didn't have time to date casually, so he guarded his heart.

After everything his brother faced as a kid: fighting the tumor, then going to follow-up visits for years, never sure when his cancer might return, Seth didn't want distractions from his family and work. Almost losing Brian still weighed on Seth's mind. He busied himself with his hospital obligations and wanted to make Open Hearts successful...but Dr. Harte...she wedged her way into a crack in his heart, threatening to break it wide open. He couldn't help it. She was hard to resist.

His phone rang and Seth glanced down to check the ID. *Mom.* "Hey mom, what's up?"

Seth's mother defined a southern belle. Nancy Broadstone had big hair and an even bigger personality. She'd never met a stranger, and she valued family and God above all else. "Hey sugar, how's my baby doin'?"

Seth fiddled with the coffee stirrer on the table and swirled his now-cold coffee. "Mom. I'm not a baby, you know. I'm a grown man." He chuckled. "And I'm doing well."

"Well, now, I know that. But you'll always be my baby. Both you and Brian. Speaking of which, he's back at work and at it like a dog with fleas. I worry that it'll be too much for him. I told him earlier today he needed to stay home and prop his feet up."

Seth rolled his eyes and smiled. His mother loved to fuss over her boys. A mild cold could ignite a full-on hospital visit. If she knew about his coffee date with Amy, his mother would launch this conversation into the Spanish Inquisition and surmise that he was engaged by the end of it. "Mom, I'm worried about Brian, too, but don't you think you might be overreacting. The doctor cleared him at the hospital, and it's been a week."

"I know, and I'm sure he's fine. However, if you were at Tech Solutions with your father, then maybe Brian could take a few weeks to rest. I know you're doing important things at the hospital and I'm sure they can't spare you for anything." His mom held a degree in dispensing what Seth termed southern guilt.

"Mom. I'm certain Brian is fine. If it makes you feel better, I'll call him later tonight to check on him…and you know I love you and dad and care about the business, but I like my job. I want to help you guys, but if I leave the hospital, no one else will push for Open Hearts. They're always looking for a reason to cut the program. It doesn't inherently bring revenue into the hospital and most of the Board only cares about the bottom line." Seth scrunched his brow in worry, thinking about his last conversation with Ed Baker.

"Ok, ok. I'll leave it for now. So, honey, what're you doing on this glorious day the Lord has made?" His mom also changed the subject like a professional when she faced defeat. She sacrificed the battle to win the war.

"Uh… I went to church…and then out to coffee. I'm still here at Joe's." Seth spoke with vagueness, hoping to evade his mother's intuition.

"Well sugar, are you drinking coffee alone? You should've called me and your father. We would've joined you. It's just a hop, skip, and a jump over there." She lowered her voice to a whisper. "Your father tried to get out of church today, the old dog, but I dragged him, and don't you know he was so glad I did. Not only did we both get a word of encouragement, but he got a few new contacts for the business. I call that favor of God."

Seth shook his head. His parents made him laugh. His dad loved Jesus, but also would never miss an opportunity to advance the family business. "I didn't get coffee alone, so no worries."

"What do you mean you aren't alone? Are you on a date? Is my sugar darlin' out on a date? Is there hope for grandchildren still yet?" His mother squealed in delight on the other end of the phone.

"Mom calm down. It's not a big deal." It was a big deal. "I ran into someone at church, and we went for coffee afterwards, that's all." Seth looked around the rapidly filling coffee house to see if anyone noticed his discomfort at his mother's prying.

"Oh, that's nice. Is it someone I know? One of those young people you sit with near the front of the church? What's their names? Jess, and something or other?" He could tell she was half paying attention to her conversation with her son and already turning her attention to something else; likely a household chore or upcoming social obligation. Still, he needed to tread with care.

"Uh... not exactly... I rescued Dr. Harte's phone from an early death at the front door to the church. So, I offered to take her to coffee... to thank her for all she did for Brian." Seth held his breath, hoping this nugget would be enough to quench his mother's appetite for information.

No such luck. She latched on like a piranha. "Dr. Harte!"

Seth could envision his mom's head whipping around.

"Isn't she the young lady who took care of Brian? The young doctor from the hospital last week? Wait, were you on a date with Dr. Harte, Seth?"

He could hear his mother clapping her hands in glee. Seth looked toward the ceiling and rubbed his eyes with his thumb and first finger, pinching the bridge of his nose. This would snowball into a family dinner; he just knew it. He loved his family and wanted to make everyone happy and keep the peace. And he loved his mother, including all her socially intrusive ways. He started to warm to the prospect of opening his heart again, but he wasn't sure he wanted to introduce Amy to the entire Broadstone clan.

He recalled one family reunion that began as a simple outdoor barbecue and ended with over one hundred neighborhood family and friends gathered around an improvised stage. By the end of the night his dad closed at least three new accounts, his brother danced around with several ladies in the neighborhood, and his mother sang a Broadway show tune on the stage. Things escalated quickly.

"I guess you could call it a pre-date or an outing with a friend." Seth dodged the question.

"Will there be another one? When can we meet her? Could this be The One? Oh, Seth, I'm so happy for you. You know life is short, and after everything your brother went through, you should know more than anyone else you can't take days for granted. Your dad and I aren't getting any younger. I want some grandbabies!"

Seth noticed Joe staring at him. He wondered if Joe could hear his mother's voice through the phone.

She shouted again.

Joe must have sensed Seth staring, because he busied himself with scrubbing a non-existent spot on the counter.

Seth's voice became stern. "Ok, if I tell you the truth, do you promise not to make a huge deal of it? Because I don't want to put too much pressure on myself. Or her."

"Promise. Cross my heart." Seth's mom fell silent.

"I asked her to go with me to dinner Friday night and then to the concert at church afterward. So, yes, there will be another date. Although, we work together, and things could get complicated...but she's great."

"Oh, Seth, I'm so happy for you! Now you must bring Dr. Harte over for dinner. I can't wait to meet her. I'll cook us up a big spread and we can all have a sit down together. She can meet me and your dad, oh, and Brian, but she's already knows him." Seth could tell he lost the war. His mom went into planning mode. Most likely, she'd already compiled a mental list of whom to invite to the wedding and suitable names for their children.

"Mom."

She continued prattling on about the Big Family Dinner.

"Mom!"

His mother stopped her monologue. "What, honey? Did you say something?"

"Mom. I'll invite Amy to dinner to meet you all, I will, but can I go out with her on Friday first? And do you promise not to go overboard with the dinner? I don't know Amy well yet, but I want to get to know her more. I like her a lot, but I'm also trying to be smart. I don't want to get hurt."

"Yes, yes. I promise to be on my best behavior and not embarrass you. Now your father, no promises there. He'll probably try to sell her healthcare software, knowing him. Oh, and you know your brother will give you a hard time, even though he doesn't mean nothing by it. I'm so excited!" His mother finally paused for a brief breath.

"Mom."

"Seth. Listen to me, sugar. This is important. You know 2 Timothy 1:7 tells us 'God has not given us a spirit of fear, but of power and of love and of a sound mind.' My sound mind is telling you not to close off your heart before you start. Give this gal a chance. You never know what God has in store for you. I want you to find love. You two can figure out the hospital working together stuff later. You're always so concerned about everyone else, which I love about you, but you deserve some happiness, too. Now if you find that happiness working with your daddy, well…" His mom trailed off leaving her not-too-subtle hint hanging in the air.

"Mom! You're a mess, you know that, right?

"Yes, I know. It's just because I love you. "

"I love you, too. I have to go. I've got to get some numbers together for the Board Meeting tomorrow. My boss is already looking for any excuse to eliminate Open Hearts and last quarter's numbers didn't look good for the hospital. I've got to find room in the budget to keep the program and show the rest of the Board how crucial Open Hearts is to the community and its patients."

"Ok, honey, well you let me know when we can shoot for that dinner and I'll fire up the oven. Oh, just think, we could have a doctor in the family…" Seth's mom went into future daughter-in-law planning mode.

Seth cut her off, "I love you, mom. Bye." He hung up his phone and rubbed his hand down his cheek, grabbing his tense neck. He sighed and looked at Joe, who wore a knowing grin, and nodded at him in understanding. Seth chuckled to himself thinking about the yet unconfirmed, but inevitable family dinner. He knew his mom was right about one thing. He needed to open his heart with no fear. He hoped Dr. Harte didn't break it. He stood and exited Joe's Cafe with the ringing bell overhead sounding more optimistic than Seth felt.

Chapter 10

July 9, 2017, Sunday evening

Amy arrived on the doorstep of her childhood home and raised her finger to ring the doorbell. She paused, wondering if this may be one of the last times she did it. She sighed, pulled her shoulders back, and stood straighter, pressing the buzzer with fierce determination. After learning about the promotion possibility at the hospital, Amy decided that no matter what it might take, she would land that job and the bonus. She had to do it. This home was all she had left of her mother.

The door flung open and Amy's dad scooped her into a big hug. "Baby girl! How're you doing, honey?" Her dad nearly squeezed the life out of her with one of his epic embraces. He lifted her feet off the ground and spun her around in the air once before planting her feet on the floor again.

She landed with a thud. "Oof. Good to see you, too, dad. I'm well. I missed you." Amy leaned in and gave her father a quick peck on his stubbled cheek.

Jeff Harte stood tall at six foot. He weighed around two hundred pounds with broad shoulders that appeared they could carry the world upon them. She raised her eyes to his and saw for the first time in the last year the toll her mother's death took on him. Dark, heavy bags formed underneath his eyes. When he smiled, it did not reach his eyes. The sallow color to his skin and overgrowth of stubble on his cheeks added to the growing mountain of evidence that her father not only grieved, he worried. It didn't look like he'd slept in weeks.

Amy put on a hand gently on his forearm. "Dad, are you getting any rest?"

"Shoot, sleep is for the dead, isn't that what they say?" Her father squeezed her arm and grinned.

"Dad, it's me. Don't do that with me. Be honest. How bad is it? Are there any other funds we can tap to pay off the loan? Or any way to get them to give us an extension?" Amy raised her eyebrows, hopeful. She sat her purse down on the floor and shook the shoes off her feet. The aroma of rosemary roasted chicken, mashed potatoes, and buttery rolls wafted through the air.

"Listen, let's sit down and eat first. There's plenty of time for that talk later. I fixed us a good meal and I intend to enjoy it. Discussing houses and mortgages and loans depresses me. Come on, let's eat." Her dad placed an arm around her shoulder and guided her to the dining room.

"Okay." Amy walked into the homey dining room that had hosted many Sunday dinners, Thanksgivings, and Christmas' over the years. She recalled hours of homework completed at the ten-foot long oak table. Her dad had prepared a feast. Amy pulled the oak high-back chair out and sat down, scraping the leg against the floor for the millionth time in her life.

Once seated, her father prayed for the meal. He thanked God for all the good times He blessed their family with, for the life of her mother and what joy it brought, and for the home He gave them filled with love.

By the time he said Amen, tears stung her eyes. She blinked hard. "Thanks, dad, that was beautiful."

"Awe, nothing to it. Now, let's eat and you tell me all about the exciting life of an emergency physician at that fancy hospital."

Amy scooted mashed potatoes around her plate with a fork. "Well, I met a boy."

"Is he a boy or a man?" Amy's dad raised a questioning eyebrow.

"Ha ha, Dad. No, he's a man. A good man, I think. His name is Seth, he's the CFO for the hospital, so he has a good job, and he goes to church and is a Christian. I believe you would approve…

but, I'm not sure I want to get involved with anyone. I'm taking my time." Amy chewed her chicken and watched her father's reaction.

"That sounds like a good start. I must meet this young gentleman and see what I think. But a good job and being a Christian are two wins in my book." Jeff winked at his daughter.

The rest of the meal went by pleasantly with the two of them reminiscing about old times. Amy grew up as an only child, but that didn't take away from the immense love within her family. They talked about dance recitals, school play disasters, Amy's mom's cookies and tea, bicycle wrecks, and the Christmas when the chimney caught on fire (despite her dad being a firefighter in the past). She doubled over in laughter, clenching her sides when recalling this last story, which was Harte Lore and repeated many times over the years.

Her dad shook his head. "You'll never let me live that story down, will you? No one got hurt. I climbed onto the roof and put the fire out within a few minutes. The house was fine. You were fine. Your mom was fine. It was all fine." Amy's dad gestured with his arms and shrugged. He did not see the big deal about the Christmas Fire of 1995.

"You don't find it even slightly humorous or at least ironic that one of the town firefighters set his own house ablaze?" Amy guffawed again. Happy tears ran down her cheeks. The two of them laughed uncontrollably and finally Amy caught her breath. She sighed. "Oh my. That was funny, dad. You're funny... hey, I wanted to ask if you still have that old picture album of me from when I was a baby?"

"Yeah, I think it's upstairs in your bedroom." Her dad chewed another bite and smiled.

"Do you mind if I grab it and take it home for a little while?" She finished the last of the chicken, thankful for her first home cooked meal in weeks.

"No problem, sweetie, I'll go get it for you. I think I know where it is. Why don't you take these dishes into the kitchen and I'll be right back?" Amy's dad rose and walked up the stairs with slow steps, holding onto the railing. It reminded Amy of the years of age upon him.

Amy carried the empty dinner plates to the kitchen and placed them on the cream laminated countertop. She returned to the staircase near the front of the home and noticed her parent's wedding picture hung on the wall above it. Amy walked up the stairs and paused midway, inspecting the photo more carefully. In the photo, her mother was laughing at her dad while holding his arm as they walked down the aisle at the end of the wedding ceremony. He must have said something hilarious to her just as someone took the picture. His face resembled a man who had won the lottery. Amy's mom had her short dark hair swept into a chignon under a fingertip length white veil. She wore a white A-line gown with a cathedral length train. They looked blissfully happy. Her father returned down the stairs carrying her baby album. He saw Amy admiring the wedding photo and stopped to reminisce with her.

"She was a beauty, wasn't she? An absolute knockout. I don't know how I convinced her to marry me, but it was the best decision of my life to ask her." Tears welled up behind her father's eyes.

"I miss her, too, Dad. I know it's hard." Amy gave her dad's arm a squeeze. "Hey, you found it!" Amy nodded her head toward the album.

"Yep, you take it. It'll be good for you to look through it. There are a lot of pictures of you and your mom, too. Good times." Jeff continued down the stairs after handing the album over to Amy.

She took one last glance at her parent's picture on the wall and the life she knew prior to a year ago. She walked down the stairs slowly, letting her hand graze across the thick, smooth, mahogany handrail. When she got to the bottom, she paused, hoping this would not be the last time she gazed at that photo and walked down those stairs. Amy had to save this house. Not just for her father, but for herself, for her memories, for the last pieces of her mother that remained so vibrant here. She would get that promotion. With this final thought, she hugged her father goodnight, and set out more determined than ever to become Metropolitan Hospital's next Chief of the Emergency Medicine.

Chapter 11

July 10, 2017, Monday

Seth strode into the hospital with a spring in his step. He hadn't stopped thinking about Dr. Harte since his coffee outing with her after church. He still worried about getting hurt, but his mother's words of reassurance rung in his ears. He knew she was right. God did not give him a spirit of fear. To that point, he planned to confront Ed Baker today to turn in the most recent budgetary report and demand continued financial support for Open Hearts for the next year.

He hoped the rest of the Board members backed him, too. Seth squared his shoulders, determined to succeed. He rode the elevator up to the fourth floor and said hello to a few colleagues and the department secretary as he walked past. Seth noticed Ed's door remained closed, and he looked down at his watch. 8:15 am. Typically, Ed arrived in the building first and left last. He could be sloppy and a blow-hard, but Seth had to admit that Ed worked hard. *Maybe he's in a meeting.*

Just as he raised his hand to rap on the door, Seth heard muffled voices. One voice belonged to Ed Baker; he heard Ed's familiar bellow and one of his often-used "son-of-a-guns," but the other voice, he felt like he heard it before. Seth searched his memory trying to recall the second speaker. The mystery voice grew louder and laughed. "Ed, you know I'm your guy. Anything you or the Board needs. Metro is my main concern. I want to help where I'm needed. It's an honor to pitch in."

The voice lowered and Ed's voice boomed. "Mark, I knew I could count on you. Now, I've set nothing in stone, mind you, and I must go through the motions. We have to put on a good show, you know. I've got a few more interviews to do... let's see, Dr. Harte turned in a resume. Dr. Harte... she's newer, right? I don't know her well. It says here she completed her residency about a year ago... plus, she's not one of us. You know what I mean?" The two men erupted in laughter again.

Seth could envision them ribbing one another.

"Now Ed, I have to say Dr. Harte is an excellent physician. I think she told me she was the Chief Resident at Carilion Clinic. So, she's sharp. But, you're right, she joined the Metro family a year ago. I think she wants the promotion, though, if I'm being honest."

It was Mark. Seth could almost hear him winking through the wall. It sounded like they were discussing the Chief of Emergency Medicine job. If so, that could violate Board protocol. Even if Ed considered Mark as a top candidate for the job, it wasn't appropriate for Ed to discuss it without the Board present. Seth wondered if Mark would take the promotion if he knew Amy wanted and needed it.

The conversation neared an end, so Seth made a quick decision and knocked on the door. The voices fell silent.

Ed Baker opened the door to his office and wore an expression of surprise on his face at the sight of Seth. "Seth, son, how are you doing this fine morning?"

After appearing flustered, he regained his composure. "Sir, I'm well. I'm sorry to interrupt, but I wanted to drop off the quarterly numbers and speak with you before the Board meeting about Open Hearts." Seth looked between Ed Baker and Dr. Blakely. "Mark, funny meeting you here."

Mark seemed more stunned than Ed and took a few seconds longer to recover, but then he pasted his usual winning smile on his face. He stretched out his hand and shook Seth's. "Seth, good to see you again. Have a nice time yesterday?"

"I did, thank you for asking. What are you doing up here on the fourth floor? It's a long way from the ED." Seth stared at Mark. He didn't know what the two men were up to, but he did not trust Mark one bit.

"I'm getting ready to head downstairs to start my shift. I wanted to check in with my good buddy Ed. We're trying to iron out some details for an upcoming golf game and he wanted to discuss some hospital needs with me. I told him I'm always a team player and here to help when beckoned. Just like you, I'm sure." Mark stepped closer to Seth and tightened his jaw.

Seth clenched his fist and relaxed it. He took a deep breath and silently asked God to calm him. He turned his attention toward his boss. "I didn't want to interrupt your meeting, Ed, but if you have a moment, I want to go over this report with you."

"Certainly, my boy." Ed faced Mark. "Mark, I'll talk to you soon. I know you've got lives to save and important work to do. Oh, don't forget the Metro Ball is soon! Better line up your date! The Board likes to see a good attendance from its staff. Good for morale, you know." Ed slapped Mark across the shoulder.

Seth's stomach dropped. Everything in life revolved around politics. Cliques. Good-ol-boys' clubs. However, you painted the barn it was still red as his mom would say.

Mark shook Ed's hand a final time. "Absolutely, sir. I'll be there. And you know I'll have one of Scottsburg most eligible ladies on my arm. I wonder if Dr. Harte has plans, yet?" Mark threw Seth a pointed look and turned on his heel. He exited the room whistling with his hands shoved in his pockets.

Seth's blood boiled. That guy knew how to get under his skin.

Ed turned his attention to Seth. "That goes for you, too, Seth. I hope to see you at the Ball."

"Uh, well, I'm hadn't really thought about it... but about the report." Seth tried to change the subject, shoving his folder in front of his boss.

"Nonsense, you must attend. You're one of my top guys. We have to show the community that Metro cares and we're a strong family unit. So, that's settled. Now, about this report. How're we doing?" Ed had already turned around and sat at his desk. He picked up an uneaten muffin and dug in.

"The numbers for this last quarter are acceptable for the annual budget, even though we purchased some new surgical equipment and included the bonus for the Chief of Medicine position. The problem is that Open Hearts has not received as many donations over the last quarter as usual. I wanted to ask you, and the Board later at the meeting, to consider letting me send out letters to the community requesting support. I think families who have benefited from Open Hearts would help promote it and may even donate themselves. Lots of our families own small businesses in town with reasonable resources."

Seth's boss had a mouth full of muffin and swallowed, crumbs falling onto his pressed white dress shirt. "I'll tell you what. You fly it past the Board later and we'll see what they say. I don't have a problem with it, but if this little project of yours doesn't grow wings of its own, we may have to put it to bed." He took the folder from Seth's hand and glanced at the first page of Seth's annual report before closing it. "I'll take a look at the rest of the report later. Thanks for dropping it by."

He walked across his boss's office, ready to leave and feeling uncertain about the future of Open Hearts and Amy's chance for a fair interview. He paused at the doorway and turned to face Ed. "Sir, I don't know if you've decided about the Chief of Medicine position, but I wanted to be upfront and let you know that I'm taking Dr. Harte out for dinner Friday night. I just want to be honest about any conflict of interest, since I have a voting seat on the Board. I know they make the final decision based on your recommendation. I'll recuse myself from voting on the matter."

"Thank you for your honesty, Seth. We can let the Board know at the next meeting, but as long as you don't vote, I don't see a problem." Ed wore a dark grey suit with a navy tie. His portly abdomen fought against the buttons on his pressed white dress shirt, screaming for help. He shoved the rest of his blueberry muffin in his overstuffed mouth, talking between bites.

"Uh, sir, I don't want to pry and it's probably none of my business, but I couldn't help overhearing some of what you and Dr. Blakely discussed before I came in… what was Mark helping you with?" Seth held his breath, hoping he hadn't stepped over bounds.

"Oh, that. Nothing to worry about. I told him I wanted to know if I could count on him to help wherever needed. And he takes the helm on organizing our golf outings. A few of the other Board members wanted to hit the links at the Country Club this weekend. That's all."

Seth could tell he was being informally dismissed. He looked back at his boss, feeling uneasy about the future of Open Hearts and the discussion he interrupted between Ed and Dr. Mark. He hoped the Board remained open-minded and that he wouldn't have to trade in his tennis racquet for golf clubs to save his philanthropic endeavor. He walked down the hall toward his office, already planning a letter pleading for help from the community for Open Hearts. He would outline all the good the charitable program did for the families with cancer. It provided weighted blankets handmade by local artisans to patients. It gave art and music therapy opportunities to patients in-house undergoing chemotherapy and treatment.

Open Hearts assisted with funding for medical treatments and copays if the cost exceeded what insurances paid. It donated wigs, scarves, and other head coverings to make the patient more comfortable. The organization even provided funds for several terminal patients and their families to take a final dream trip. Seth thought about all the pain his family endured when Brian sat in a hospital bed, night after night, helpless to make him better. Having the encouragement and support of an organization like Open Hearts lifted both the family's and patient's spirits. It mattered.

Seth resolved that no matter what, he would save the organization. He owed it to his brother, to all the other families to come, and to his community.

Chapter 12

July 14, 2017, Friday

Amy held up a fifth dress in front of herself, studying her reflection in the full-length mirror inside her bedroom closet door. The body skimming wine dress had cap sleeves and a peplum. She scrunched her forehead. *Too business casual.* She held up a sixth choice: dark denim leggings and a satin, blush colored sleeveless blouse. She shook her head and tossed it aside. *Too 'datey'.*

Next, Amy selected a long maxi length dress with three quarter length sleeves and a tangerine ikat print on a charcoal background. *Nope, too church-y, plus too long.* At five-foot two-inches tall, she'd need at least four-inch heels so the dress wouldn't drag the ground. Four-inch heels meant a high likelihood of falling. She huffed and threw the long dress on top of a growing mound on her bed.

Amy scanned her room. Immaculate earlier that morning, it now looked like the day after a Barney's sample sale. *Wrecked...like tornado wrecked.* She sighed, blowing her freshly trimmed bangs out of her eyes. Why was choosing an outfit to wear for an evening with a handsome man so difficult? She wanted to look pretty. *No, that was a lie.* She wanted to look gorgeous, not like she was attending a business meeting.

She skimmed through her closet one last time, willing a

clothing inspiration to come to mind. Her eyes landed on a turquoise blue, short, flowing summer dress she bought a month ago. It still had the tags on it. It cinched in at the waist and boasted ivory lace across the upper back. If she added her brown belt and cropped dark denim jacket it would be perfect. Amy squealed and pulled her new camel lattice wedges off the closet shelf fresh out of the box. Nothing matched the joy of wearing a new pair of shoes. She grabbed the dress and jacket and shimmied into them quickly.

She dashed into the adjoining bathroom and looked at herself in the mirror. Her outfit was adequate, but her hair needed desperate help. She turned on her pink curling iron to create the perfect size curls for her chest-length hair. While it warmed up, she pulled out her makeup bag. Applying foundation, bronzer, peach blush, light pink lip gloss, mascara, and a subtle swipe of auburn eyeshadow across her eyelids calmed her. She dusted illuminator on her cheeks to give the illusion of a full night's sleep like a normal human being. Her makeup looked good. She moved on to her hair — the hard part.

Ever since high school, Amy struggled with hairstyling. She was a smart girl. How hard could it be? Very hard, it turned out. She recalled a time in high school when she took on the challenge of hot rollers. Instead of creating supermodel-type waves, she burnt all ten fingers and her forehead, while tangling one small roller in the underside of her hair. It took her mother two hours to remove it, and she nearly had to cut it out. *So, hot rollers were out.* Amy chuckled and picked up the curling iron and got to work.

Several minutes, and one near singe later, Amy's hair behaved. She did a final finger comb through her soft, beach-inspired waves and smiled at her reflection. *Good.* No, better than good. She looked... pretty, hopeful, and happier than in a long time.

After one last glance in the mirror, she turned off the light, snatched her phone from the nightstand, and shut her bedroom door, leaving the clothing bomb behind. As she started down the stairs, the doorbell rang. She took a deep breath to steady her nerves, crossed to the front door, and pulled it open.

Seth greeted her with a smile and look of admiration. "Wow! You look great! Are you ready to go?"

"Yeah, let me lock the door, and then I'm all set." Amy dug

through her small black and brown leather hobo bag, searching for her keys. Her purse resembled a labyrinth. "Sorry, I know they're in here somewhere… got it!" She locked her door, then turned around and smiled again. "Ok, ready."

Seth escorted her to the passenger side of his black SUV and held the door open for her.

Wow, chivalry lives. "Thanks." She slid into the soft, grey leather bucket seats and noted the immaculate state of his car. Her lips formed a half-smile.

Seth slid into the driver's seat and glanced at her with a quizzical look. "What's so funny?"

"Oh, I noticed how clean and well-kept your car is, and thought about how terrible my bedroom looks after trying on about twenty different outfits for tonight." She laughed. "You'd probably die if you saw it."

Seth chuckled and started the car. "No way. I'm tidy, but not pathologically clean. I wanted to make a good impression, so I dropped my car off earlier today at the detail shop. Your messy secret is safe with me." Seth sent her a grin and looked over his shoulder, backing out of the driveway. "Are you hungry?"

"Starving. I had a crazy busy day at work yesterday, and we were short staffed, so I had to stay and pull a second shift. I didn't get in until 7:00 this morning and then I crashed for most of the day. In the medical world, sleep takes precedence over hunger." Amy mused at this truth. When she woke up from her nap earlier, she only took time to consume a granola bar before beginning the process of nervous preparation for the evening. Her stomach growled, confirming her story.

Seth met her gaze and laughed. "You'll love this place." He made several careful turns, merging into traffic. "They usually have a live salsa band on Friday nights, and the food is amazing." Carrying on with easy conversation, Seth navigated around slower moving cars.

Amy studied him. Seth made her comfortable, as if she had known him her whole life. He felt a lot like home. "That sounds great." They pulled into the parking lot of the restaurant. An oversized, bright orange, neon light-up sign emblazoned with the words La Casa hung over a rustic, wood-paneled shanty. Small, spherical twinkle lights draped in a canopy above an outdoor space, where several diners sat chatting, eating, and laughing. A warm, enchanting glow welcomed them. "Wow! This place is beautiful. It looks magical."

Seth gestured for Amy to go first. "Wait until you taste the food." He walked up to the hostess stand and waited patiently to give the greeter their name.

"Hola! Buenos noches, amigos. How many?" The greeter wore a grey v-neck t-shirt and crisp dark denim jeans. He held several menus and smiled at Seth, waiting for a response.

"There's just two of us." Seth turned to Amy and held out a hand.

She hesitated for a moment but took it and smiled. Amy tried to concentrate on walking instead of Seth's warm skin pressed against hers.

"Perfect, follow me, right this way. I have the perfect table for you two." The host guided them to the outdoor dining area, and Amy followed behind him. She surveyed the space and noted several other couples present who were probably on dates. The place exuded a romantic vibe. She inhaled the scent of honeysuckle. Looking around, she found the source of the pleasant fragrance: several beautiful, red flowering plants covering a stone wall which ended at the beginning of a small stage. On stage a guitar, microphone, keyboard, bongo drums, and a horn rested, awaiting their turn in the spotlight. No performers joined the instruments yet. Amy's stomach flipped with nerves and excitement.

The host stopped in front of a small, two top table and pulled out Amy's seat for her. "Here you go, amigos. A seat for the beautiful lady." She eased herself into it, careful not to miss the landing and create a spectacle of herself. Grace was not her strongpoint. "Gracias." Amy, now planted, flashed a grin at the host.

The host left and Seth took his seat. "Do you speak Spanish? Your accent sounded good."

"I do. Not well, like I used to, I'm sure. I studied abroad in college for one summer at a small university along the northern coast of Spain. I love the language and the culture. It was one of the best experiences of my life. I took class during the day. Then, we explored the city in the evenings. A few times I went to the local salsa clubs there…I used to love dancing."

Seth placed his napkin in his lap and grinned. "That sounds amazing! I wanted to study abroad in college, but I couldn't take time away from the tennis team in college."

Amy returned his smile and unfolded her napkin, laying it across her legs. "It's a shame you didn't get to go somewhere, because I enjoyed that summer so much. Several days a week after class I took a towel and a book to the local beach and camped out on the sand for the rest of the day. My parents freaked out when I first told them I wanted to go to Spain. My mom worried about me traveling alone."

Seth chuckled, picking up a menu. "Believe me, I know about worried mothers. Mine's a professional."

Amy rolled her eyes and smiled. "That was my mom, a fretter. She meant well and loved me lots. I remember calling my parents halfway through the summer and telling them I wanted to live there forever. I think they panicked. Obviously, the summer ended, and I returned home. I adored it, though. That summer developed my love for travel and adventure, and it made me braver."

"Did you go alone?" Seth raised his eyebrows and waited for her response.

"Yeah. At the time I didn't have a lot of confidence. I think the summer in Spain gave me a chance to gain perspective. Before that trip, I lived each day ensuring my life looked immaculate from the outside. It drained me, trying to keep up an imaginary ideal."

Seth nodded.

"I wanted someone to love me. To think I was perfect and beautiful. I hadn't stopped in years to search my heart and listen to what God wanted for my life and who he wanted in my life. When I spent that summer on my own with God, I learned I could rest in Him, in knowing my identity was just that…being a child of God." Amy paused for the first time in several minutes, analyzing Seth's face to see if he was ready to run for the hills. This must all sound kind of crazy, huh?"

Seth shook his head. "No, I get it."

Amy feared she'd divulged too much too soon. She shrugged her shoulders. In the past, she would've beaten herself up, and started an internal monologue over-analyzing every word. Not now. Amy released perfectionism, so she counted it one victory won. No, her current battle lay solely with residual anger at God over her loss, her own guilt, and the grief. A fresh wave of tears threatened to expose her thoughts, so she turned toward the stage.

"Hey, are you ok?" Seth placed a comforting hand on hers.

"Yeah, I'm fine." Amy feigned interest in the musicians as they sound checked their equipment. Once the threat of full-on crying subsided, she met Seth's eyes again. "Anyway... to answer your question... I went alone to Spain. Things ended with my boyfriend before I left, and I didn't know anyone else on the trip, but I decided I wanted my life to be an adventure. I didn't want to live the rest of it paralyzed by fear, afraid to jump. So, I leapt."

Seth sent Amy an admiring gaze. "I think that's awesome! Even though I never studied abroad, I traveled to Europe right after college graduation. I did the backpacking and discovering-yourself-thing." Seth glanced at the stage as the horn player tested out his instrument.

Amy noticed slight stubble on Seth's cheeks, as if he missed a day or two of shaving. It gave him a rugged look she didn't mind at all. She loved how the edges of his eyes crinkled and formed slight lines around his temples when he smiled. Overall, she found him handsome, trustworthy, and full of wisdom. "Where'd you go?"

Seth's deep indigo eyes twinkled, and he became animated as he spoke about his college-era trip. "Everywhere: Rome, Pisa, Florence, Paris, London, Dublin, Edinburgh, Berlin, Switzerland. I love to travel, too. I think it opens your eyes to see the world and how other people live. You realize that as much as we're different, we're very much the same. And that God loves all of us."

Amy paused as the waiter came to the table to take their order. She ordered her favorite, a burrito superior. *Mmm, what food couldn't be improved by pouring melted, white cheese on top?* Seth ordered an exotic rice dish, which Amy believed secretly housed octopus within it. She debated mentioning this but decided against it.

The waiter walked away toward the kitchen with the orders, just as the rest of the band took their places on the small stage. "Hey amigos. Let's get this party going. Grab your lady and make your way to the front. Let's see some salsa heat in your feet!" The lead singer bellowed into the microphone with a strong Spanish accent. Seth looked at Amy and raised his eyebrows. "You game?"

If there was one thing Amy loved more than coffee, it was dancing. She took dance lessons as a child, but feared her skills were rusty. Medical school and residency had a way of interfering with fun. She sent Seth a half-smile and met his encouraging gaze. "Ok...you're on!"

Amy accepted Seth's hand and followed him to the front of the room where a small opening below the stage welcomed dancers. It soon filled up and she turned to face Seth as the singer belted out the words to the first song of the evening.

"Dejame Amarte... Dejame Amarte, mi corazon." The singer crooned as the drummer beat rhythmically on the bongo drums. The bass player strummed in the background and the horn bellowed several long, smooth notes. The music swelled.

Amy stepped backward with her right foot as Seth stepped forward with his left, beginning the familiar dance. She moved easily with him.

Seth caught Amy by surprise and spun her around.

She twirled and laughed throughout the rest of the song, and by its conclusion wore a permanent grin. The song ended, and all the restaurant goers erupted in applause for the band. Amy glanced at their table and noted the waiter had brought their food. "Hey, all that dancing made me hungry." She nodded toward the table. "Let's eat!"

Seth smiled and squeezed her hand. "Sounds good to me." He led her back to the table, his hand still interlocked in hers.

An unfamiliar feeling of warmth spread from Amy's stomach through her chest and settled in her face, betraying her feeble attempt at nonchalance.

Seth pulled out her chair and she took her seat.

Amy picked up her fork to dig in to her first bite when Seth cleared his throat. Her eyes flicked up to his.

Seth grinned and reached across the table to take both her hands in his. "Hey, let's pray."

He continued to surprise her. Amy prayed at home alone in the past without other people watching her. She talked with God a lot more before she had gotten so angry over losing her mom last year. Since then, most of her prayers consisted of tagging on an amen to the end of her father's dinner blessings.

Amy found it easier to avoid pain if she put God in a box. Letting Him out into all of her life, well, that could get messy. Her cheeks burned with uncertainty and embarrassment, but she obliged Seth, taking his hands in hers.

Seth closed his eyes and bowed his head and Amy followed suit. "Dear God, thank you for this time together. Thank You for the chance to know this beautiful woman better and to learn about her heart. Thank You for this food, for Your grace and love, and for making all things new. Amen." Seth concluded and looked up, serious, but smiling. He let go of her hands, grabbed his fork, and shifted gears, diving into his complicated seafood dish.

Amy raised her eyebrows in surprise. "Wow. That was some prayer. I don't know if I've ever said that many words out loud in front of someone else to God. Actually, I don't know if I've ever said that many words out loud to God period. You make it seem so… easy." She picked up her fork and picked through her burrito trying not to appear too eager. Her stomach grumbled betraying her pretense of civility and manners, so she shoveled melted cheese and chicken into her mouth. Three bites into her meal, she took a breath and spoke again. "Have you always been that comfortable praying?"

Seth chuckled, shaking his head. "No. Not always. I think it got easier and more natural with time. When I grew up, we went to church, but not every Sunday. Definitely for major holidays. Easter, Christmas, Mother's Day. Maybe Thanksgiving weekend. Sometimes for Vacation Bible School, but that was more like a week of games, crafts, and junk food. Then, I went away to college and my roommate disappeared every Friday night. He'd leave the dorm room around 6:30 pm and stayed out until midnight. I didn't know him well and didn't want to intrude, but I also didn't know many people at college."

Amy raised her head and paused, her fork in the air. "Sorry to interrupt, but where did you go to college?"

"I went to the University of Virginia. All the Broadstone's went to UVA. It's a family tradition. Then, I got my Master of Finance at Vanderbilt. Very prestigious. Very serious. Very expensive." He made a stoic face like a statue.

Amy laughed. "Not your scene?"

"No, I loved both schools. I don't want to sound ungrateful or anything. I studied business and finance and got a wonderful education. I also made amazing friends and connections for work. Status never was important to me, though. Going to a fancy, expensive, big name school wasn't my dream. Now, my parents...it mattered a lot to them. That's how I landed at UVA."

She scraped the last piece of tortilla off her plate. "You didn't want to disappoint your parents." Amy stated this as a fact rather than an observation.

Seth's brow furrowed and he murmured, "Something like that."

She hoped she hadn't upset him. Amy wiped her mouth with her napkin and steered the conversation toward a lighter topic. "So, where did this roommate run off to on the weekends?"

Seth relaxed his face. "So, my roommate seemed to have a blast every weekend. One week I asked him where he went every Friday night. He dared me to come with him if I wanted to find out. Now, I have never been one to turn down a dare." Seth wore a challenging grin. "So, I tagged along. I honestly thought as cryptic as he was being about the whole thing that it had something to do with a fraternity or secret society. I thought maybe a hazing event for freshmen awaited me."

"Imagine my surprise when we pulled into the parking lot behind the science and engineering building at school. We parked and walked into the oldest building on campus to the large teaching auditorium. It floored me when I opened the door and found it filled with hundreds of students. I turned to him and asked what he'd dragged me to, but I couldn't hear his answer over the roar of everyone laughing and talking. Then, I noticed a band at the front on an ancient stage. The lead singer started playing a song about thanking and praising God during both bad and good times." Seth sang softly the final few words to a song vaguely recognizable to Amy.

The words sounded soulful. He had a rich, thick voice, and it surprised Amy. "I didn't know you could sing!"

Seth shrugged his shoulders, his face flushing, "I'm not great, but I love it."

"Stop it. You're amazing! I can't sing at all. That was great!" Amy's eyes locked with Seth's and she marveled at how he drew her to him. Fine goosebumps prickled her arms and her spine tingled.

Seth's neck turned crimson. "Well, I've sang with friends at school functions or family get-togethers most of my life. I started singing for the church about a year ago. I only join the worship team one Sunday a month, though."

"I think you're great! Seriously, I'm super impressed." Amy mentally added singer and dancer to Seth's list of admirable qualities.

He cleared his throat. "So, I sat in this auditorium and the band sang a killer rock song talking about how great God is, even when things don't go the way we want them to in life. I thought to myself, this doesn't make sense. Why would someone be happy if things went badly? There were hundreds of college students jumping, clapping, and agreeing with the words. It was a crazy scene."

Amy sent a half-smile to Seth. "It sounds like a party."

Seth nodded his head. "It looked like one. The song ended and the main speaker took the stage. He welcomed everyone to Collegiate Christian Assembly, CCA for short, and everyone cheered. I'd never heard of the group before. I'll be honest, for a second I considered running for the door." Seth laughed as he recalled the memory. "But, the more the speaker talked, the more I heard the truth in what he said. His words got through to me, you know?"

She nodded in agreement but remained close-lipped.

Seth sat his napkin on his plate and took a sip of water before continuing his story. "The leader talked about how none of us can do life well alone. He said we all make mistakes and mess up but all we need to be happy is to know Jesus. I'd never heard it put that way before. I knew he was right. So, at that exact moment, I gave my heart to Jesus. It totally changed my life." Seth rubbed his hands together. "It wasn't all rainbows and butterflies from then on. I struggled in my walk with God and wrestled with hard stuff…but my life was good because I knew I wasn't alone, and I always had God. That made all the difference for me." Seth finished his testimony and looked at Amy, searching her face for understanding.

Amy's eyes welled up again. A single tear streamed down her cheek. "Wow. That's beautiful. I'll be honest, I got saved when I was eight years old, but…" Amy drew in a deep breath. "I've had a hard time this last year having a relationship with God. It's hard for me to understand why a God who loves me, a God who knows my heart, would want something so awful to happen in my life. To lose my mom, who I still needed, on the same day of my graduation... it's hard to process experiencing your best day on your worst one." Amy shook her head.

Seth smiled sympathetically, encouraging her to continue.

"I'd be lying if I told you I understand, or that I've accepted it yet. I've been so angry that I cut off all communication with God until recently. Until a few weeks ago when I came to church. And you know what? It feels good. Hard, but good." Amy finished her heartfelt speech and clamped her mouth shut, embarrassed by her emotional outburst.

Seth smiled with reassurance and placed a hand on top of hers.

She welcomed his touch and looked down at her plate, astonished to find it empty.

The waiter returned to check on them. "All done here? Can I get you anything else?"

Seth raised his brow at Amy, and she shook her head. Seth looked up at the waiter. "No, we're good."

Amy glanced at her phone to check the time. "Oh, my gosh! It's almost time for the concert to start. I didn't realize it had gotten so late!"

"You know what they say. Time flies..." Seth smiled. "We'd better get going. You don't want to miss this band. They're crazy good, especially the drummer. I used to play in high school and this guy kills."

"Well, let's go. I can't miss this killer drummer." Amy gathered her bag and brushed a few residual crumbs off her lap. She watched Seth dig in his wallet and questioned why she had shared so much of her heart with him after spending the past year avoiding her feelings. She feared letting him in to her life. She couldn't bear to lose someone else she cared for but seemed unable to shut him out. He made her feel safe, and the more time she spent with God, the more she wanted to let go of her fear, pain, and grief.

Seth reached his hand out for hers. He dropped sixty dollars on the table, enough to cover the meal and a large tip.

Amy made a mental note. Check generosity off the list, too. In junior high school, Amy made a checklist of future-husband-qualities and hid it in her ancient Bible, now falling apart at the seams. A seventh grader wrote it, so it read more like a Christmas wish list. Amy shook her head at the ridiculousness of it. She wrote it one summer at a vacation bible school. She had read and reread it many times over the years and now had it memorized. The List likely contributed to her current singleness. Her best-friend-in-the-entire-world, Beth, often scolded Amy's unrealistic expectations. Amy kept high standards and with college, then medical school, and residency, she didn't have time for… nonsense. She smiled.

Seth looked at her with a lopsided grin.

Yes, The List. At the top of it read Must love God and follow Jesus. The rest of it included being generous, kind, a good listener, a hard worker, and a musician. Seth checked off all of her list.

"What's on your mind." Seth squeezed her hand as they exited the restaurant.

Amy's pulse quickened and she felt like a junior high girl again. Butterflies flitted inside her stomach and her palms sweat. *Why did Seth make her so nervous?* Because he promised long-term potential, and it both exhilarated and scared her.

"Oh, nothing, just thinking about how great dinner was and how much I enjoyed dancing with you." Amy peered down at their hands, still clasped together, and never wanted to let go. She arrived at Seth's car and he dropped her hand to open the door for her again. *Gentleman. Check.* That wasn't on her list, but she should add it. Amy turned toward him.

He stepped closer. Seth brushed a loose strand of hair off her cheek and his fingers lingered for a moment. He paused, and for a moment Amy thought he might kiss her.

A few short weeks ago she feared letting God and Seth into her heart and life. Standing with mere inches separating them, staring into his piercing eyes, she willed him to press his lips against hers.

Seth leaned in at the same time a car alarm started blaring nearby in the parking lot.

The sound startled Seth and his hand fell from her cheek. He laughed and squeezed her hand. "Thank you for coming with me and sharing your heart. Now, we better go, or we'll be late. Also, if we stand here any longer, we might go deaf."

She sunk into the car seat and took a deep breath. The car alarm screamed for attention, but Amy only heard the beating of her own heart. Their near kiss sent it pounding like the drum in the restaurant.

Seth slid into the driver's seat, started the car, and headed toward a new adventure.

Chapter 13

July 14, 2017, Friday

Seth pulled into the church parking lot, now rapidly filling up, and a volunteer wearing an orange vest guided him to an open spot. He speculated that at least five hundred people came tonight, maybe more. Seth parked the car, hopped out and walked around to Amy's side, opening the door for her. He reached for her hand and she exited the car, pressing in close to him to gain her balance and smooth out her dress. Seth drew in a breath, surprised at how she affected him. He wanted to put his feelings into words to tell her, but instead murmured, "Ready?"

She straightened and turned her attention to the growing crowd funneling into the church building. Amy opened her mouth and closed it again with hesitation. She nodded her head, "Ready."

He smiled and led her into the large church auditorium which held up to nine hundred people. It provided stadium seating and a huge, professional looking stage. Hundreds of flashing lights in various colors filled the backdrop of the stage, each strobing in rhythm to the music funneled through the sound system. The band waited in the wings of the stage and people stood elbow to elbow trying to find seats.

On a normal Sunday, hundreds of people came. All ages filled the church, but the majority included young adults, families with children, and teens. It looked like everyone who usually attended brought at least one to two guests tonight. Seth shouted over the roar of laughing, talking, and chaos. "Where do you want to sit?"

Amy cupped her hands around her mouth to make her voice heard. "Wherever you want is fine with me!"

"Let's go to the front. I see some of my friends there and we can view the band better." Seth, with his hand pressed in hers, guided her to the front of the church. He couldn't wait to introduce Amy to some of his church friends.

The evening was going better than he imagined. He'd enjoyed hearing about Amy's childhood and college years, and he loved dancing with her. It remained the highlight of the evening. He confessed holding her close, even if only for a few minutes on the dance floor, ignited something inside his heart and made his pulse quicken.

Despite facing a tough year with losing her mom, Amy seemed to soften. When she shared with him her grief and the struggle to continue her walk with God, it touched him. He knew the difficulty of trusting God in the middle of a storm, or even in the aftermath of it. He still wrestled with the fear of losing Brian or someone else he loved. Seth hoped to talk with Amy more about Brian and introduce her to his family soon. He continued to make his way toward his friends and the front row of the auditorium.

Chapter 14

July 14, 2017, Friday

Great. The front row. Amy was not shy, not really. However, she preferred to avoid the front row at church. She took into account the bright light beaming down and the preacher staring at her and speaking soul-piercing truth. It made her feel like she was standing trial and should walk on stage and confess all her sins. Just get them out of the way. She gave a half-smile. Also, standing near the front of anything involving a bright spotlight invited her to make a fool of herself by falling, tripping, or otherwise mismanaging her limbs. Never mind the risk of a wardrobe malfunction. She shuddered, then she pasted a forced smile on her face. "Great!" *Just great.*

Seth and Amy weaved through the maze of bodies, hands still clasped, and arrived at the front. Two guys with dark black hair and a girl with long blond, beachy waves stood next to two free seats. Amy guessed they were close to her age.

Seth introduced her with a wave of his hand. "These are my friends, Jordan, Jessie, and Matt. Guys, this is Amy."

"Hey, it's great to meet you!" Jessie, the girl with the effortless blond waves, stretched her arm out to shake Amy's hand. She experienced a twinge of jealousy, but Jessie smiled so warmly that Amy immediately regretted it. Jessie gave her a hug and Amy's shoulders relaxed.

Amy shook hands with Jordan and Matt next. "Nice to meet you, too." They both smiled and she instantly felt grafted into the group. She glanced at her phone and saw the concert was about to start. The lead singer took the stage and everyone in the auditorium jumped to their feet and clapped. A clamorous patron yelled, "Woohoo."

The lead singer waved. "Thank you. My band and I feel blessed to be here tonight. It's an honor to worship with you and give God all the praise He deserves. Are you guys ready for an awesome night?" He raised his hands and clapped.

The audience responded, and then some. "Yes, yeah, woohoo."

Excitement coursed through Amy's veins. She hadn't been this enthusiastic about church and God in years. She jumped to her feet, and the guitarist strummed the first intro chord to a song Amy recognized about the power of faith and encouraging people to persevere. She looked over at Seth and smiled at him, and he reached over and took her hand. The words pierced her heart. She appreciated the truth of them deep in her soul, as if God had placed them there for her. Warmth and peace washed over her. Song after song, Amy heard confirmation of God's love for her and the promise of hope for a good future. *Beauty for ashes*. Amy's mom always told her when life got hard, God would give her beauty for ashes. She never understood what that meant before now. The concert flew by and when the band finished the final song, Amy hungered for more.

She said goodbye to Seth's friends and followed him outside. She got in his car and rode home in comfortable silence.

Seth pulled into Amy's driveway and turned off his car. He got out and walked around to Amy's door, once again opening it for her.

She slipped out, and he shut the door behind her before walking her to the front door. She fumbled around in her purse, in another frustrating search for her keys. It took her several seconds of digging to find them buried in a deep corner of her bag. She pulled them out and paused before placing them in the lock. Amy turned toward Seth. "Thank you for tonight. Seriously, it was one of the best evenings I've had in a long time. I had a great time at dinner. The food was amazing, and the dancing was fun, but the concert at church blew me away. I feel lighter, changed... in the best way…and thanks for listening to me. You're great." Amy stumbled over her final words and looked down at her feet.

Seth put his right hand on her cheek, gently lifting her face up toward his while sweeping away a tendril of hair with his left hand. He gazed deeply into her eyes.

Warmth spread from Amy's chest up to her cheeks. She closed her eyes and waited.

Seth tenderly grazed her forehead with his lips. "I think you're great, too." He took a step away from her. "Let's do this again. Next Saturday?"

She pondered the forehead kiss. Confused, Amy simply smiled and bobbed her head up and down. "Saturday. See you then." She opened her door and entered her home. After shutting the door behind her with a thud, she leaned against it, taking a deep breath. *Saturday.*

Chapter 15

July 14, 2017, Friday

Seth drove home and marveled at how well the evening went. He kicked himself for not kissing Amy on the lips. He wanted to, for sure. His relationship with Amy meant a lot to him and he wanted to take his time and do everything right. Plus, there still stood the complication of working at the same hospital. He didn't want to rush anything. Seth always guarded his heart and built up walls, but Amy tore them down each moment they spent together. He couldn't wait to see her again. Saturday seemed like a month away instead of a few days. He wanted to take her to one of his favorite spots in town and talk with her more about Brian and his family. Seth gave a half-smile as he turned down the road leading to his townhouse.

In the meantime, he needed to focus on fundraising efforts for Open Hearts. He ran the numbers again yesterday and unless a miracle happened, he couldn't make the balance sheet equalize for the next year. The Board planned to meet in the next week or two to discuss the current year's budget and the next year's fiscal projections. If he couldn't find a way for the hospital to fund Open Hearts, then outside donations provided the only other option to salvage the non-profit organization.

He knew Ed Baker wanted him in attendance at the Metro Ball to support the hospital. He had considered inviting Amy to accompany him, but he didn't want to pressure her by inviting her on a second date to such a high-profile event. Also, the Metro Ball presented networking possibilities and Seth needed to focus on schmoozing the Board members and other higher-ups at the Ball to woo them to support Open Hearts. Perhaps a generous benefactor might be empathetic to the organization's needs and goals. Based on the amount needed, it might take several benefactors. He shook his head. He wouldn't worry about it tonight. He had until the next Board meeting to find a solution and until then he wanted to enjoy thinking about the way Dr. Amy Harte's smile made him his heart pound.

Chapter 16

July 15, 2017, Saturday

Beth, Amy's down-to-earth, spunky, tell-it-how-it-is best friend ticked items off on her fingers like a shopping list while she talked. "So, you mean to tell me you guys had a romantic dinner, danced, shared meaningful moments together at church… and he does all this chivalrous, manly stuff like opening doors for you, paying for the date, and walking you to your front door, but then he kissed you on the forehead?!?" Beth's mouth hung open and then shut in obvious disbelief and disapproval.

Amy finished chewing her bite of a delicious chocolate muffin, swallowed, and muffled a matter of fact, "Yeah."

Beth stared at her with expectation. Her pixie short platinum blond hair further emphasized the striking color of her aqua eyes. At five feet tall, most people underestimated Beth. She was, however, a powerhouse in every sense of the word. Years of teaching intense hour-long cycling classes combined with her regimented vegan diet produced a small, yet mighty, frame. Beth clocked in at a size two, but that didn't take away from how intimidating she could be when necessary. When required, she meant business… and her current business included grilling Amy about her recent romantic entanglement. Beth wanted all the details and Amy knew her friend well enough to know Beth would pursue the information tenaciously until satisfied with the answers.

She sent Beth a blank look. "What?"

Beth scanned Amy's face with suspicion in her eyes. After a long pause, she planted her hands on her hip. "What do you mean, what? That will not fly with me and you know it, sister. Come on, cough it up. I know there's more to this story. I mean, all this romance and that's how the night ended?"

Amy raised her right hand as if taking an oath. "I'm telling you a hundred percent the truth. He kissed me on the forehead. That's it. Then, he left. Nothing else to tell."

Beth clasped her hands together, begging for more details. "But, how does that make you feel? What kind of kiss is a forehead kiss? My grandma kisses me on the forehead. My dad kisses me on the forehead. I think my pastor might have even kissed me on the forehead once when I was four years old. But, never, and I mean ever, has a romantic date concluded with a (Beth made air quotes) Kiss On The Forehead! At the very least, I feel a hug would've been a better choice. Or no kiss at all? Leave you wanting more kind of thing. Some mystery. So, does this mean you guys are just friends? Does he think of you as a little sister? Was this an appreciation meal for taking such good care of his brother? Like a payback kind of thing?" Beth finally stopped her rapid-fire questioning to take a breath. Unfortunately, she was as neurotic as Amy. Typically, Beth stood on the receiving end of the exposition on the do's and don'ts of first date etiquette.

Honestly, Amy didn't know why she wasn't more upset about the forehead kiss. Perhaps the events of the past few weeks had left Amy too exhausted to review the recent episode in the "life of Amy" thoroughly. Or maybe all the stuff about seeking peace and letting go of anger and worry was taking effect. Amy shrugged her shoulders. "Dunno." Amy took another bite of muffin and a swig of coffee. "It didn't feel like a (more air quotes) 'just friends' kind of kiss, but it also didn't land anywhere near my lips or even on my cheeks. Maybe it's for the best. This way, if we never go out again, or only as friends, then I'll harbor no feelings of humiliation or regret. And if we go out again and something more develops, then I'll know it's real... not just a physical thing. You know?"

Beth stared at Amy as if she sprouted a third head. "Well, it's your funeral. Sounds like a wonderful way to make a relationship (again with the air quotes, those were annoying) 'Dead On Arrival' as you doctors like to say. Besides, what about Mark? I see how he looks at you at work. How is Dr. Ruggedly Handsome? Hmm?" Beth smiled behind her favorite mug, which she insisted on bringing with her from home. It read "The Tears of My Enemies" across the front. She took a sip and waited for All. The. Details.

Amy swatted away her friend's prying with her hand. "Oh, would you stop? There is nothing going on with Mark. He works with me daily. So, that's complication number one. I'm fairly confident he finds fault with my newfound interest in God, so there's complication number two. Oh, and rounding out the situation is complication number three: He. Dates. All. The. Women. How could I trust his intentions? He's never had a relationship that lasted longer than a loaf of bread." Amy snorted and spewed coffee on her pristine white t-shirt. Well, that's what she got for gossiping about someone. She grabbed a napkin off the table and blot the stain, her cheeks warming with remorse.

Beth's eyes widened, and she leaned in. "Yeah, but you have to admit. He's super cute. Beyond cute. Drop dead gorgeous comes to mind. And he's medical, so he loves blood and guts and all the gross stuff like you do." Beth made a face of disgust and stuck out her tongue. "And he likes you. It's so obvious. Didn't he ask you out a few weeks ago?"

She threw the napkin on the table and tossed her hands up in frustration. "Oh, come on! You love the drama. Yes, it's true, he asked me out on a date in his own carefree way several weeks ago and I said no. I don't think he meant it and even if he did, I don't want to go. Can you imagine that date? It would be me watching him flirt with another girl by the end of the night, probably a tall blond who is not me. No. No, thank you. I have enough problems to sort out in my life. I don't need more." Amy sucked in a breath before continuing her speech when she noticed a funny look on Beth's face.

Furrowing her eyebrows, Beth sent Amy a pointed stare. She nodded her head toward the counter behind Amy.

Amy clamped her mouth closed. She turned around slowly in her chair, pretending to get the coffee barista's attention. She came face to face with Mark. Right then she knew Mark likely heard a lot of her tirade. Nausea washed over Amy. *Well, that's just great.* Heat surged up her neck. She wanted to vanish, or at least slink down her chair and under the small table between herself and Beth. Instead, she pasted a forced smile on her face. "Ma-arrk, how's it going? Funny running into you here, again! You must love coffee." *What a silly thing to say. Of course, he loves coffee. Who doesn't love coffee? It's coffee. The most glorious substance God ever created. Wait, that's not true. Chocolate was the most glorious, but coffee remained a close second.*

"Amy, who's your friend here? She looks familiar. Have we met before?" Mark stretched out his hand towards Beth.

Beth shook it. She appeared delighted by the turn of events and wore a mischievous grin. "Not officially. I started work as a respiratory therapist at the hospital a month ago, but I spend most of my shift on the medical or critical care floor. You've probably seen me around the Emergency Department, but we've never been formally introduced. Amy told me all about you, though."

Amy glared at her best friend, sending daggers her way. Amy's face burned, both from anger and embarrassment. "Beth," she said through gritted teeth. She turned toward Mark again. "She's kidding. She likes to kid. She just means I've told her a lot about work and so, you know, your name came up from time to time because of that." Amy stopped talking and mentally made a list of ways to torture Beth once he left.

Mark clutched his hand to his chest. "I'm flattered either way. I'm glad I ran into you here."

"Oh, really, why's that?" Amy leaned back, concerned about Mark's motives for his visit.

"I wanted to see if you would accompany me to the hospital's Metro Ball. If it makes you feel better, you can call it a work outing. I'm sure I could use a chaperone to ensure my good behavior. Plus, Ed told me he'd love it if you and I attended together as the face of the Emergency Department." Mark winked at Amy. "He's supposed to make a preliminary announcement about the next Chief, too."

Just say no. Just say no. Just say no. "Uh, I'll think about it." *Agh!* When would Amy learn to keep her mouth shut? No, that wasn't the issue. Amy found Mark attractive. He was wrong for her for many reasons, but still, there it was; he was handsome. She chided herself for admitting it to herself. "Isn't this event a big deal? Like black tie big deal?"

"Exactly! See, I win on two accounts. One, I'll have a responsible date who'll keep me in line for most of the evening. And two, I'll get to escort the most beautiful woman in the room." Mark threw another wink her way.

Amy sighed. *What was with the winking? Did he have something in his eye?* "I'll think about it, but only because technically it's a work function. It wouldn't be a date. Also, if I say yes, you must be on your best behavior. Professional." Amy shook her finger at Mark like a parent to a child requiring reprimand. *Well, let's face it. He behaved like a child sometimes.* She laughed.

Mark raised his dark eyebrows. "What's so funny?"

"Oh, just imaging what everyone in the hospital would say if they saw the two of us at the Ball together. I'm sure the rumor mill would fire up in no time." Amy set her mouth in a firm line at the thought of the ensuing gossip if she accepted Mark's invitation.

"Who cares what other people say? Besides, maybe it won't all be a rumor." Mark leaned in closer to Amy and threw her a devilish grin.

Amy shifted away from him. "Mark! It's not a date. Professional!"

"Ok, ok. I'll try to behave myself, but no promises. Pick you up Friday night, one week from now, at 7:00 p.m.?"

"Let me think on it a little more… I'll let you know by early next week at work. Ok?" Amy hoped Mark accepted this morsel and might allow her to postpone a final decision for now.

Mark nodded in concession. "Ok, Amy, I'll let you off the hook for now, but think about it. It'd look good for the hospital's two top ER docs to show up together at the Metro Ball and I'm sure it would please Ed. Don't forget about making an impression on him for the promotion. I'll check in with you later this week." Mark waved goodbye to Beth and winked one final time at Amy before heading out the coffee shop door.

Beth grinned. "Why aren't you going with Seth to this shindig?"

Amy fiddled with her mug. "Well, we haven't told Human Resources at the hospital anything about our relationship because I'm not sure if there's anything to tell. So, if I go with Seth what does that mean? Are we a couple? What will the hospital say?"

Amy shook her head. "I don't want to create problems at work until I know how he feels about me and the promotion is finalized. I can't do anything to jeopardize it right now. If I go to the Ball with Mark at Ed's request, then it would be only as colleagues."

"You realize Mark came in here just to talk to you, right?" Beth raised her cup and took a sip of her drink.

"What are you talking about? You're crazy. It's a coffee shop, Beth." Amy sat up straighter and squared her shoulders.

"Yeah, and did you see him get any coffee?" Beth wore a smug grin on her face.

"Oh." *Hmm. No, this was not good... and likely to get complicated.*

"Uh-huh, oh." Beth took another sip of her green tea and smiled behind her cup to hide her amusement from her best friend.

Chapter 17

July 17, 2017, Monday

Amy walked past the nurse's station in the Emergency Department during her lunch break with fierce determination in her eyes and purposeful direction in her steps. She was a woman on a mission. She awoke that morning with the realization that only a few weeks remained to save her childhood home. The idea made her stomach churn.

Her mother's memory felt slightly more distant each day. After her date with Seth, the impulse to call her mom and tell her about the date struck Amy. The pang of grief that she would never talk with her mom in this lifetime washed over her. She wanted to share with her mother what Seth said, where they went, how much she liked him, and how she enjoyed singing at the concert and spending time in God's presence. Amy imagined her mom teasing her about her atrocious singing voice.

She wore her comfortable green scrubs with her worn black clogs but tried to walk with her head held high to look like she had her life together. She still felt lost without her mom. Hot tears burned her eyes and her throat tightened. She glanced at her phone and contemplated listening to one of the few remaining messages on her phone from her mother. She couldn't bring herself to delete them. Knowing she carried her mom's voice with her was a small comfort. Seeing the time, Amy realized there was no time for that now. She arrived at the elevator, pressed the button, and waited. Staring down at her feet, she took a deep breath. *It would be ok. It had to be.* The elevator door opened, and Amy stepped in, heading toward her destination: Ed Baker's office.

By the time she arrived at Ed's office door, rings of sweat formed under her arms causing her to look like a marathon runner. She wiped beads of perspiration off her forehead and knocked on his door with a shaking hand.

"Come on in. Door's unlocked." Ed didn't value pretense.

Amy pasted her most convincing smile on her face and opened his door.

Ed raised his head as she entered the room. "Dr. Harte, to what do I owe this unexpected pleasure?" He sat at his desk eating the largest hero submarine sandwich Amy ever saw. He took a bite and pieces of shredded lettuce fell from his mouth to the paper on his desk below. Miscellaneous forms scattered the desk in what resembled a disheveled mosaic. Golf clubs leaned in the corner of a mahogany bookshelf holding books stacked with no clear organization. The towering bookshelf matched his imposing desk. The entire office smelled of musk cologne mixed with salami. *Fun.*

Amy stepped in further.

Ed gestured for her to take a seat.

She planted herself in a brown tufted leather chair opposite his desk, facing him. "Um… I'm sorry to come by unannounced… but, I hadn't heard if or when you planned to hold interviews for the Chief of Emergency Medicine position… and, um, I wanted to make sure you received the copy of my resumé… and knew how interested I am in the job, sir." Amy stopped talking and stared at a lone piece of lettuce now wedged between Ed's two front teeth.

"Well, now, I believe I saw your resume here somewhere on my desk." Ed rifled through about thirty pages and pulled out one housed under his precious sub. The paper now appeared to have oil stains on it and was wearing part of Ed's lunch. "Ah, here it is. Right where I thought I'd left it. So, nothing to worry about. I've got it right here." Ed patted her form and resumed shoveling bites into his already half-full mouth, as if the conversation ended.

"Uh, well that's great, sir. The thing is, I hadn't heard about the job. So, I didn't know if you would have formal interviews?" Amy raised her eyebrows.

"Well, now don't you worry. I'll let you know. I'm more of an on-the-job evaluator, know what I mean? I'll tell you what. I'll take another look at your resumé, and swing by the Emergency Department later. I like to talk to the other employees that work with people in consideration for a promotion. Get the team evaluation and all that. And I think it'd go a long way if you plan to attend the Metropolitan Hospital Ball. You'll be there, right?" Ed wiped some mustard off the corner of his mouth.

Amy's mouth felt glued shut. "Well, I hadn't decided for certain... I know most staff will attend it."

"Nonsense, you must come. It looks good for the hospital to have its lifesaving doctors there. I think it sends the message to the community that the hospital cares. I know Dr. Blakely will be there. Why don't you two come together and represent the face of the ED? I'll think about this promotion more and like I said, I'll talk with the staff. Also, when you're at the Ball, it'll give you a chance to talk with the other Board members, which never hurts."

"Ok-okay, sir. I'll plan to be there. But, sir, about Dr. Blakely, I don't know—" Ed cut her off mid-sentence.

"It's settled then. You and Dr. Blakely will attend together. I'll look for you and we can discuss this promotion business more then. Now, I'd love to sit here and shoot the breeze with you, Dr. Harte, but I've got to get ready for an important meeting in thirty minutes." With his final word on the matter, Ed turned a more serious eye toward his sandwich, dismissing her.

Amy rose from the chair, spun on her heel, and scurried out the door. The turn of events confused her. Whether she wanted to, she was going to the Metro Ball. Perhaps she could meet Mark there. Maybe Ed Baker wouldn't be any wiser. Hopefully, once he spoke with the staff in the ED and reviewed her brief, but impressive, resumé, he would give her a shot at the Chief job. She convinced herself she had a chance, because the Chief promotion held her last hope to save her parent's home. Amy shook her hands out and walked back to the elevator.

As the elevator doors parted, Mark exited. He smiled and gave her one of his winks. "What is Dr. Amy Harte doing on the fourth floor? Checking up on the Chief Financial Officer?" Mark's eyes clouded.

Amy placed her hands on her hips and tilted her head. "Not

that it is any of your business, but I met with Mr. Baker." Amy didn't know why, but she preferred Mark not know the details of her meeting with her boss.

"Well, that's a coincidence. Old Ed told me to meet him, too." He walked past her toward Ed's office, but paused and turned around. "Oh, I wanted to see what time I should pick you up for the Ball? You didn't think I'd forget, did you?"

Amy shifted her weight. "Uh, funny you should mention that Mark, Ed just told me he hoped he would see us there and how great it would be if we came together, you know, to put on a good front for the ED and the hospital. So, yeah, I guess it's on." Amy's cheeks burned.

"Great! It's a date! I'll probably see you later this week, but if not, I'll pick you up Friday. 7:00 pm." Mark threw her another wink and headed down the hall, whistling to himself.

She marveled that Ed had dismissed her for a meeting with Mark but tried to move past it. "It's not a date! It's a work outing!" Amy shouted at Mark as he walked away.

Chapter 18

July 21, 2017, Friday

Since her first evening out with Seth, they had shared two more casual coffee dates and one lunchtime stroll. Now, Amy prepared for her first and only intended evening out with Mark. She blew her bangs off her forehead and sighed. Standing alone once again in her bedroom amidst a clothing tornado, she weighed her options. This time she took a different approach.

Although she didn't want to look hideous, Amy also didn't want to give Mark encouragement. He didn't require much. The Metropolitan Hospital Ball demanded professional attire, too. Tomorrow morning the aftermath of the fancy-shmancy hospital event would be the talk of the town. All the big wigs attended the gala, including the hospital's CEO. Ahead of her lay an evening fraught with complications layered by added pressure to attain a crucial work promotion and finished with the pièce de résistance: evening wear. So, no stress.

Amy wondered how an evening gown stunned in a department store mirror, but later resembled a shiny potato sack once donned at home. She exhaled and picked up her wardrobe selection for the evening: a deep plum satin one-shouldered concoction. Stepping into the frock, her fingers trembled. Once in place, she scrutinized the effect. It draped across her chest and gathered with ruching around her waist before flowing outward in an A-line skirt. She tilted her head. *Not bad.* It flattered her natural hourglass shape, and the color complemented her complexion, offsetting her pale skin and accenting her blue eyes. She smiled at her reflection in the mirror.

She splurged today and went to her favorite salon in town, The Last Strand. Two hours in a salon chair produced billowing, soft waves. Next, Amy spent an hour on makeup application. That was a lie. Makeup application took thirty minutes, but Amy found the initial result appalling. A reasonable aesthetic outcome resulted after wiping it off and starting again. Light brown shadow graced her eyelids. Three coats of waterproof mascara (she couldn't trust herself these days not to cry) covered her lashes, and a nude gloss across her lips completed her "look" for the evening. *Perfect.* Well, maybe not perfect, but good enough. She looked pretty, but not too encouraging. Professional, but not stuffy.

She nodded and teetered into the living room in her high heels to wait for Mark's arrival. After planting herself on her grey couch, Amy rubbed her fingers back and forth across the cushion next to her. Five minutes later, she'd nearly eroding a hole in the spot on the sofa next to her when the doorbell rang.

Amy rose from the safety of her couch and smoothed out her long gown. She walked to the door, drew in a deep breath, and opened it. Amy froze. *He was handsome... and he knew it.*

Mark tossed her a mischievous grin. "Hey, gorgeous. Ready to have the time of your life?"

She squirmed.

He chuckled at her obvious discomfort.

She nodded her head. "Ready or not." Amy still held serious reservations about this date. Mark was an ok guy. Fine to work with. A reputable doctor. He was fun. But sincere with women? No, probably not...and she suspected he didn't share her belief in God. Or if he did, she never heard him talk about it. A year ago, Amy questioned her own faith in God after losing her mom. But now... things felt different. She still questioned the justice of life and death, and dealing with anger over her loss, but she felt closer to God.

Mark rubbed his chin and leaned against the doorframe. "What are you thinking about? You look too serious for that dress."

Amy glanced around her living room for an excuse to cancel

the evening. "Oh, I'm wondering how many people will be at this thing. Maybe we should bail. It'll probably be boring and stuffy. And politicky."

He laughed and extended a hand to Amy. "Politicky is not even a word... You aren't nervous to go out with me, are you? I won't bite... unless you ask me."

Amy stared at his outstretched hand like it might bite. "No, no, it's not that." It was that. "It's just... I'm not sure that us going together is the greatest idea, what with us working together and all. And the Metro Ball... well... it's a public event, that's all."

"I thought this wasn't a date... what did you call it? A work outing?" Mark turned on his heel and sauntered to the car, whistling as he walked. He reached his side of the car and slid into the driver's seat.

She followed him to the car and stopped in front of her unopened door, staring at it. Mark started the ignition and then realized Amy hadn't entered the car. He rolled the passenger side window down. "You ok? You coming?" He smiled, oblivious.

Well, chivalry wasn't extinct, but it seemed endangered. Bonus mental check mark for Seth. She pulled in a deep breath. "I'm coming." She opened her car door, slunk into the seat, and buckled up for the impending bumpy ride of an evening. Amy clenched her teeth. "Let's go." She closed her eyes and prayed for an uneventful night.

Chapter 19

July 21, 2017, Friday

Amy willed the ride to the Metropolitan Convention Center to last longer, thus delaying the upcoming evening. Unfortunately, Mark drove as fast as he changed dates and ten minutes later, his car pulled into the Convention parking lot. Feelings of dread crept into Amy's heart and a tinge of worry clouded her mind. Maybe more than a tinge.

The Metropolitan Convention Center held the unofficial title of the town's singular convention center and The Place To Have Any Important Event. The Metropolitan Hospital Ball ranked at the top of that list. The Convention Center buzzed with activity as couples in tuxedos and evening gowns exited expensive foreign cars and limousines and walked into the acclaimed Ball. Amy watched the impressive scene unfold as everyone entered two by two. Not exactly what Noah envisioned when he worked on the ark.

Amy got out of the car and met Mark in front of it. He handed his keys to the valet. Mark reached out his hand to her, and she paused before accepting it. His hand felt much different from Seth's; rougher and courser.

She climbed the long set of marble stairs leading to the entrance of the town's highly talked about event and surveyed the crowd. Amy gasped. At least four hundred or more people awaited in the ballroom below. It was a collection of a Who's Who of

Scottsburg. So much for discretion. Amy pasted a smile on her face and squared her shoulders back, stepping inside. "I can't believe how many people are here."

Mark grinned and waved at several of the Board Members. "I know. Isn't it great?"

Amy's mouth settled into a flat line of displeasure. "Yeah, great."

Mark pointed to the side of the room. "My dad's over there talking to Ed Baker. I'm going to grab a glass of champagne and say hi to them. Do you want me to bring you a glass?"

"No, I don't drink—" Amy stood with her mouth open as Mark dashed away before she could finish her answer. "Right," she muttered to no one in particular. Amy scanned the room and her eyes landed on Mark's father and Ed. She contemplated how they knew one another.

A waiter carrying a silver tray of canapes distracted her. Amy made a beeline toward the waiter. As she shoveled her third canape in her mouth, Beth arrived, rescuing her waistline. She hadn't seen much of Beth the past week. Gratitude rushed through Amy at the welcome sight of her best friend.

"Hungry much?" Beth laughed, stealing an appetizer away from Amy.

She scowled at her spunky best friend. "Don't judge me. I've eaten nothing since eleven am and I'm nervous-eating now." Amy took in Beth's attire. She wore a short, red sheath ending four inches above her knees. "You look great!"

"Thanks." Beth popped another bite in her mouth and smirked. "So, where is Don Juan?"

"Haha, funny. Amy gestured over to the gaggle of women surrounding her date. Two other gentlemen stood with Mark amidst his entourage. "He's hunting for bubbly liquid courage and schmoozing with all the 'it' people from the hospital."

The two other men's backs were turned away from Beth's line of sight. Beth raised her eyebrows. "Who are the two other guys?"

"Oh, that's Ed Baker, CEO and Head Of The Hospital And My Entire Professional Life As We Know It. No biggie. And the other guy... apparently that's Mark's dad." Amy scrunched her face in deep thought. "Does he look familiar to you? I keep thinking I've seen him around the hospital, but I can't put my finger on how I know him."

"I've never seen him. I assume the rest of the women are part of the Mark Fan Club?" Beth watched Amy reach for another hors d'oeuvre.

Amy crammed a fourth canape in her mouth and grabbed another one. "Yep. Typical."

Beth nodded her head toward the fifth tidbit in Amy's hand. "So, I'm not judging you at all, but you might want to slow down girlfriend."

Amy glared at her brutally honest friend.

"Also, um, Mark seems to be hitting the champagne hard. While you and I stuffed our faces with these appetizers, he's done the same with champagne flutes. I think that's number four for him, in a matter of," Beth glanced at the large, regal clock on the wall of the convention center, "about fifteen minutes?"

Amy frowned. "Well, to be fair, the glasses are small." She trailed off, shrugging.

"Yeah, but still. That won't be fun to manage all night." Beth patted Amy's upper arm. "Have fun with that."

She sent a half-smile to her friend. "Wow, thanks Beth. You're always so helpful." Amy sighed. "I guess if I'm honest, you're right. I'm not judging him, but drinking is not my thing. Then, he didn't open my door either time tonight. Also, he thinks my hope for a relationship with God is a fairytale. So, we're zero for three. Oh, and then there's all the competition for his attention." Amy gestured again toward Mark's adoring fans.

Beth stared directly at her friend. "So... what are you going to do?"

Amy let a sigh slip out again, blowing a few escaping tendrils off her forehead. "I don't know, Beth. But not this." Amy took a swig of her own non-alcoholic sparkling cider, set her glass down on the server's tray, and marched off toward the balcony and into the night.

Chapter 20

July 21, 2019, Friday

Amy stood on the balcony of the Metropolitan Convention Center and looked out at the city lights below. A gentle breeze blew, and the late July night air had turned unusually crisp. She rubbed her bare arms and shivered. Someone caressed her shoulders from behind. She spun around and faced her date for the evening, Dr. Mark Blakely.

"Hey, gorgeous. Where've you been hiding?"

Amy stiffened. "Well, I didn't want to interrupt your admirers, so I came outside to get some fresh air."

"Ah, it's not like that. They're professional acquaintances." Mark winked. "Why don't you come inside and dance with me?"

"I don't feel like dancing right now."

"Oh, come on. Just one dance. Then, we can go if you're tired of the high society." Mark grabbed her hand, tugged her inside, and led her to the center of the ballroom. He moved one hand to the small of Amy's back, grasped her other hand in his, and waited for the next song to begin.

She shifted, wishing the music would start. Several jazz musicians stood on a black stage that contrasted against the light hickory wooden floor waxed to a brilliant shine. The band included a pianist, guitarist, lead singer, saxophonist, and a trumpet player. The horn player lifted his instrument to his lips as the lead singer tapped the mike and crooned. Mark swayed Amy back and forth, moving her around the grand room with easy steps, perfectly timed to the music.

For once this evening, Mark surprised her. He got half a point for his dance prowess, despite his consumption of endless flutes of champagne. Mark leaned in closer, and her stomach tensed. She drew away from him and dropped his hand. Thankfully, someone tapped her on the shoulder.

Amy turned and found Ed Baker, CEO of Metropolitan Hospital and Head of the Good Ol' Boys Club, standing in front of her.

Mr. Baker, rotund and wearing a black tuxedo with a burgundy pocket square and coordinating tie, slapped Mark across the back. "Mark, son, great to see you here with Dr. Harte. Glad the Emergency Department is making a good impression on the community... and the hospital's donors." Ed winked.

Was winking contagious? Amy noticed a slight tickle in her own eye.

Mark grinned and returned Ed's thump on the back. "Well, I reminded Dr. Harte the hospital required her presence at this important event."

Amy's face burned. She feared her acceptance of Mark's invitation as his date to the Metropolitan Hospital Ball sent the wrong message to him. With his dark hair and blue eyes, he never lacked female attention and required little encouragement.

"Dr. Harte, I hoped I'd speak to you tonight. As you know, I'm looking for a replacement for Dr Bowers since he retired to captain a boat around the world, or some other such nonsense. The Board of Directors will vote on it, but they always endorse my recommendation. I've reviewed the applications and narrowed my choice to two people." Mr. Baker paused, looking around the ballroom.

Amy held her breath.

Ed waved at a fellow Board member. "Where was I?"

"You said you narrowed down the Chief of Emergency Medicine position to two people." Amy clamped her mouth shut.

"Oh, that's right, so, I've narrowed it down to you and Dr. Blakely. It surprised me when Mark said he'd be interested in the job, because I thought only women interested him." Ed guffawed at his own joke for a few seconds.

Amy's mouth dropped open. "What do you mean, he'd—"

Ed interrupted her. "But the more I thought about it, I could see Mark as a leader. The staff speaks highly of you, Dr. Harte. You do great work. But Mark's been with us a little longer. It's a tough call. So, you're both still in the running." Ed turned his attention to Mark.

Mark avoided Amy's gaze and smiled at his boss. "Thanks, sir. I think I speak for both myself and Dr. Harte when I say that it's an honor that you're considering us for the job."

"Good, happy to hear it. Oh, Mark, I saw your dad earlier tonight. I told him I missed him at the last Board meeting and to make it to the next few. They'll be important." Ed winked again and ribbed Mark in the side with his elbow. "Well, enjoy the evening, Dr. Harte." He nodded at Amy, then staggered off to schmooze a potential donor.

Amy clenched her hands and turned to Mark. "So, you're trying for the ED promotion as well? After you told me about it? After you suggested it as a way for me to save my family's home?"

Mark put his hands up. "Listen, it's not like that. The other day Ed called me to his office. He asked if I'd consider leadership at Metro, and I said yes. I never told him I wanted Chief of Emergency Medicine outright. I knew you were applying, so it's not like I went behind your back." Mark refused to meet her eyes.

"Ok, fine. So, maybe you didn't apply for the job, but you didn't tell me Ed talked to you about it. I saw you head to his office days ago. You could've said something. And what's this about your dad being on the Board of Directors? Is he good friends with Ed? Another tap on her shoulder stopped Amy, and she turned.

Seth Broadstone stood before her. "Would you like to dance?"

Amy drew in a breath at the sight of Seth. His dark hair, deep chocolate eyes, and welcoming smile caused her to tremble. She liked him. He was kind, handsome, and a Christian. She hadn't mentioned her date with Mark to Seth because she didn't want to upset him. Now she wished she'd told Seth of her plans. Amy closed her eyes, hoping when she opened them the whole mess vanished. She opened them again. Nope. Both men remained, eyeing one another. This was no good. No, worse than that.

Horrific defined this situation.

Amy took two steps away from Mark. "Seth! What're you doing here?"

Seth's expression softened. "As the Chief Financial Officer for Metropolitan Hospital, it's part of my job to present a smile and handshake to the community on behalf of the hospital."

Amy cleared her throat. "Well, you know Mark, right?"

Seth eyed up his competition.

"We're here on business, too. Uh… the hospital administration encourages the physicians to attend the Ball. They think doctors add humanity to the event. You know, the face of the hospital making a difference, one patient at a time. And all that." Amy fumbled through her response. She smoothed out the skirt of her gown and looked down at her shoes.

Mark stepped closer to Amy. "Well, we're here for the humanity endorsement and also because Dr. Harte couldn't resist my invitation." He smirked and crossed his hands in front of his chest.

Dropping her face into both hands, Amy willed the entire night to disappear. She peered between one finger to assess the damage. Seth hadn't fled yet. She fake-yawned, covering her mouth with her hand. "Mm… well… I'm getting tired. So, uh, if it's ok with you, Mark, I think I'll grab a taxi and head home. I've got to work tomorrow, and I need to get some rest." The band picked up their instruments again, starting the chords for a slow ballad.

"No way! It's still early. Plus, you only danced with me once." Mark grimaced and reached for Amy's hand.

She pulled her fingers from his. "No, I'm leaving, but you stay and have fun. I don't want to spoil the evening for you. Besides, I'm sure your adoring female fans can entertain you."

Seth placed a hand gently on Amy's arm. "Wait. What about my dance?" He smiled and waited for Amy's answer.

Glancing at Mark, she and saw him already chatting with a young, blond nurse. "Well, I guess one dance couldn't hurt." Amy smiled. "Ok, but then I have to go."

Seth scooped up Amy's hand and led her to the other side of the ballroom. He placed one hand behind her back and pulled her a little closer.

A pleasant, tingling sensation traveled down her spine, and faint goosebumps rose on her arms. Staring into Seth's brown eyes awoke a yearning deep within her heart. Warmth spread from her chest and flooded her cheeks. She smiled, laid her head on his shoulder, and inhaled a blend of the masculine scent of tangerine and cedar wood. Amy's insecurity melted as she leaned into his strong, broad chest.

Seth guided her around the room and by the end of the song, stirrings in Amy's heart heralded the start of something epic. She shook her head and forced her thoughts to the present. "Thank you for the dance and for saving me from Mark. Sorry about that." Amy squeezed Seth's hand.

He gave her a broad grin, still holding her hand. "Happy to rescue you. Thanks for dancing with me. Why don't you let me take you home?"

Amy nodded and smiled. "That'd be great. Let me grab my bag and I'll meet you outside." The evening promised to end better than it began.

Chapter 21

July 21, 2019, Friday

Amy rode to her house with Seth in comfortable silence.

Upon arrival, he turned to her and grinned. "I'll walk you to the door." He got out of the car and opened Amy's door.

She slid out, ducking her head so not to embarrass herself by bonking it on the car roof.

Seth shut the door behind them, and he reached for her hand.

Amy accepted it and breathed in fragrant lilacs planted outside her townhouse. She noted the ebony night sky speckled with twinkling stars overhead, blanketing them in a warm glow.

Seth walked her to the front door, then stopped.

Amy turned and faced him. He was handsome, and as she looked at his full lips, she imagined the touch of them against her own.

Seth interrupted her daydream, still holding her hand. "Hey, thanks again for the dance. I had a great time. I wanted to tell you how beautiful you looked tonight." Seth brushed a loose tendril of hair off Amy's forehead and placed a hand alongside her cheek.

Amy's pulse quickened. She closed her eyes and tilted her chin upward.

Seth leaned his face closer to hers.

With an inch separating their lips, the growl of a roaring engine yanked Amy from the enchanted moment. Her eyes flew open.

Amy's phone chimed as her best friend's car pulled into the driveway. She watched in horror as Beth hopped out of her car with her phone to her ear.

"Amy! Amy! I know you're here. Pick up." Beth screeched into her phone, not yet realizing Amy stood only feet away within earshot. "Amy, why did you leave so ear—" Beth's gaze connected with Amy's, and her mouth dropped open. "Oh."

"Yeah. Oh." Amy released a soft sigh and stepped away from Seth.

"Hey, Beth, good to see you." Her boisterous best friend had terrible timing. Amy pasted on a smile and turned back to Seth. "Thanks again for saving me tonight." She tried to hug Seth at the same time he patted her arm, and their limbs entangled like toy monkeys in a barrel. She laughed and Seth corrected the encounter by giving Amy a brisk squeeze.

"Thanks for letting me rescue you, and for the dance." Seth's eyes crinkled as he smiled. "Maybe I'll see you at church on Sunday?"

Amy fiddled with her dress. She glanced at Beth to see a teasing grin. "Yeah, save me a seat." She sent Seth an encouraging smile.

"For sure. No problem. Ok, I'll see you soon. Good seeing you, Beth." Seth, a gentleman, turned toward the source of their interruption, and stiffly shook Beth's hand.

"Be safe!" Amy called, then smacked her forehead. Be. Safe. What was she thinking? She wasn't his mom. She whirled around and faced her friend. "Beth! Won't you come in? Since you're here and all?"

Beth fluttered her eyelashes. "I thought you'd never ask."

Amy opened the door and walked inside. Beth followed her, and Amy slammed the door with a resounding thud. She huffed out a breath and flopped down on the couch. "Well, that was a spectacular disaster."

"Oh, I don't know if I'd call it a disaster. Maybe a mishap or even a debacle, but not a total disaster." Beth smiled and sat down on one end of Amy's couch, folding her hands in her lap.

Amy flopped onto the other end of her grey sofa and flung a white, fluffy pillow at her best friend's face. "You're the worst."

"Well, now that's not a nice thing for a church-going gal to say." Beth put her hands on her hips in indignation, only half-kidding.

Amy sighed and flew her hands in the air. "What can I say? I'm a work in progress."

Beth stared at her distressed friend. She dropped her hands and raised her brow. "Ok, seriously, what's the deal? What happened tonight?"

Amy pulled in a deep breath. When she exhaled, tears came to her eyes. "Sometimes I don't know which way to go or why I'm making certain decisions. I'm struggling with what to do in my life without my mom in it. She was my guidepost so I wouldn't get derailed. Now that she's gone, and I can't pick up the phone and call her to get her advice...I feel lost and alone."

Beth sent her friend an empathetic smile. "You're not alone. Not only do you have me, a fantastic friend in your life to encourage you and keep you on course, but you have God."

Amy nodded her head as a tear trailed down her cheek. "I know the answer is to make God my beacon, but some days I can't see it through the haze of guilt and anger. I should've been there with her the day she passed, not at graduation... I'm mad at myself that I couldn't save her. Isn't that egotistical of me?"

Her friend shook her head. "You can't control everything. Even as a doctor, you don't have the ultimate say over who lives and dies. You did your best. You need to lay your guilt and anger at His feet."

Amy gave a shuddering breath. "I give it to God one day, only to pick it up again. I don't know what to do next. Take tonight, for example. I accepted a date, no a work outing, with a man I know isn't a good choice for me. He doesn't share my life values, he's not ready to settle down, and he wouldn't know what chivalry was if it knocked him on the head."

Beth shrugged her shoulders. "Why did you go with Mark? Other than for my amusement."

Amy sent her friend a withering gaze. "Because I wanted to make a good impression on my boss to get the promotion to Chief of Emergency Medicine? Maybe. I think part of the reason I said yes to Mark is that I didn't want to sit at home in silence, alone with my thoughts about the unfairness of life and how much I miss my mom. I still needed her to help me figure out the rest of it, you know?" Amy wept, sputtering words and phrases in between sobs.

Beth bobbed her head up and down. "I know... I know."

Amy continued her catharsis, "And then I have Seth, a true gentleman who seems to care for me, and what do I do? Oh, I go on a date with a yahoo to the town's biggest event and bump into him. Then, he witnesses the train wreck of a date I am on with another man. So, not only did I go out with another guy, but I went out with an egocentric ladies' man only interested in the chase. I bet Seth thinks I'm flaky or into complete imbeciles. Or both." Amy wiped tears from her eyes with the back of her hand and caught her breath. "Then there's the fact that I am still $52,000 shy of saving my parent's house."

Beth handed her a tissue from the box on the end table.

Amy took it and blotted her eyes before blowing her nose. "I ran into Ed Baker tonight at the Ball and he told me he plans to give the promotion to me or Mark. He still hasn't decided, but him and Mark looked chummy tonight."

Beth already had another tissue prepared and passed it to her friend. "I'm sure things are not as bad as you think. I think it is good news that you're in the final running for the Chief position at work. Let's focus on the positive. Ed hasn't made a final choice, and you still might get the job and the raise."

Amy considered this possibility for a moment. "Focus on the positive... ok, you might have a point."

Sitting up straighter, Beth shifted into full-on motivational speaker mode. "Also, from what you've told me about Seth, I doubt he would judge your character on one encounter at a company party. Plus, you left the party with Seth, not Mark. You weren't the one downing champagne and then flirting with anyone in a skirt. I saw you and Seth together on the front porch tonight and it definitely looked like he likes you... a lot." Beth nodded her head to emphasize her point.

Amy's tears had stopped, and she gave her face one final swipe. "I guess you could be right... I still wish I'd gone to the Metro Ball with Seth... and I hate to think what Mark will be like at work on Sunday. Ugh."

Beth redirected the conversation to a happier topic. "So, are you really going to church again Sunday?"

Scanning the room, Amy's eyes settled on a photo on the

coffee table of her with her mother on Easter. Amy wore a white tulle dress in the picture and had her arms wrapped around her mom's neck, gazing at her with the unconditional love of a six-year-old. "I don't know... I think so. I've only been a few times, but so far it feels right. It's nice to have someone remind me that life can be good again, and everyone at church is welcoming. When I leave, I'm closer to God and less angry about mom. Plus, there's free coffee." Amy threw Beth a mischievous grin.

Her friend took her turn at whipping the white pillow at Amy's face.

Amy put her hands up in defeat. "Kidding, kidding." But seriously, I love my coffee." She cackled and multiple pillows flew between the two best friends until a red ceramic vase Amy had bought on clearance at Dock Two six months ago met its demise.

Beth gasped and covered her mouth with one hand. "Oh, Amy, my bad. So sorry."

Amy jumped up and picked up the pieces. "It's ok. That thing was a steal. It gives me an excuse to go shopping to find something to replace it. Hey, I know how you can make it up to me." She turned to Beth and smiled.

Her friend sent her a scowl. "I'm afraid to even ask."

"Well, I was thinking about shopping for some new things. I haven't freshened my wardrobe since mom died. She and I always went together, and it hasn't felt the same without her. So, I could use some new clothes, new shoes, and apparently a few new items for the house, including something for my end table, which is now barren thanks to your pillow shot. Please come with me and help me find a new look and you can make it up to me by buying coffee afterwards." Amy placed her hands together in a pleading gesture.

Beth rolled her eyes but succumbed to the guilt trip laid upon her. "You won't take no for an answer, will you?"

She shook her head with vigor. "Nope. Not a chance. Besides, you know you love shopping, too, and you love coffee even more. We could go Monday afternoon after you get off work. Hopefully, Joe will still have some of his famous cinnamon rolls to go along with our cafe lattes." Amy wagged her eyebrows.

Beth put a hand up. "Stop. You had me at cinnamon rolls. Those are the best. I don't know what he puts in them, but it can't simply be sugar and flour. Ok, I'm in. I'll meet you at Dock Two? Then, we can head down the street to that cute clothing boutique, Southern Charm. I think they carry clothes, shoes, and bags. All that shopping should work up an appetite." She clapped her hands together, growing excited about the upcoming outing.

Amy knew the way to her best friend's heart was caffeine and sugar. The shopping was a bonus. "All right, I'll see you Monday around 4:00 pm. Now, as much as I love you, and you know I do." She smiled again and fluttered her eyelashes at Beth. "You've got to go!" Amy flung one final pillow at Beth's head with perfect aim. She punched both arms in the air. "Score!"

"Ouch." Beth frowned for a second, but then erupted in a fit of giggles. "I let you hit me because you had a tough night and you're going through a difficult and confusing time. Ok, I'm out of here. Love ya, babe. Hang in there. You're on an upswing. I know it. I'm praying for you and I think God's got some great things ahead for you." Beth stood up and hugged her friend as she headed out the door.

Shutting the door behind Beth, Amy's smile waned. It saddened her to see her effervescent friend leave. Perhaps Beth knew best. Maybe God had some good things planned for her future. With tomorrow being Saturday, she wanted to clean, do laundry, and then plant herself on the couch in her favorite cotton pajamas and hunker down for a movie night binge. She hoped once she righted her house and rested herself, Sunday would bring a fresh start.

Chapter 22

July 22, 2017, Saturday

Seth woke early on Saturday morning, unable to turn off his mind and its racing thoughts. He got in late last night after his evening at the Metro Ball and tossed and turned most of the night. He remembered the near kiss between himself and Amy. Her lips taunted him mere seconds from meeting his when Beth arrived interrupting them. The disappointment of not kissing Amy and expressing how he felt hung heavy over him.

He turned his attention his computer in front of him and the task at hand. He needed to finish a fresh prospectus this weekend to have it ready by Monday. He hoped to submit it for the Board of Directors regarding his proposal for further fundraising efforts for Open Hearts. He continued to rework the numbers, but the simple answer was the non-profit organization needed one new, generous financial donor. The Board meeting to discuss Open Hearts, the upcoming year's budget, and the confirmation of several new positions, including the Chief of Emergency Medicine, lay ahead within the next week or two as long as all the Board members schedules allowed.

Ed made it clear to him multiple times that if the funding lacked, the Board would cut the program, and soon. Seth promised his boss he would find a solution by the next official meeting and the threat of losing something close to his heart weighed on him.

Seth started typing and the image of Amy with Mark at the Ball flashed through his mind. He grimaced. He didn't trust that guy. For starters, Mark and Ed seemed too close for a boss and employee. Seth learned at the Ball that Mark's father held a voting seat on the Board of Directors. Apparently, he didn't regularly attend meetings, but Seth suspected he wouldn't miss the next one regarding his son's future as Chief. Seth feared Amy didn't have a fair shot at the promotion but hoped Ed and the Board proved him wrong. He knew the Amy needed the bonus to save her family's home. Also, Seth didn't enjoy seeing Mark and Amy together one bit. He suspected Mark only wanted to win Amy's heart for bragging rights, not because he honestly cared about her.

Seth shook his head, trying to clear his thoughts. He inhaled and imagined the sweet scent of Amy's perfume intermixed with the lilacs at her house. He usually approached life and love with a thoughtful, planned manner, but something about Amy made him bolder. She made him helpless to defend against her ability to reach into his heart, making herself at home. It scared him how quickly he came to care for her. He didn't want to get hurt, or lose her, but he couldn't deny it; though he'd only known her a few weeks, he believed he might be dangerously close to falling in love with her.

As he stared at the blank screen in front of him and resolved to focus on his work, his phone rang.

His mother's syrup-laden, Southern-coated voice broke into his inner debate about his relationship with Amy, the interloping Mark, and what to do about salvaging Open Hearts. He was thankful for the interruption. "Well, sugar, I've been worried sick about you!"

"Mom, why were you worried about me?" His mother's dramatics did not faze Seth.

"Well, I hadn't heard from you in days and I thought you might be dead!"

Classic mom. Seth grabbed a pen from his desk and doodled on the white-lined notepad next to his computer. "I talked to you this past week. I know we're a close-knit family, but we don't always talk every day." Seth made repetitive circles with his pen. His thoughts returned to Amy and the brilliant blue color of her eyes and how soft her skin felt when caressing her face. He hoped to see her at church tomorrow, which seemed like an eternity from now. His mom must have spoken without him realizing it because she screamed his name into the phone.

"Seth! Seth! Did you hear what I said?"

"What, oh, yeah, sure. No problem." Seth did not understand what he was agreeing to, but when it came to Nancy Broadstone, the answer was always yes if you didn't want to stir up trouble.

"Wonderful. So, you'll ask Amy to come to dinner with us? Perhaps Friday night? I have a new recipe for chicken I've been dying to try, and you know no one can resist my famous sweet tea. Best in the south." Seth's mother prattled on about the menu, table setting, and her to list to ready the house for company. He knew she'd clean it to a spotless sheen. His mom loved entertaining and took family dinner's seriously.

Seth wondered if his family might overwhelm Amy. Plus, their relationship seemed to barrel ahead at a locomotive pace, which both exhilarated and terrified him. "Uh, this Friday? Coming up? I'll ask her... but... that might be short notice."

"Nonsense. It's all settled. You told me last time we talked we would have her over, and this is it. Now, I need to run and get started on the grocery list for this feast. I love you sugar, bye-bye."

With a click, his mother hung up and probably already headed to the supermarket, planning their meal. Seth stared at the quiet phone. He ran a hand through his hair. Placing the phone down, he gave a half-grin, and rolled up his sleeves ready to work. He'd ask Amy tomorrow if he saw her at church. Shaking his head again, Seth hoped Amy was ready to meet the Broadstone's.

Chapter 23

July 23, 2017, Sunday

Amy's alarm rang on her phone resting on her nightstand, and she jumped out of bed wide awake. Saturday proceeded without event as Amy achieved her goals of clean clothes, a cleaner house, and nothing else accomplished other than rest. She felt rejuvenated. Sunday held the promise to make all things new: with God, herself, her friends, family, her job, and even with Seth. She longed to let go of all anger and fear, to trust God again, and to open her heart up to Him. She hoped to let down her walls with Seth and be brave. *Now, for the important question of what to wear to be brave?*

She tapped her foot in her fuzzy pink slippers and smiled to herself. She couldn't wait to shop with Beth tomorrow, as her wardrobe begged for attention. She let more than her relationship with God go while grieving her mother. Regardless of that, she still loved clothes. Her mom loved all things retail, so peering into storefronts and hunting for new finds reminded Amy of her mom.

Amy planned on seeing Seth at church, so she wanted to look nice, but not as romantic as the Big-Mexican-Dinner-Salsa-Dancing-Date. She walked to her closet and rifled through her extensive, although worn, collection. Her hand stopped short on a top she hadn't worn in over a year. The white blouse fit snug through the bodice and had stretch, lace sleeves. It flattered her hour-glass figure well and complemented her favorite pair of black skinny jeans.

The last time she wore it, she'd been with her mom. They went on an epic marathon day of shopping, hitting all the best stores. Loaded down with multiple shopping bags and unable to carry any more, they grabbed a meal at their favorite restaurant featuring large slices of cheesecake. They talked, laughed, reminisced about Amy's childhood, and ate at least a pound of cheesecake each. Neither of them wanted the day to end, so Amy's mom suggested they drop off their bags at the car and take a stroll to the big fountain in the middle of the outdoor shopping mall.

They ducked to the car, unloaded their treasures, and sauntered down the faux cobblestone street toward the fountain. Amy remembered feeling like a kid in that moment and grabbed her mother's hand in hers. They approached the fountain and sat down on the bench in front of it. The fountain looked beautiful, made entirely of enormous grey stones and surrounded by three rows of varying colored blooms. Nearby, honeysuckle trees stood, and the sweet smell welcomed them. They sat on the bench and discussed everything and nothing.

"Amy, I'm so proud of the woman you've become. You're smart, strong, and kind. And you have a big heart for God. Don't lose that." Caren, smoothed her hand over Amy's hair. She leaned in and hugged Amy.

Amy buried her face into her mom's soft, brown hair and inhaled the familiar scent of her floral perfume. "I won't mom. I won't. I love you. This has been the best day. Promise me it will always be like this. Promise." Amy squeezed her mother's shoulders tighter.

Caren pulled away from Amy and gave her a kiss on the top of her head. "Oh, Amy, I hope so. No matter what happens in life, I'll always love you. I cannot wait to see what God has in store for you. Big things, I know it. Big things."

Amy's mom told her she couldn't wait for Amy to meet the man she would marry and provide at least one, if not more, grandchildren to spoil. Her mom had been a kindergarten teacher and loved kids. Amy told her how great life had been growing up and how she appreciated their friendship now. She recalled sitting by the fountain, staring at the water flowing out from the top, inhaling the scent of honeysuckle, and thinking to herself the moment seemed perfect.

After talking for at least an hour by the fountain, the sun started to set. "I guess we should head home. It's getting late and if we sit here any longer, I think the security officer will get suspicious." Amy giggled

Her mom chuckled, too. "You're right. We should go. I hate for it to end. You're right. It's been the best day. Let's remember it always. Our special day." Caren's eyes twinkled. "Do you know what would top off this perfect day?"

Amy grinned. "What mom?"

"How about we stop by Joe's on the way home for a late-night cookie and coffee fix?" Caren, stood, knowing her daughter would follow suit.

"Do you even have to ask? Chocolate and coffee? You're on!" Amy jumped up, the pre-caffeine buzz kicking in already, but halted to squeeze her mom in one last tight hug.

About a month after that outing, Amy's mom fell sick, and they never went shopping or had another "girl's day" again. That white shirt still carried the vague scent of her mom's perfume and honeysuckle. She hadn't worn it since. She started to pull it out to wear, but paused, thinking better of it.

Instead, she moved over to the next item, an old standby: a simple, long, black maxi dress that she could dress up or down depending on the occasion. It had a scoop neck, short sleeves, a fitted bodice, and wasn't so long that she might trip and make a complete fool of herself. *Perfect.* She added her silver bohemian statement necklace, some plain stud earrings, and her black patent leather sandals to finish the ensemble.

Glancing at her clock, Amy realized only thirty minutes remained for her to get ready and leave if she didn't want to arrive at church late. After a flurry of activity, she made it out of her house on time and pulled into the church parking lot with one minute to spare.

She hopped out of her car, slammed the door shut, and scurried to the front entrance as the greeter started closing the door for the start of service. No time for coffee this morning. She hated coffeeless mornings. Amy searched for Seth, and as the door shut behind her, her eyes landed upon him.

As if he felt her gaze, he looked up from his seat in the third row, waved, and smiled. She raised her eyebrows and mouthed, "Any room?"

"Yes," he mouthed back. He nodded his head toward the seat next to him.

She made her way down the right aisle of the church and took her spot. Dropping into her seat, she grinned. "Hi. Sorry I'm late."

"Hi, yourself. And you're not late. You're exactly on time." Seth clamped his mouth shut as the lead pastor took the stage and made announcements.

"I'm glad everyone came today and I'm excited to see all these smiling faces. Are you ready for something good to happen today? Can we give God praise?" The pastor roused the crowd with encouragement, and everyone cheered, clapped, and gave a resounding, "Amen!"

The worship team took the stage and launched one of the best musical sets, Christian or mainstream, Amy ever heard. They played four contemporary Christian songs and finished with a modern rock version of "It Is Well With My Soul." She never thought much about that song before, but she believed God planned for her to hear it today. Every word spoke to her soul. She knew she hadn't arrived at her destination on her journey of grief and faith, but God continued working on her heart to heal it. It was becoming well with her soul.

The pastor took the stage again and continued with the same theme. "There will be times when you feel like giving up, when you feel like quitting. When anger and pain and grief stop you in your tracks. There will be times when you want to turn away from God and close off your heart to avoid the pain. Don't do that. Turn to God in those tough times. Ask him to carry you, tell Him you love and trust Him, press onward in the fight of faith, and feel the peace that He gave you deep in your soul." The pastor finished the service, and the room fell silent.

Amy smiled and a single tear slipped down her cheek. Taking a deep breath, she turned her head away from Seth, self-consciously wiping the tear away. She turned back around with only the smile planted on her face.

Seth placed a reassuring hand on top of hers. "It's ok to cry."

"I wasn't crying, not really." Amy swiped her cheek once more with the back of her hand.

Seth looked her with a raised brow.

"Okay, maybe a tear or two, but that was it."

"Like I said, it's fine. I get it. That was a big message. Powerful stuff. I'm glad you came, and I got to sit with you."

"Me, too."

"Do you have plans or do you have time to grab a coffee and take a quick walk?" Seth sent her a hopeful expression.

Amy looked at her phone to check the time. 11:00 am. She agreed to cover a half-shift for a colleague but didn't have to work today until 2:00 p.m. "Sure, that'd be great! I don't have to get to the hospital until 1:45 p.m., so I have time. Plus, I missed my morning caffeine infusion, so it's a patient safety issue. I don't think they'll want me working in a medical capacity without my coffee. I think a walk and coffee is mandatory."

Seth rose from his seat. "Great! Okay, how about we meet at Joe's and grab a quick cup to go, then hit the rail trail right down the road?"

"Perfect. I'll grab my car and meet you there." Amy stood and wiped one final tear, ready for something good to happen today.

Chapter 24

July 23, 2017, Sunday

Amy pulled up to her familiar coffee hub and turned off the ignition. She hopped out and shut her door. As she opened the cafe door, the small gold bell overhead chimed. She approached the counter and the waft of blueberry scones intermixed with hazelnut roast.

Seth stood a few feet ahead of her in line, arriving ahead of Amy. He wedged his hands in his pockets and talked easily with Samantha Matherly.

Samantha. Amy cringed. She knew God said to love everyone, but some people made it easier than others. Samantha was in the "others" category. Extra grace required, or EGRs, as her father liked to say.

Samantha, the town gossip, had long, silky golden hair, bright blue eyes that often appeared surprised in a coquettish manner, and full red lips. She towered over Amy at five foot nine inches tall, and her long, tan legs, touted an athletic physique.

She also attended Seth's church and was a single Christian girl's nightmare. Samantha garnered male attention everywhere she went, and it appeared she intended to capture Seth's. She had one hand placed on her chest and another one draped on Seth's forearm. Watching Seth and Samantha chat aroused the green-eyed monster within Amy.

Seth threw his head back and chuckled.

What was so funny? Amy's relationship with Samantha went back to their elementary school years. The first altercation happened during a junior high talent show. Samantha chose the same song as Amy, but ensured she went first during the performance. The result made Amy look like a copy-cat and Samantha ended up winning the Best Overall Award for the evening. Then, in high school, Amy arrived at a Friday night football game and found her boyfriend lip-locked with Samantha on the first row of the stadium in front of everyone. She went home and cried into her pillow for hours, while her mom stroked her hair. Amy hadn't forgiven Samantha for that (something else to discuss with God). Seeing her proved unpleasant, especially with her standing so close to Seth.

Amy stepped forward and cleared her throat. "Ahem. Am I interrupting something?"

Seth smiled at Amy. "No, not all. I was standing in line ready to order when Samantha came up and introduced herself. She said she goes to our church. How great is that?"

"Great." Amy's mouth settled into a flat line. *Just great.* Amy needed to curb her enthusiasm at seeing her arch nemesis standing next to the objection of her affection...and right after hearing a sermon about loving other people. No, this was definitely not "well with her soul". This wasn't well with her anything.

She put on her most dazzling smile and turned to Samantha. "It's great to see you again. It's been, what, almost ten years? I guess the last time I saw you was at a high school football game." Guilt washed over Amy. She shouldn't have brought up the memory. She looked to the floor before meeting Samantha's gaze again. "What I meant to say is, I'm sure I've seen you around town, but just not had the chance to talk. How have you been?"

"Bless your heart. I'm wonderful. I opened a little shop down the road a few months ago. So, things are busy but exciting."

Amy questioned the sincerity of Samantha's southern drawl and the words behind it. Samantha and Amy grew up together, and while their community produced a southern accent, Samantha's sounded overdone.

Samantha wore a devilish grin. "But it hasn't been long since I saw you last. Unless my eye's deceived me, I think I saw you the other night at the Metro Ball."

Aha! Amy knew it. She thought she saw Samantha at the Ball. She probably witnessed the spectacle of "Amy and Mark" that night. Samantha knew everyone and everything happening in town. Amy gritted her teeth. "Oh, right. I was there. What a beautiful event. Did you enjoy yourself?"

Samantha inched toward Seth. "I sure did. It impressed me to see you there with the Town's Most Eligible Bachelor, Dr. Mark Blakely. It looked like you two had a great time dancing."

"Well, Mark and I work together. It was more of a work outing. We only danced together once, the same as Seth and me. And I don't know if I'd call Mark the Town's Most Eligible Bachelor. I'd say there are a few other gentlemen in the running for that title." Amy flicked her eyes toward Seth and smiled. "I hate to cut this short, but Seth and I planned to grab a coffee and take a stroll before I have to head to work at the hospital."

Samantha frowned for a second before replacing it again with a forced grin. "Oh, well that sounds nice. Maybe I could join you sometime?" She fixed her gaze on Seth.

Amy scooted closer to Seth. "Hmm, that'd be...something. Well, it's been a surprise bumping into you. I'm sure we'll see more of you at church?" At least those words held truth. She didn't say it was a pleasant surprise running into Samantha. Just a surprise. Amy grinned again. Samantha's arm finally released Seth's at the same Amy considered prying it off with her bare hands.

"Oh, most certainly. It's been a pleasure. Now, Seth, if you need anything at all, you know another member of the church body. Call me anytime if I can help you or you need some companionship for a coffee or a stroll." Samantha batted her eyelashes.

Could Samantha be any more obvious?

Samantha exited and somehow the ding of the bell sounded more sensual when she made it ring.

Amy sighed and faced Seth. She smiled, despite wearing a furrowed brow. "Funny running into my old school acquaintance, huh?"

Seth laughed and took a step closer to the counter, ready to order. "I take it there's no love lost between the two of you?"

Amy moved forward in the line. "Well, I wouldn't go that far." She would go that far, and beyond. "It's just silly schoolgirl stuff from so far back that it shouldn't even matter now. I'm sure Samantha is a kind girl. I haven't talked to her in ages. People change as they grow up. I know I'm not the same person I was ten years ago."

"Hey, I get it. God calls us to love everyone, but that doesn't translate into being everyone's best friend. Remember the verse about being wise as a serpent and gentle as a dove? It's ok, I understand." Seth grabbed one of Amy's hands.

She squeezed his hand. "I'm sure she was just being friendly. Besides, I can understand why she'd want to talk with you. You're a great guy."

"I'm sure she's nice, but that's all. I've got my mind on someone else." Seth's eyes twinkled.

Amy's cheeks warmed. She nodded toward the counter. "You're up."

"Huh? Oh, thanks! What do you want?" Seth dropped her hand and turned to Amy.

"Um, anything with caffeine is fine. Maybe… a vanilla cafe latte?"

"You got it. That sounds good. Make it two vanilla cafe lattes and two scones, please." Seth gave the barista the order and reached in his back pocket for his wallet.

She shuffled down the line to wait for the order. Two minutes later, Amy followed Seth out the door, hands full with a latte and scone. She strolled with Seth down the sidewalk and crossed the street toward the nearest walking trail. Slowing her pace, she walked in silence for a few minutes.

Seth ate his pastry and sipped the hot beverage.

Amy broke the silence, "I can't believe fall is around the corner. You can almost smell it in the air. I love when the leaves change on the trees and things become still… like God reminding us to slow down, too, and spend time together."

Still finishing his scone, Seth nodded his head. He took another drink while Amy continued reminiscing.

"My mom loved Thanksgiving, which is funny because neither of us cooked well. Every year we divided up the dishes to make. My dad made the turkey and stuffing, which turned out well. Mom handled the side dishes, but often tried to make them healthier, so the result could be unpredictable. I made baked goods, like rolls and cookies. My family thought since I loved bread and sweets so much, I could handle those without creating a disaster. Some years they were right, other's tragedy struck." Amy laughed.

Seth tossed his cup and wrapper in a can nearby and they continued walking down the paved path. "So, if we cook together, I should plan to do most of the heavy lifting?"

"Um, yeah. Probably a safer bet." Amy's stomach growled. She dug into her scone and finished it in a few bites before turning her attention to her latte. She picked up her pace and fell silent for several minutes.

He took her scraps and threw them in another container before reaching for her hand. "You still miss your mom a lot, don't you?"

Amy nodded. "Yeah. It's funny… you expect as time goes on the missing will be less. And it is easier in some ways. I don't cry every day, not even every week anymore. Sometimes I remember special times, like Thanksgiving dinners, with fondness now instead of sadness. It seems like the simplest things make me miss her most."

Seth bobbed his head up and down. "I get that. The small things in life are often the most memorable."

"I'm going shopping with Beth tomorrow and thinking about the shopping trip is harder than remembering the Thanksgiving dinners. My mom and I used to shop together all the time. We'd try on silly things and laugh at ourselves until we couldn't breathe. It was the best. I also miss talking to her in the mornings. I used to call her on the phone on my way to college and then medical school. We chatted about everything and nothing. It's funny what you take for granted until it's gone. I think that's why it's important for me to save my parents' home. It's the last big piece of my mom I have left."

He stopped in his tracks and changed the subject. "I want to show you something." He guided her up a hill to a bench perched at the top of a knoll on the trail. The bench accommodated them both and overlooked an opening in the trees, revealing the entire city below.

Amy gasped. "Wow! I never realized this was here." She marveled at how small the buildings and people below appeared.

"I know. It reminds me how small I am in this world and makes some of my problems seem even smaller. I come here to think. The week after my brother's car accident I came here and thanked God for protecting Brian. Even though life is unpredictable, God never changes." He toward his body toward Amy. "You know?" Seth scooted closer to Amy and wrapped an arm around her shoulder.

"I'm understanding it more. I still struggle with losing my mom. Losing my parent's house...well, I can't even consider it...but I'm trying to open my heart to God and people again. It's hard and scary. I'm still angry, but I do remember God loves me. I'm holding on to that right now." Amy looked up at Seth and felt tears brimming to the surface.

He lifted his hand off her shoulder and ran it through her hair. "You know, Amy, you're amazing. You're smart, beautiful, and even though the last year has been tough, you still have a heart for God."

"Wow, thanks Seth. I think the same about you. I honestly don't know how you're still single. You're kind, thoughtful..." Amy paused, and Seth raised his eyebrows, "and handsome! That's a given."

Seth erupted in laughter. He locked eyes with her and fell silent.

She leaned in and a soft breeze caressed her cheek.

Seth tilted her chin up towards his mouth.

Amy closed her eyes and her stomach flipped. Just as Amy's lips were about to meet Seth's, her pager interrupted the moment with a loud beep-beep-beep. She jerked her eyes open and groaned

"No!" The sound still struck anxiety within her after many years of disrupted sleep by the dreadful thing while on call. She pulled the pager out of her pocket and pressed the button hard. The brief message flashed across the screen. *Staff low. Need you sooner. 8213. Mark.* Amy's shoulders sagged. She looked up at Seth. "Seth, I'm so, so sorry. I cannot believe this, but I have to go. Raincheck?"

Seth shrugged and grinned. "Yeah, yeah. No, big deal. Duty calls. Right? I'll walk you back to your car. Go save a life." He grabbed her hand and led her back to where her car awaited in front of the coffee shop. Seth gave her a long hug and kissed the top of head. "I enjoyed talking with you. I had a great time. Maybe we can get together again later this week?"

She wanted to blurt out yes but used every bit of willpower to appear calm. "Sure, that would be fun. Call me this week and we'll figure something out. I have to work on Wednesday, but I'm off Thursday and Friday night."

Seth snapped his fingers. "Hey, I have an idea. My brother told my mom about you after the accident, and she would love to meet you. I didn't want to spring my entire family on you too soon. They can be a lot." Seth laughed. "My mom wanted me to invite you over for dinner. Would you want to come Friday night?"

"Friday night." Amy tried to tamp down an impending wave of excitement mixed with panic. "Yeah, that sounds great. Let me know the details and directions, and I'm there." She arrived at her car and opened the door, pausing before getting inside. Amy turned to face Seth.

He held her door open while she slid inside. "No way. I'll pick you up. It's a date."

She grinned. "Ok, it's a date."

Seth shut her door and sent her a quick wave.

Amy drove as fast as her car would carry her to the hospital, with a wide grin the entire way. She suspected the time between now and Friday night would drag. Amy rolled her eyes imagining Beth's reaction to her upcoming family dinner date. She'd never hear the end of it. Amy shrugged. At least Beth could help her find the perfect "meet the family" outfit tomorrow.

Chapter 25

July 31, 2017, Monday

Amy took off Monday from the hospital. She slept in, awakening to the sound of her stomach growling instead of the annoying alarm from her smartphone. She shuffled into the kitchen, wearing fuzzy white slippers. Reminiscing of childhood Saturday mornings, Amy made her father's famous waffles, which created a tornado of batter in her kitchen.

She languished in a syrupy daze for hours, clicking through a series of tv shows. Her favorite program involved people hiring a realtor to find the perfect home in a foreign country. The customers packed up their entire lives to make a drastic intercontinental move. Amy laughed out loud at people's unrealistic expectations. The most recent episode concluded with an enthusiastic couple passing on all the homes. Amy felt sorry for the realtor. All that work for nothing. She sighed and turned off the television.

Glancing at the time, she realized Beth would arrive in one hour. Amy peeled herself off the couch and hurried around the kitchen and living room in a whirlwind; flinging dirty dishes into the dishwasher, scrubbing countertops, and straightening pillows on the couch. She ran the vacuum over the floors with a few quick swipes, and her place looked reasonably righted. She dashed to the shower and welcomed the warm water to wash away the stress of the last few weeks.

Last night she saw more patients in six hours than in two normal shifts at work. Several of her cases challenged her. A pediatric patient arrived in anaphylaxis from an accidental nut exposure. Thankfully, he made it to the emergency department in time, and after oxygen, epinephrine, and antihistamine, he improved.

Amy relished in the hot spray beating on her tense muscles in her upper back. The water turned cool, signaling Amy to hop out of the shower. She wrapped herself in a fluffy, oversized white towel, and wrapped a smaller one around her hair.

Nearly one hour later, taking much longer than necessary, Amy stood clean, dressed, and ready to go. She looked at her phone again and realized she had five minutes to spare. She flopped on her couch again and reentered the world of home seekers on tv. The latest couple's hunt for a home in the countryside of France absorbed Amy until she heard rapping on the door. Opening the door, she smiled. "Hey, I have so much to tell you!" Amy looked up into the eyes not of her best friend, but of Mark. "Mark! What are you doing here?"

Mark sent her a half-grin and leaned his forearm against her doorframe. "Hey Amy, nice to see you, too."

Amy held the door with a firm grip and planted her feet. "No, I mean, seriously, what are you doing here? We didn't have anything scheduled. What's up?"

"Well, I was sitting at home this morning, and I couldn't stop thinking about our evening at the Ball. So, I hopped in my car and drove over here to take you out for round two." Mark grinned as if giving her a gift.

She shifted her weight and crossed her arms. "Um... well, I'm flattered... I really am...but I have plans with Beth today, Mark. Besides, we are just friends, right?" She held her breath.

"Well, I thought we could become better friends. Like maybe friends who do this." Mark stepped forward and placed his hand on Amy's cheek, leaning in to kiss her. Thankfully, Beth arrived at that moment, confused, but entertained by the latest development in Amy's tumultuous romantic life.

Beth wore a bemused grin. "Well, well, well. What do we have here? Am I interrupting something?"

Mark turned toward Beth, his back to Amy, while Amy made

wild gestures with her hands behind his back trying to get Beth's attention.

She mouthed the words "Help Me." Amy laid her hands together in prayer.

Beth smiled wider in response. *Oh no.* Beth loved the drama.

"Mark! So good to see you again. Amy and I were getting ready to go out, but did you two have plans?"

Staring daggers at her best friend behind Mark's back, Amy mouthed, "Don't You Dare," and prayed Beth would have mercy upon her.

Beth raised her eyebrows.

"We didn't have plans yet. How about it, Amy? Want to grab a bite to eat?" Mark winked.

"Uh… well…Beth and I made plans to go shopping and grab coffee days ago. And… I'm not the girl to break plans with a friend for a guy. It's a strict policy of mine. Girl code and all," Amy stammered, but nodded her head with determination. "I hope you understand. Besides, I'm sure you have a ton of girls waiting in line to seize the opportunity to date the eligible Dr. Blakely." Amy clamped her mouth shut, hoping she made her case.

Mark laughed and stepped back. He raised both hands in concession. "Hey, no sweat. And you're right. There are a ton of girls waiting for me to call them, but they aren't as interesting and challenging as the evasive Dr. Harte. Don't worry, Doc. I'll be back. I don't give up easily and I get what I want, but I'll let you off the hook today." Mark finished his speech with his trademark wink and left.

Amy sighed and dropped her arms to her side. She glared at Beth. "I could strangle you; you know."

Beth cackled hysterically. "I know, but then who would provide your life with all this entertainment?"

"You better be glad I love you. That was a close call. What if I couldn't have gotten him to leave?"

"But you did darling, you did," Beth spoke in a theatrical, British accent.

"You are certifiable. You know that, right?" Amy's anger eased now that her fight-or-flight response dissipated. Her shoulders relaxed.

Beth flung an arm around Amy's shoulder and squeezed it.

"I know, but you still love me. Plus, if you didn't have me, who would you take shopping and on all of your caffeine runs?"

Her friend made a point. Coffee always tasted better with company. "True. Ok, you're off the hook. Just don't do that to me again. Come on, let's go. We're wasting precious retail therapy time." Amy grabbed her bag and shoved her best friend out the door. "I'm driving. You've scared me enough for one day."

Beth started to object but realized the truth in that statement. Beth was a horrendous driver. She conceded the argument and settled into the car.

Amy shook her head. God broke the mold when He made her best friend.

Chapter 26

July 31, 2017, Monday

Amy parked downtown, amidst many local boutiques, each one known for its trademark merchandise. Uncle Owl's Candies, a wonderful shop that made the most delicious chocolate bark, beckoned customers with its sweet aroma. The Treasure Chest, a handmade jewelry store, specialized in engraved leather cuffs with vintage broaches attached to them.

Bessie's Bags sold, well, expensive leather bags, but the craftmanship made the price tag worth it. In the middle of the row of stores stood The Shoe Shack, an establishment with a mundane name that carried exquisite shoes at competitive prices. Joe's Coffee shop, a retail therapy must, marked the central point of downtown.

Sam's Closet, unfortunately owned by Samantha Matherly, offered an assortment of breezy summer frocks, inventive bohemian tops, and the softest, yet most expensive, jeans. The jeans felt like butter and created the illusion of looking five years younger and ten pounds lighter. They were denim perfection.

Living in a small town, boutiques provided the mainstay of shopping. Sure, Amy could drive an hour north to Richmond to the mall, but aside from having to face horrid traffic to get there, the boutiques on Main Street offered not only convenience, but novelty not found in the mainstream department stores.

Beth raised her eyebrows and gestured to the row of shops before them. "Where to first?"

Amy met her friend's gaze, paused, and smiled. She announced, "coffee," at the same time Beth did and Amy chuckled. She nodded her head toward Joe's and started walking down the street.

Within minutes Amy opened the door to Joe's, and the little golden bell dinged overhead. She immediately relaxed into the familiarity of the smell of steaming milk, baking bread dough, and brewing dark roast.

Joe lifted a hand and waved a greeting. "Hey ladies!"

"Hey Joe! It's been forever since I've seen you. How have you been?" Amy scanned the bakery glass case, willing herself to skip the sugary delicacies for once.

"I've been great Doc. I just got back from a quick trip to North Carolina. I'm thinking about opening a second Joe's there and franchising. It's all about branding yourself, you know." Joe sat his hands on his hips. He wore a Joe's Coffee Shop white apron, and he looked like a little kid trying to portray a superhero. Amy giggled.

"Wow, Joe, when did you get so trendy?" Amy cocked her head to the side. She wondered about Joe's age. If Amy had to guess, she would speculate Joe to be in his mid-thirties. He wore his dark hair in a faux hawk, had a cross tattoo on one forearm, and a single hoop earring in one ear.

On the outside he resembled a roughneck, but within Joe was a big heart. He worked hard and showed God's love to others. Joe donated food weekly to the local homeless shelter. Amy knew this because one of the regular staffers at the shelter came through the emergency department and mentioned it during the visit. He also attended church regularly and volunteered where needed. With deep brown eyes to match his tanned skin, he wasn't bad on the eyes either.

Now that Amy thought about it, Joe and Beth hadn't taken their eyes off one another. Amy loved a good scheme. "Hey Beth, I'm sorry I won't be able to go with you to see that new movie this weekend. I hate to miss it, too. I love that series about the compound with all the dinosaurs that break loose. Then it shocks everyone when the scientific plan for farming dinosaurs with modern genetics goes awry. I know you were excited about it, too." Amy frowned.

Beth stared at Amy with a furrowed brow.

Amy raised one finger and pointed at Joe. "Hey! I know! Joe, weren't you telling me last year when the second movie came out how much you loved it?"

Joe didn't take Amy's hint. "Yeah, I mean, I think they're good action films." He continued wiping off the counter and then readied Amy and Beth's large, black mugs.

Beth's eyes widened and she shot daggers with her eyes at her plotting best friend.

Amy grinned at Beth and turned her attention back to Joe. "Great. That's perfect. It's settled, then." Amy nodded.

Joe looked up and met Amy's gaze, raising one brow. "Uh, what's settled?"

Amy placed her hands on her hips and shook her head. "You and Beth, silly. Going to the movies. Friday night. To see the newest, most epic dinosaur film. Movie three in the saga. You guys will have a blast, and I won't have to disappoint my best friend. It's a win-win." She secretly started planning her best friend and favorite barista's nuptials in her head.

Beth sent a quick glance to Joe.

A slow smile spread across Joe's face. "Well, what do you think? Critics are calling it the action movie of the year. I wound hate for you to miss it."

Beth returned Joe's smile and her wide-eyed expression relaxed. "I guess that could work. I was excited about going." Amy and Beth had not discussed seeing this movie previously at all, however that fact seemed to have escaped Beth's memory.

Amy grinned. "Great! You guys will have a wonderful time, I won't feel like a heel for letting my best friend down, and I'll still get to take care of my… prior obligation."

Joe turned to Beth. "Ok, so I'll meet you at the movie theatre Friday?"

Beth batted her eyes at Joe. "Sure, sounds perfect."

Amy interrupted the budding romance. "Perfect, now that you guys have your weekend plans ironed out, can we order? I'm severely under-caffeinated and fear for the lives of those near me if

I don't rectify this situation, stat."

"Sure, what'll it be today ladies?" Joe spoke to both women, but Amy noted he only looked at Beth. His grin expanded to wider than before.

She surveyed the drink menu, although Amy knew most of it by heart. "Uh, I'll have a vanilla cafe latte with extra foam, and an additional shot of espresso on the side."

"Wow, Amy, don't hold back there. That's a heart attack in a cup. Um, I think I'll have an herbal green tea, no sugar." Beth stepped back from the counter, finished with her order.

"Green tea! Who drinks green tea? I'm appalled. It's an insult to coffee beans everywhere." Amy raised a fist for emphasis.

Beth scooted to the side, making room for the next customer to order. "Unlike you, Ames, I would like to live to see my 40th birthday. I'm trying to make better lifestyle decisions." She lifted her chin.

Suspecting her bestie read an article in some fitness magazine emphasizing the importance of antioxidants, Amy snorted.

A frown formed on Beth's lips. "What was that about?"

"Nothing. Honest to goodness. Cross my heart." Amy made an "x" shape across her heart with her hand. "Now, can we sit down now? I have a ton to tell you about my last encounter with Seth. I need your opinion."

Beth raised her hands up in concession. "Okay, okay. Truce."

Grabbing the caffeinated and green decaffeinated (yuck) concoctions from Joe, Amy carried them with care to her favorite table by the large bay window. She recalled the recent run-ins with Samantha and Mark. From this vantage point, Amy could see customers entering the cafe and take cover under the table if needed.

Beth took a cautious sip from her steaming beverage. "Okay. We're caffeinated, well you are anyway, we're alone, and we have the best seat in the house. So, spill. What's up?"

"Well... I invited you shopping because you broke my vase—"

"Hey, it was an accident—"

Amy held up a hand. "And I wanted to spend time with you, but also because I need a new outfit to wear to dinner with Seth and his family Friday night. I'm freaking out about meeting his entire clan. What if they don't like me? What if I don't like them?

What if they are stoic and find me neurotic and annoying? And then there's the whole thing with this promotion at the hospital. Beth, if I don't get this job… that's it for my parent's house. I don't know what I'll do." Amy drew in a breath.

"Whoa, whoa, whoa. You've got to calm down!" Beth placed one index finger on the other, ticking off reasons to ease Amy's panic. "First, you are neurotic and annoying."

Amy sent her friend a frown.

Beth laughed.

Leaning across the table, Amy slugged Beth in the arm. "Thanks a lot."

Clutching her heart, Beth hammed up her speech. "But those things contribute to the complex person I know and love." She ticked off her next finger. "Second, you will get that promotion because you're a talented physician and an excellent leader. Third, Seth's family will think you're wonderful. Why wouldn't they like you? What do you think is wrong with you?"

"Oh, you know… it's just…here I am…a Christian who, until recently, exuded a lot of angry grief and is still working through her relationship with God. Also, there's the fact that I'm a doctor. Maybe they won't want Seth to marry someone in medicine. I've heard it all over the years. They might wonder how I'll be a wife, mother, and physician. The whole, how do you do it all, and do it well thing? What if that's how they feel?" Amy took another deep breath.

"Listen, as usual, you're overthinking everything. Seth hasn't gotten down on one knee yet. This is a dinner to meet the people who shaped and molded him into the hunky man you love but won't admit you love. It'll be fine. More than fine. Seth is a kind, generous man who loves God. I doubt his family will be anything less. The evening might be enjoyable." Beth finished her speech and took a long draw on her hot tea.

Amy relaxed her shoulders and eased back into her seat. "Maybe you're right. I get myself worked up over nothing, and I over-analyze everything." She lifted her latte to her lips and swallowed, letting the warmth soothe her.

Beth shook her head side to side in exaggeration. "No, not you… and in the matter of the Chief job… you trust God to work out whatever is best for you. The hospital, and Ed Baker, would be crazy not to put you in charge. You're definitely bossy enough."

Amy slugged Beth again with her free hand, still holding her drink in the other one.

"Ow! That one hurt! You've got to stop doing that. Or else, I'll encourage you to buy something horrendous to wear to The Big Family Dinner. Bahaha." Beth sent Amy a devilish grin.

"Okay, okay. Deal. No more punching. In all seriousness, thank you for coming with me today. I want to make a good impression on Seth and his family. I don't think I've ever felt this way about someone before." Amy gasped and reached across the table to grasp Beth's forearm. "I totally forgot to tell you!"

"Agh, the clutching, girl you don't know your own strength. What, what is the big news?" Beth rubbed her arm.

"So, remember how Seth and I went for a walk after church on Sunday?" Amy paused for dramatic effect.

Beth stared at her friend and took another sip. "Yes?"

"We went for a walk on the trail for a long time, maybe an hour or more. We talked about what we wanted out of life, where we wanted to travel, our hopes for the future, and how we felt about God. Everything, really. I explained about Mark. Seth seemed to understand. More than understand. We were both open with one another. So, we arrived at a clearing in the trail, and sat down at a bench overlooking the city. The view was stunning."

"Wait. Did he sit close to you? Hold your hand?" Beth's hand flew to her mouth and she paused before dropping it. "Did he kiss you?"

Amy blew out an exasperated breath. "I'm getting to that part! So, we sat on this bench barely big enough to hold us both, and we talked more. I turned to Seth, and he stared into my eyes, and it felt like a magnet pulled us together. Just as I closed my eyes for Seth to kiss me, my pager went off!"

Beth leaned forward. "No! It could only happen to you. You have the worst timing. So, did you get your kiss? What happened after the pager?"

"Well, I wanted to stay, but it ruined the moment. Plus, there was an emergency. I had to jet. So, we walked back to Main Street, he gave me a hug goodbye with the promise to see me Friday for the family dinner, I hopped in my car, and left." Amy took another long drink of her now cold coffee.

"So, now what? We hit the stores and try to create a look that says, 'Marry Me Darling' to Seth and 'Trust Me with Your Son' to his parents?" Beth threw a hand to her chest and wagged her eyebrows.

With one final shove at her best friend's now-pummeled arm, Amy drained the remaining few drops of caffeine. "Exactly. Let's go."

Chapter 27

July 31, 2017, Monday

Amy strolled down the street, plotting her upcoming date ensemble with Beth. Turning to her best friend, Amy grinned. "So, what do you think about Joe?"

Beth grabbed the curved, golden handle attached to the impressive cream baroque style door at the entrance of Samantha's Closet. The sweet scent of honeysuckle and lavender perfume wafted through the air.

Despite Amy's resistance to show enjoyment with anything related to Samantha, she inhaled the intoxicating aroma and breathed a sigh of satisfaction. *Dang it. The girl had style and taste. Please let her not be working today.*

Scanning the room, she saw no sign of Samantha. Amy's gaze landed a kind, local teenage girl with an athletic build who she recognized from church. The girl wore her hair in a short blond bob and Amy thought her name was Megan.

Megan smiled and opened her hands in a welcoming gesture. "Hello, ladies! How can I help you today?"

Beth flopped down in an oversized white wingback chair. "Well, my friend Amy has a date to meet her new boyfriend's parents Friday night. So, we need to create a look that straddles the line between demure future daughter-in-law and fabulous hot tamale. What have you got?"

"You guys got here at the right time. We just got a new shipment in today of beautiful, flowing dresses that I think would be perfect. Want to check them out?" Megan looked at Amy and waited for her answer.

Beth clapped her hands together. "That sounds perfect!"

"Great, what size do you need, Amy?" Megan surveyed Amy's petite, yet toned frame. "I'm thinking a two? Maybe a four? Would that work?"

"Yeah, that should work. Just make sure it's not too flashy. I'd much rather err on the side of understated." She wrung her hands. Thinking about the upcoming family encounter brought beads of sweat to the nape of her neck. Swiping them away with the back of her hand, Amy hoped Megan and Beth didn't notice.

Beth raised her eyebrows and gave a half-grin. "Nervous?"

"Oh, be quiet! Why do you have to know everything?" Amy raised her voice, "Yes, I'm nervous. I told you I was nervous earlier. It's getting worse the more I think about it."

Megan emerged from the back of the shop with her arms loaded down with at least thirty dresses. "Here we go."

Amy gulped. "I thought you were going to bring me back one or two?"

"Well, I figured, since you're here and these are all new, we might as well have a little fashion show. The more you try on the better chance of finding the perfect one. That's what my grandma says about clothing and guys. Not that I agree with her." Megan chuckled.

Amy stepped closer to the daunting stack of clothes. She reached out and lifted the first dress off the mound. "Ok. If we're going to make it through this pile by midnight, we better get started."

"All right. I'll set these up in a changing room for you and you can take your time. When you get one on, though, show us. There's a pedestal and the three-way mirror out here." Megan nodded her head for Amy to follow her.

Sighing, Amy conceded. It was two against one. She followed Megan into the open changing room and threw her bag down on the empty chair in the corner.

One hour, fifteen dresses, one minor fall, and approximately a pound of sweat later, Amy exited the dressing room wearing an exquisite creation. The blush pink frock had darker mauve colored small flowers sprinkled throughout it. It had narrow, but not spaghetti-thin, straps. The middle cinched at the waist with slight ruching, and flowed downward to her calves, ending with a slight flare. The dress flattered Amy perfectly. It emphasized the warm, rosy glow in her cheeks and accentuated her curves, while still remaining modest. As soon as she stepped onto the pedestal in front of the mirrors, Megan and Beth both gasped.

Beth hopped out of her seat. "Oh, my! That's it!"

"It really is a lovely dress, honey," a familiar southern drawl interrupted Amy's excitement.

Her stomach plummeted. Amy turned and placed a forced smile on her face. "Samantha, I didn't think you were here today."

"Well, honey, I stepped out for a minute to run some clothes to the women's shelter that the church ladies' group collected to donate. It pleased me when I returned to my little shop to find Dr. Amy Harte here. I must say that dress looks stunning on you. What's the occasion?" Samantha stepped closer to Amy.

She debated telling Samantha the truth. "I'm looking for a dress to wear to a family dinner." Amy tried to remain vague and avoided Samantha's eyes in the mirror.

"Oh really, well that one there would be perfect. Is it for dinner with your father? Or perhaps Mark's family?"

Stalling for time, Amy looked down at her mangled cuticles and picked at them. "Uh, no, not exactly. It's for... dinner with Seth and his family. He wanted me to meet his family." Amy glanced up in the mirror's reflection and saw a brief scowl come across Samantha's face. Just as quickly as it appeared it fled and Samantha's wide, overly whitened smile replaced it.

"Well, that sounds positively wonderful. I always say you can never have too many friends in this world," Samantha emphasized the word friends.

Amy looked at Beth and expected steam to start pouring out her ears at any moment. "Yeah, I guess I would have to agree with you."

"Samantha, I have to agree with you. Seth is so blessed to be dating my best friend, one of the kindest and smartest women I know," Beth said in a syrupy sweet voice.

Samantha wore a brief look of disgust on her face before

remembering her southern manners. She reached out and patted Amy's hand. "Well, bless your heart, Amy. That is great. Really, great for you. Well, that little dress is darling. Let me know if I can do anything else for you gals." She sniffed and scurried away.

Amy locked eyes with Beth in the mirror and suppressed a giggle.

Beth snickered.

Taking a breath and squaring her shoulders, Amy tried to remain serious. "Beth, stop. Seriously. You have to stop."

Beth's eyes widened. "What?"

Wearing a slight smirk, Megan watched the entire exchange. "Ahem. I take it there isn't a lot of love lost between you and Samantha?" She chuckled.

"That's not exactly true. I want to like her and get along. We have some history with competing for things in school, from activities, school awards, to boys. I need to let it go. I'm asking God to help me embrace his peace and let go of the past. I want to have God's heart and love everyone...and I'm sure that somewhere, deep down, she means well. At least with some things she does...like the clothing donation. I need to seek the good in people. What can I say? I'm not perfect." Amy sighed.

"Then there's the fact that Samantha has probably been plotting for weeks how to attain the title of Mrs. Broadstone for herself." Beth cackled.

Amy raised her finger to her lips. "Shh. Beth, she'll hear you. Be nice."

"Hey, the truth is the truth. And what was it your dad or grandma or somebody always used to say to you? EGRs? Extra Grace Required. I'd say she'd be one to earn that title for sure."

Amy gave a slight nod. "Okay, fine. You might be right, but let's strive to be better people. Would it kill us to be kinder?"

All three women looked at one another in the mirror before erupting in a fit of laughter.

Wiping tears of laughter off her cheeks, Amy attempted to catch her breath. "Let's get out of here. Before we gossip any more. So, what do you think? This is the dress?" Amy spun once in a circle.

Beth nodded her head again. "Yep, it's perfect. They'll love you."

She hoped so. Amy liked Seth a lot. Maybe more than liked him. She gasped.

Beth turned her head sharply. "What's wrong?"

"What if these people, Seth's people, what if they are... fancy?" Amy shifted her weight.

Her friend scrunched her nose. "What do you mean fancy?"

"You know... fancy. Like, what if they set dinner at an impressive wooden table with candelabras that are lit, with linen everything, and polished silver utensils with five different forks, three spoons, and a gazillion different shaped knives? Oh, and that little bowl of water that you're never sure if it's for drinking or washing? What if there are multiple courses? I know nothing about airs." Amy made quotes with her fingers.

Beth wrinkled her brow. "I'm sure they're normal, down-to-earth people excited to meet their son's new girlfriend, or whatever you are. Besides, who eats like that nowadays?"

"But what if they do? Do I have manners? I would think the fact I have to ask you would tell me I don't." Amy placed her hands on her hips.

A guttural belly laugh slipped out from Beth that spread to Amy.

Seconds later, Amy doubled over gasping for air with fresh, joyful tears streaming down her face in the middle of the classy dress boutique.

"I... don't... think... either... of... us... have... manners," Beth guffawed.

Amy stood up and wiped the tears away. "I...guess...you're...right."

Beth regained her composure. "How about you follow the Miss Etiquette rule of starting from the outside and working in with your eating utensils?"

Amy giggled again and grinned at her best friend. "I think fancy people call it cutlery?"

Placing a hand to her chest, Beth spoke with an exaggerated southern drawl. "And, remember, darling, never, ever drink the water from the finger bowl."

Chapter 28

August 3, 2017, Thursday

Seth Broadstone stood in his office with his hands crossed in front of his chest. He surveyed the mountain of paperwork yet to complete for the Open Hearts Foundation. He loosened his tie and ran a hand through his hair, sighing.

The fiscal year ended in October and he needed to have a proposal to submit to the Board of Directors well before then. He stayed up the night prior well past midnight agonizing over the numbers.

A knock on his open door interrupting his thoughts. "My boy, you ready for this meeting?" Ed Baker tapped on his gold wristwatch to hurry Seth along.

Seth glanced at the clock on the wall and shook his head. "11:45 am already? I've been working nonstop since seven and the time got away from me. I'm ready." He hoped.

Ed surveyed the room, not meeting Seth's eyes. "Good, good. Glad to hear it. You're presenting the hospital budget for final approval today, right?"

"Yes, sir."

Ed smoothed his navy satin tie. "Well, great. I assume you have a plan for Open Hearts?"

Stalling for time, Seth rambled, "Uh, well… I'm still ironing out some details… waiting to hear from a few donors I spoke with at the Metropolitan Ball."

"Cutting it a little close, aren't you? I don't want to be the bearer of bad news, but if your horse isn't riding, maybe you need to get a new one. Understand?"

Seth nodded, but rarely understood his boss's southern colloquiums. "Sir, this organization does so much good for the families here. As you say, I think it is a horse that can ride. I'll see you at noon at the meeting and lay out my plan for the upcoming year."

"Fine, fine. Better get a move on it, though. Don't want to be late. The Board hates tardiness." Ed focused his gaze on Seth now and sent him a pointed look.

"Understood." Seth shuffled his papers into his briefcase and straightened his tie. When he looked back up Ed Baker had disappeared. Seth shook his head and muttered under his breath, "Understood."

Seth gathered his suit jacket, briefcase, and a packed lunch and dashed down the hall to the elevator. He stepped on it and recognized a gentleman he had seen at the Metro Ball and perhaps one other Board meeting. He thought the man held a place on the Board, but rarely saw him at the meetings. Seth stared at the numbers above the elevator door and the two men rode it up to the fifth floor in silence. The man exited and Seth followed him to the conference room.

A projector attached to a laptop lit up the whiteboard at the front of the room. A few of the other Board members sat at the table with their lunches spread before them. Seth placed his briefcase down next to a seat near the front. He unpacked his ham sandwich and water and pulled a thumb drive and several copies of the budget from within his briefcase.

Ed Baker strolled into the room, his rotund belly leading the way. He found a place at the long brown table with the gentleman from the elevator and leaned his head toward the man in a hushed discussion.

An agenda laid before each seat, so Seth turned his attention to it. He noted two items for discussion under new business. One was the annual budget. The other was the Chief of Emergency Medicine promotion.

Standing up, Ed cleared his throat. "If everyone's ready, we'll get started. First order of business is the annual budget. I'll turn that over to our Chief Financial Officer, Seth Broadstone." Ed sat down and zeroed in on his foot-long Italian combo sub sandwich.

Seth grabbed his zip drive and sauntered to the front of the room. As he plugged it in to the computer, he assessed his audience. There were four main Board members who he knew well and encountered at the hospital daily. Ed Baker, the CEO, was present, along with the Chief of Operations, and the Chief of Medicine. The other member was an administrator who oversaw the lab, radiology, and pharmacy departments. That left two remaining silent members of the Board. Seth suspected they secured their seats through generous funding. One of those members was the man from the elevator.

Seth stood straight and sat his shoulders back. "Good afternoon. I'm passing around a copy of the hospital budget for the next fiscal year for final approval. As you can see, the hospital funding overall is healthy, and I project growth of five to ten percent for the following year. That includes pledges from community donors for specific areas of the hospital, but most of the hospital's billing and collections sustains itself."

Ed raised a hand.

He raised his eyebrows. "Yes, sir. You have a question?"

Ed furrowed his brow. "Yes, sorry to interrupt. I don't see the Open Hearts Foundation listed on here in the liabilities column."

Seth rubbed his cheek with one hand. "Ah, well, you see I wanted to discuss that today with all of you. As of now, Open Hearts is shy of balancing its budget by $100,000 for the next year. I know that sounds like a lot."

The man from the elevator jumped into the conversation. "It is a lot. Now, where exactly is that amount of money going to come from in this report? Not from the hospital's main budget? It would break the bank. And for an organization that brings nothing fiscally to the hospital?"

Seth opened his mouth to speak, but Ed cut him off. "Mr. Blakely's right. I don't see how you'll find that sum of money in the next few weeks. We need to have the entire budget completed by the end of August."

Despite standing at the front of the room, Seth raised his own hand. "Gentlemen, I'm waiting to hear from a few more donors.

Could I ask that you give me a couple more weeks? I promise to fund Open Hearts without dipping further into the hospital budget. Please. Can we finalize the budget with a clause about this matter?"

Ed paused between bites, a piece of meat hanging from his lips. He chewed thoughtfully and swallowed. "Tell you what. You find some additional funding that doesn't pull from the hospital's allocated resources and I'll support it." Ed turned to face the mystery Board member next to him. "Mr. Blakely, what do you think?"

The older man smoothed out his lapel. "Well, I don't suppose a few more weeks will make a difference. Now, can we please move on to more important matters? We need to decide on the Chief of Emergency Medicine. I can't stay here all day. I have my business to get back to at 1 pm."

Ed nodded his head, talking between bites. "Yes, yes. Thank you, Seth. Let's put this budget to a vote, except for Open Hearts. I move to approve it with the clause about the Foundation. Do I have a second?" He looked at his comrade, the elder Mr. Blakely.

"I second the motion." Mr. Blakely took a bite out of a cucumber sandwich.

"Very well. Do we have any objections?" Ed looked around the room, and facing no opposition, took another bite from his sub. "There you have, son. It's settled. Now, about the Chief of Emergency Medicine position."

Shifting his weight, Seth retrieved his thumb drive from the computer. He raised his hand one more time.

Mr. Baker glanced at him with a slight frown. "Yes, Seth, what is it?"

Seth moved to the seat where his briefcase laid and met his boss's gaze. "Sir, I'd like to recuse myself from this discussion and vote. I have a conflict of interest. I know one of the applicants on a personal level."

Mr. Baker's face relaxed. "Thank you for your time on the budget. Keep us posted in the next few weeks about the Foundation."

Seth picked up his briefcase and walked to door. As he exited the room, he heard the discussion begin about the Chief job.

Ed spoke with confidence, "Now, I think the best man for the job is Dr. Mark Blakely..."

Stopping in his tracks, Seth reflected on meeting the mystery Board member today from the elevator. *Blakely.* The gentleman's last name was Blakely. Could that man be Mark's father? If so, why didn't he recuse himself from the vote? Ed and Mr. Blakely seemed fairly chummy, too. Seth considered rejoining the meeting, but he'd already taken himself out of the discussion and vote because of his personal ethics. Instead, he walked down the hall and took the elevator to the fourth floor with trepidation.

Seth settled in his office and began calling the list of donors, trying to find help for Open Hearts. Firing up his laptop and digging out his cellphone, Seth readied himself to make pleading calls. His shoulders tensed. Ed Baker's words about Mark rang in his ears. Seth rolled his sleeves up and loosened his tie, ready to work. He had to get a lot accomplished today, so he could take tomorrow night off for his date with Amy. The thought of seeing her again made him smile. Seth sighed. He prayed the Board gave Amy a fair chance and that he was wrong about Mr. Blakely's connection to Mark.

Chapter 29

August 4, 2017, Friday

Beads of sweat formed across Amy's forehead as she bent over, trying to squeeze the unrelenting strap of her new sling back shoe over the heel of her foot. Others might unlatch the strap like a normal human, but not Amy. No, she liked a challenge. Her whole afternoon went this way.

Oversleeping that morning, Amy missed her 8:00 am spin class. She arranged her schedule at the hospital so she could take off the entire day so she might spend it preparing for her dinner with Seth's family and obsessing over what to wear and say tonight. Determined to get in a workout to burn off some pre-dinner calories and stress, she threw on her workout clothes and went for a jog.

Sweaty and short on time, she skipped a much-needed shower and instead went for a pedicure, a luxury in which Amy rarely partook. She hoped it might boost her confidence and relax her. In that right, it had been a success, but while rushing to buy Seth's family a small gift, she smudged her left toe against the car floorboard.

She drove like a maniac to the grocery store and bought a large glass vase filled with billowy white peonies. Amy hoped Seth's mother liked them. While selecting the flowers, she knocked over two other vases. She offered to pay for them, but the store clerk kindly declined. Stooped over with her smudged toenail and sweat-drenched clothes, Amy helped mop up the water from the vases, shaking her head. She wondered if flowers were enough of a gesture. After finishing sopping up the watery mess, Amy asked the clerk to direct her to the baked goods aisle. She glanced at her phone which read 2:00 p.m. and started to panic. She still needed to shower, get dressed, fix her hair, and put on makeup.

Amy ran toward the bakery aisle and found walnut brownies and then headed to the checkout with her white peonies, brownies, and an impish grin from reflecting on the disastrous mess she'd made in the flower aisle. By the time she got home it was 3:00 pm. Seth promised to pick her up in two short hours. She hopped in the shower and took a deep breath. The hot water and steam melted away the stress of the morning, and her shoulders relaxed. Flying through the rest of her beauty routine, Amy spackled makeup on her face.

She slipped into her new flowing, floral A-line dress from Samantha's shop and giggled thinking about her retail outing with her best friend earlier in the week. Beth was a great friend, and Amy hoped things worked out between Beth and Joe. Amy knew there were sparks between them. Maybe she would head to the coffee shop Sunday after church and give Joe a nudge. She shook her head. *Back to the matter at hand.*

With her new dress in place and her makeup and hair complete, Amy wedged her heel into her second shoe. She stood to take in the final effect in front of the mirror in her room. Amy smiled at her reflection. Samantha's dress flattered her well, accentuating her waist and gliding over the curves of her hips. The soft blush color of her heels matched the small flowers in her dress. She checked her phone one final time. 4:55 p.m. *Perfect.*

Amy sunk into her couch and released a sigh. She said a quick, silent prayer for the evening. A few minutes later the doorbell rang, and she stood up, squared her shoulders, and walked to answer the door. Upon opening it, she met Seth wearing a broad grin.

His eyes lit up. "Wow, Amy, you look amazing. I love that dress."

Amy smiled before looking down and smoothing the skirt. "Thanks, Seth. It's new. I'm glad you like it."

Seth extended a hand to her. "Are you ready to go?"

She paused before taking his hand. "I guess so. If I'm being honest, I'm nervous. What if your family doesn't like me?"

"What're you talking about? How can they not like you? You're beautiful and smart." Seth's face reddened.

Amy grinned and grasped Seth's hand. "Thanks, I hope you're right... Ok, I'm ready." She walked hand in hand with Seth to his car, and he opened the door for her. Sliding into her seat, she prepared herself for the big night.

Chapter 30

August 4, 2017, Friday

Amy fiddled with her dress while she listened to Seth talk about his hospital budget meeting. She tried to focus on the words coming out of his mouth. Seth continued the conversation as if she responded appropriately, but her mind wandered to the dinner ahead. She vaguely heard him mention that a man named Mr. Blakely attended the meeting, but before she could ask him about it, they arrived at Seth's parent's house. *Stay calm.*

Seth turned the ignition off. "We're here." He came around and opened her door, guiding her by the hand to his parent's front door.

Taking in her new surroundings, Amy's jaw dropped. Symmetrical pear trees lined the driveway. She inhaled and the scent of honeysuckle greeted her. Eight by four-inch pavers separated by pebble river rocks created an intricate patterned walkway leading to the impressive residence. Stately might be a better word. It stood at least three stories tall. The brown brick colonial with two large white columns in the front welcomed guests onto a wrap-around porch.

The mahogany door stood at least twelve feet tall. A golden, lion-faced knocker sat in the middle of the door and matched the doorknob. Amy looked to the side for a doorbell but found none.

Seth wrapped the door with the grandiose knocker. "Ready?"

"Yeah." Amy turned around to take in the expansive,

manicured green lawn cut into a checkerboard pattern. These people had money. Amy's palms dampened. She had no time to think about it because the grand mahogany door flung wide open, and Amy came face to face with the Broadstone matriarch.

"David! David! Seth is here. Hey baby, get over here and give me some sugar." Seth's mom engulfed him in a hug and Amy appraised her. She was tall like Seth, probably five foot ten inches. She styled her jet-black hair in a flattering, youthful pixie cut. Her skin appeared well-tanned, and she spoke through plump, bright red lips. She reminded Amy of someone... maybe from Broadway?

Mr. Broadstone stepped onto the porch. "Seth, my boy, good to see you!" He was about the same height as Seth's mom, but seemed more subdued. He smiled and slapped Seth on the back and then shook her hand. His copper and grey flecked hair curled and ended at his shoulders.

Seth pulled Amy closer. "Amy, you know my dad, David, and this is my mom, Nancy. Guys, this is Amy."

Nancy leaned in and wrapped Amy in a hug. The scent of red roses and orchids surrounded her. "We've heard wonderful things about you! Well, don't just stand there, come in, come in. I hope you're hungry. I made enough food to feed an army."

Walking through the doorway, Amy encountered even more opulence. She looked up and saw a large Waterford crystal chandelier hanging overhead, catching rays of sunlight and sprinkling flecks of rainbow throughout the entryway. To the right sat a massive cedar sideboard with intricately carved, curved legs supporting its polished tabletop.

Amy noticed a grand mirror hanging above it on the wall with a circular center and thin columns of glass radiating outward from the center like the sun. The combination of it inter-playing with the chandelier and the sunlight stunned. She noted a plush white and grey toile patterned rug underfoot. Coordinating toile wallpaper covered the hallway, further accenting the intricate dentate crown molding painted ultra-white overhead. The decor reminded her of a French chateau. Amy swallowed hard.

Seth's mother reached for Amy's purse, breaking the silence. "Sugar let me take your bag. We'll put it right here in the parlor and get you both settled at the table. Dinner is just about ready."

Amy cleared her throat. "Ahem, th-thanks. That sounds great! I'm starving!" She shuffled further down the hallway and smiled at Seth's mother.

Nancy escorted Amy to the dining room, which did not disappoint. Evening sunlight poured through large windows flanking a set of French doors, which opened to a quaint outdoor patio that looked like an English garden. Two small black wrought-iron tables with matching chairs caught Amy's attention. They held five place settings encircling a crystal vase of fresh pink tulips in the middle of the table. Squarely cut boxwood hedges surrounded the property and provided the home with intimacy.

Amy's mouth fell open in awe. Long, flowing sheer curtains abutted either side of the windows, creating an ethereal feel. The simple flat, cream-colored walls created a blank canvas for two Moroccan shaped mirrors on the opposite wall from the French doors to shine. The mirrors had a champagne metallic finish and complemented the pattern in the cream and gold rug below. The showpiece of the room, however, was the dining room table. It seated at least twelve people. The table was also metallic, with mirrored insets on top. Ten wooden champagne painted chairs surrounded both sides of the table, while two oversized, tufted black wingback chairs sat on either end. Perched above the center of the table was another glistening crystal chandelier. Although smaller, it looked just as opulent as the first. The overall effect was very glam French country. Self-consciously, Amy smoothed down her dress, instantly regretting she hadn't selected something chicer for this dinner.

She turned toward Seth's mother. "Mrs. Broadstone, your home is beautiful. Are we eating outside? That patio is breathtaking."

Smiling, Nancy put a hand to her chest. "Well, bless your heart. Thank you so much. I thought we'd have supper in here first. I set the patio table thinking we might enjoy after dinner coffee and dessert outside. Will that suit?" Nancy raised her eyebrows.

Amy wiped her palms on her dress and nodded. "That sounds perfect." She followed Seth to her seat for the upcoming debacle. He pulled out her chair and Amy cautiously sunk into it, trying not to break anything. She sighed, grateful to sit down. How much damage could she do in a chair?

Seth's mother poured water into Amy's goblet at the same time Amy reached for her napkin with a grand flourish to place it in her lap. Unfortunately, the napkin was precariously close to the glass. Amy collided her right arm into the water pitcher and sent the entire contents of it onto the wood table, floor, and fancy wool rug. She gasped and her hand flew to her mouth. "I'm so, so sorry!"

To her credit, Seth's mother remained cool. "Oh, my!" Any residual exclamations Nancy wanted to say, she graciously kept to herself.

Amy made an unsuccessful attempt to blot the water with her linen napkin. "Please, let me help you clean this up. I apologize. Sometimes I can be such a klutz." She didn't understand why a company produced dinner napkins made from a material completely repellant of liquid. Instead of improving the status of "The Water Incident," Amy scooped the water puddle from the table into the floor to the join the rest of its company from the pitcher.

Meanwhile, Seth's mom kneeled on the floor, wearing her expensive, form fitting sheath dress and black kitten heels. She continued dabbing at the enlarging water puddle due to Amy's futile efforts.

Realizing that the mess required more than linen napkins, Nancy excused herself to find something more substantial.

As soon as she left the room, Amy covered her face with both hands. "Seth, I feel terrible. I've been here for ten minutes, and already I'm destroying your parent's home. They'll hate me."

Seth patted her on the arm to reassure her. "Would you stop that? It's fine. It was an accident. And besides, it's just a little water. Harmless really."

Her face warmed, but she took a deep breath and tried to regain her composure.

Seth's mother returned with several fresh, white rags and made quick work of blotting up the remaining mess at Amy's feet.

Amy offered to help but Nancy waved her away. "Now, hush, sugar. I've got this. It's just water. Not anything to make a big fuss about."

Exhaling a sigh of relief, Amy's shoulders relaxed a bit. Strike one. Hopefully, she wouldn't make any more blunders. By this time the rug looked like new and the table was dry.

David entered the dining room carrying a tray of cut crystal glasses filled to the brim with lemonade. He sat the tray down on the sideboard and passed out pre-filled glasses one by one. When he placed Amy's lemonade in front of her, he winked. "Thought it might be better to leave the pitcher in the kitchen this time. Less volume." He chuckled.

She relaxed her shoulders and smiled at him.

At that moment, Seth's brother came into the room. Amy last saw Brian in the emergency room at the hospital after his car accident. At first glance, Seth and his brother looked nothing alike. Seth stood taller, with dark hair and chestnut eyes. Brian was shorter by a few inches and had curly blond hair and blue eyes. Both had smiles that welcomed people immediately.

Brian walked up to Amy, and she outstretched her hand to shake his, but he lifted her into a big bear hug. "How's my future sister-in-law who saved my life? Long time no see."

He sat Amy back down on the ground, and she grunted. "Oof." After landing on her feet, she tried to regain her balance. "Uh, hey Brian, it's good to see you. How have you been? How's your head?"

Seth slapped his brother on the back. "Just as broken as ever." Some friendly shoving ensued, which escalated quickly. Amy feared they might break one of the many precious items in the Broadstone's grand dining room, when Seth's mother interrupted the scuffle.

Placing her hands on her hips, Nancy shouted, "Boys! Is that any way to act with company present? As grown men, is this any way to act at all? I mean, really. Let's remember our manners." She spoke with a smooth southern drawl and shook her head. "Now, let's all settle down and take a seat. Dinner's going to get cold if we leave it any longer, and I don't want any of it go to waste. Sit." Nancy pointed to the chairs and gave the two boys the same pointed expression with her pursed red lips that Amy suspected she had used on them since their birth.

The brothers took their seats after their mother's prompting and Nancy disappeared into the kitchen.

Seth took his place at Amy's side.

Brian smiled at her from across the table and tapped his hands on the table. "Seriously, Amy. Thank you for all you did. I have a few scratches still healing, but otherwise I'm doing great. The important thing is that I can still swing a tennis racquet well enough to whip up on my big brother on the court." He sent a devilish grin toward Seth.

Seth crossed him arms in front of his chest. "Well, I would say Brian's in fine physical condition, but obviously, he's delusional after his wreck, because the last time he beat me on the tennis court was... um... never. In the history of time."

Brian cracked his knuckles and snorted. "Have, too."

Chuckling under her breath, Amy wondered if the two men behaved this way as children and speculated that despite growing into functional adults, sibling rivalries ran deep.

Seth's mouth settled into a straight line. "I'll make a bet with you."

Brian's eyes flashed with a competitive look. "What kind of bet?"

Returning Brian's steely gaze, Seth said, "A bet that I can still wipe the court with you."

Brian furrowed his brow. "No way! Because it's not true! I'll wipe the court with you! Let's have a match. A friendly family tournament. Winner gets permanent bragging rights and free coffee for a month at Joe's."

Seth nodded in agreement. "Just name the time and the place, and I'm there."

Brian stretched his hand out to Seth. "You're on. Prepare to be destroyed. How about next Friday night, at the country club? We can have a celebration dinner at the club afterwards to commemorate my victory."

Seth took Brian's hand and shook it. "It's a deal. I can taste the fresh-roasted coffee beans already."

Both men stared evenly at one another until Brian broke the silence. "Deal."

Nancy sauntered into the room carrying the largest tray of food Amy ever saw. "Dinner's ready!" Nancy broke the tension and ended the animated debate between her children. Nancy placed the tray on the table and handed Amy a fresh napkin.

Amy smiled, sighed, and placed it in her lap. The dinner would have put Paula Southerly to shame. Nancy made fried chicken, mashed potatoes, green beans, thick chicken gravy, tomato and cucumber salad, corn on the cob, and yeast rolls the size of cantaloupes. She cooked everything from scratch and the house smelled like Sunday dinners at Amy's grandmother's house. She forgot the last time she ate a homemade meal.

Everyone bowed their heads and Seth's father said the grace, "Heavenly Father, thank you for all the blessings you've given us. Thank you for this food and the hands that have prepared it and thank you for the gift of new friends." He looked up at Amy and smiled kindly as everyone else at the table proclaimed a resounding amen. "Now, let's eat!"

Welcomed silence ensued with everyone digging into the food. Amy picked up her fork, thankful there was only one, and pierced her first bite of chicken. After struggling for a moment to disassemble it, she glanced at Seth and then Nancy. She noted everyone tore into the chicken with their bare hands. *Thank goodness!* She put her fork down and dove into the fried deliciousness.

Amy's mouth watered. The crunchy exterior of the chicken consisted of a spicy blend of sea salt and black pepper. The mashed potatoes tasted smooth and creamy and the green beans exploded with a garlic flavor. The tangy tomato and cucumber salad complemented the buttery, sweet goodness of the corn on the cob, and the rolls tasted like soft, sweet pieces of heaven.

She sighed with pleasure. Dinner for Amy usually included a microwavable frozen entrée or, worse, a peanut butter sandwich. She surveyed the room and embraced the comfortable sense of family. Amy had been nervous earlier, especially after her water debacle, but Nancy put her at ease.

Nancy placed a hand on top of Amy's. "What made you want to become a doctor?"

She gave Nancy a half-smile. "Well, when I was a little girl, I always wanted to help people. At first, I thought about becoming a veterinarian because I loved animals so much. When I turned eight years old, I developed terrible allergies to most animals, so vet school looked like a bad idea."

Everyone at the table laughed and Amy continued her story. "So, I thought, well, now what am I going to do? I talked to my dad one day after school and told him, 'I want to help people, but I don't think I want to be a vet anymore'. The next day I fell off my bike; like a total wipeout wreck. I braked too quickly and flew headfirst over the handlebars. My parents took me to the emergency department to have my right elbow and shoulder x-rayed. I was scared, but the doctor entered the room with a balloon made from an exam glove and put me at ease." She paused with her story and looked around the table.

Seth gave her an encouraging grin.

"Fortunately, I only had a few scrapes and bruises, but I never forgot how that doctor treated me. He took time to see things from the perspective of an eight-year-old kid. It impacted me. The next morning when I got up, I told my dad I knew that when I grew up, I wanted to become a doctor. After that, I did whatever it took to make it in medicine."

Amy took another bite of chicken and swallowed before continuing, "I studied late nights, took on several extracurricular activities, clubs, and graduated high school at the top of my class. After college I headed to medical school at Vanderbilt to focus on emergency medicine because I wanted to help others when they were the most vulnerable. So, the rest is history." Amy finished her monologue about her life and looked over at Seth again to see him beaming.

Nancy disrupted Amy's reverie. "Sugar, that's admirable, but I imagine it must be hard helping all those sick people after losing your momma to cancer."

Seth whipped his head around. "Mom!"

Nancy lifted her eyebrows, oblivious. "What? What did I say?"

Scrunching his forehead, Seth glanced at Amy, as if to see if his mother offended her. "That wasn't tactful... or considerate."

Amy waved away Seth's concern and sent Nancy a smile. "No, no, it's fine, really. I know you don't mean any harm by asking. It was hard... at first. My personal involvement with medicine at the time my mother got sick made the entire experience surreal. I lived in denial throughout most of her illness. I reviewed her labs, listened to her symptoms, and understood as a clinician what might lie ahead, but I never anticipated she'd have such an aggressive disease. She went from perfectly healthy to frail in a matter of months, and while my doctor mind understood it, my daughter's heart refused to believe it."

Nancy squeezed her hand. "That must have been a terrible time."

Nodding, Amy returned Nancy's squeeze. "The first few months after she passed, I cried every day, sometimes multiple times a day. Anger settled in my soul until a few months ago. I blamed myself for not getting her help sooner, and God for letting it all unfold. I took a hiatus from church because hearing the songs of hope and about the goodness of God broke my heart." She drew a shuddering breath.

"Sugar, are you ok?" Nancy asked, wearing a sympathetic smile.

She paused before answering. "Yeah... I recently learned that my dad might lose my childhood home if I can't help him raise enough money soon. I'm hoping to get a promotion at work, which would cover the cost but it's not a sure thing. I've lived with anger and guilt for over a year now and thinking about losing the house made me realize how much I missed having a relationship with God. So, I went back to church." She looked around and everyone gave her their full attention. "The first day back I bumped into Seth and we shared a coffee together, and now I'm here with you all." Amy clamped her mouth shut and felt her cheeks warm after unloading her life story upon Seth's family.

Seth's dad cleared his throat. "Ahem, I tell you what. Why don't Nancy and I clear the table and you sit here and have another glass of iced tea? Or I can make some coffee if you like?"

"Oh, yes, David, that sounds wonderful. We can enjoy it on the veranda. It's so lovely out there this time of year." Nancy jumped to her feet, already assembling an armload of dishes to transport to the kitchen like a tower of Jenga.

Amy grinned and her mouth watered in anticipation of more caffeine. "Thank you. Are you sure you don't need help?" She raised her eyebrows.

Nancy continued stacking plates on one arm and waved Amy's help away with her other hand. "Nonsense!"

Seth got up from his seat and took a step toward his mother. "Here mom, give me that large platter. I'll take the rest of the chicken to the kitchen. That's too heavy for you to carry."

Amy clasped her hands and rested her chin on them, gazing at Seth. She marveled at his kindness toward his mom.

Accepting the assistance, Nancy smiled at her son. "Well, thank you, honey. You're such a gentleman." She side-squeezed her firstborn and Nancy, David, and Seth headed into the kitchen, their arms laden with every dish from dinner.

Brian remained behind. He sat across the table from Amy. Turning his attention to her, he rested his elbows on the table. He folded his hands together as if praying and placed his chin on the tips of his fingers in an almost ceremonious fashion. In an exaggerated southern accent, he joked with her, "Well, sugar, tell me, now that it's just you and me, when is the wedding date?" He batted his eyelashes at Amy.

A volcano of embarrassment erupted up Amy's neck, spreading to her cheeks. Several seconds passed before she responded. "Uh... I don't know, Brian. I care a lot about your brother. More than a lot... but, we haven't known each other for long. So, there's that. Honestly, we have talked little about the future. Um, I think he likes me a lot... he might love me, too, but... uh... so... no wedding discussion." Amy sealed her lips.

She smacked a hand over her eyes and counted in her head to five. When she dropped her hand and looked at Brian, he wore a devilish grin.

"Awe, I'm just kidding with you Amy. I wasn't serious. But I'm glad to know you care about my brother, although sometimes I wonder why?" He grinned wider.

Amy balled up her water repellant napkin and threw it at his head. "Listen, don't you dare say a word to him about any of it. I don't know why I told you all that... and stop picking on me." She tried to scowl, but it turned into a slow smile. They shared a brief look and started cackling. By the time Seth, Nancy, and David returned, tears of laughter streamed down her face.

Seth's head snapped toward his brother. He sent him a pointed look. "What did you do?"

Brian put a hand to his chest and his eyes widened. "Who? Me? I've been an angel." He batted his eyelashes again and him and Amy erupted into another round of laughter while Seth looked on, baffled.

Seth rolled his eyes and shook his head. "Yeah, I'm sure. An absolute angel."

Chapter 31

August 11, 2017, Friday

Amy inhaled the bleach-laced scent of the hospital and looked at her phone. Almost time to leave. Somehow, the week whizzed past. Between working multiple twelve-hour and sixteen-hour shifts at the Emergency Department and squeezing in a coffee date with Beth, both exhaustion and satisfaction enveloped Amy. Before she knew it, Friday arrived bringing with it the Broadstone tennis tournament. She sighed. As an only child she did not understand Seth and Brian's' sibling rivalry.

A voice called Amy's name, "Hey, Dr. Harte! I need your signature on this final patient chart and then you should be good to go." A clipboard holding a T-sheet with charting information on it appeared in front of her on the counter.

She met the warm smile of Julia, one of her medical students. "Hi, Julie. Thanks for all your hard work today." She reviewed the student's assessment notes and then filled in her attending physician exam. She agreed with Julie's recommendations, so one last signature completed her shift.

Taking the clipboard, Julie placed it in front of her chest. "Any big plans this weekend?"

Amy shifted her weight. "Actually... tonight I'm going to a tennis match with a close... friend and his family. It should be fun."

Julie narrowed her eyes and pressed her lips tight.

Amy avoided her gaze and suspected Julie knew the date held more significance. Thankfully, protocol dictated that Julie, as a student, respect her superiors. This included Amy.

Breaking into a wide grin, Julie said, "Well… great! I hope you enjoy it! I'll see you next week, I'm sure."

Amy ambled out the clear sliding glass doors of Metropolitan Hospital at 2:00 pm. Driving home, she smiled thinking about seeing Seth later that evening. She arrived at her house and opened the door to find the typical remnants of dishes and clothes strewn about from getting ready in a hurry that morning. She scanned the room and paused, considering the mess. A quick glance at the microwave clock confirmed it; no time to clean now. Amy shrugged her shoulders to and headed to her bedroom.

She showered and changed clothes and her stomach growled, reminding her she last ate six hours ago. Black coffee provided the main fuel she had at the hospital. Then she topped that off with a handful of chocolate kisses. Over the last year, Amy learned life is short, so eat dessert. She chuckled.

Grabbing her bag, she took one final glance at herself in her foyer mirror. Amy nodded at her reflection. The light blue sundress she wore brought out the aqua color of her eyes and her hair cooperated for a change. She left it down in long, soft waves.

Amy dashed out the door and drove in a hurry to the country club to make the match on time. She could not wait to see how Seth fared against Brian. She arrived at the Scottsburg Country Club, stopped her car in front of the circular driveway, and held her breath. Her family never belonged to the club as members, so she only visited it a few times in the past.

The club imposed an impressive figure. Large white columns flanked double wooden doors at least ten feet tall. The white exterior contrasted against a black slate porch boasting several white rocking chairs in the summer. Rows of green boxwood hedges wrapped around the front and sides of the building and encased the tennis courts and first hole of the golf course in the back. A maze of golf cart trails wound its way across the property.

She exited her car, and a valet welcomed her at the club entrance. Amy never knew whether to toss the keys to the valet like in the movies or to place them in their hand with gentle care.

She wrung her hands.

Amy, not confident in her throwing arm or her aim, carefully placed the keys, along with a few dollars in the young, blond man's hand greeting her. He looked like a high schooler, and she considered if she could trust him to drive her car, but she was in a hurry and honestly, her car was not fancy. At almost ten years old, it boasted several scratches and dings. She shrugged and decided not to worry about the fate of her vehicle and tried to walk with grace into the club lobby.

Southern charm, chandeliers, and marble abounded. The place smelled of cigars and money. Lots and lots of money. Meeting Seth's family the week prior at dinner eased Amy's nerves a little. They followed some pomp and circumstance, but also were kind, down-to-earth people. She walked through the lobby and down a narrow, red carpeted hallway that opened on the other side to the back balcony. It overlooked an expansive green lawn below that abutted both red clay and hard tennis courts. From the balcony, Amy saw Seth and Brian on the courts, stretching and warming up for the match. They heckled one another, although good-naturedly from what she could tell.

She walked down concrete stairs on the side of the balcony to the tennis court entrance. Long, metal bleachers awaited at the closest end of the court and Nancy and David sat perched on the top row.

Nancy waved at Amy with enthusiasm using both hands.

Amy smiled and waved back, walking toward Seth's parents. "Nancy, David, I didn't know you two would be here today." She reached out to shake their hands, but Nancy engulfed her in an unexpected, although not unwelcome, hug.

"Oh, sugar, it's so good to see you again. Isn't it great to see Amy, David? You're such a sweet young lady. Now scoot over David and make some room." Nancy shooed her husband over with her hands. "Honey, you sit down here and get ready for the bloodbath."

Amy whipped her head up in concern. "Bloodbath? Is it really going to be that serious? I thought they were just giving one another a hard time. Joking around." She furrowed her brow.

Nancy swatted away Amy's worry with a flick of her wrist. She peered out to the court, intently watching her boys. "Oh, well, they are. But my boys are competitive." She shook her head. "Now, look here, they're fixin' to begin." She pointed toward the court.

Raising her head, Amy witnessed the two men taking wide-leg stances at opposite ends of the court. They both held their racquets in front of them.

Seth spun his racquet between his hands several times and took a yellow tennis ball out of his pocket. Both Broadstone brothers wore determined looks on their faces. Seth's jaw clenched and his eyes narrowed. He bounced the ball a few times and then held it in front of him against his racquet. Staring at his brother, he paused. "You ready?"

Amy held her breath.

Brian spun his own racquet and nodded. "I was born ready."

Cracking the first smile of the match, Seth nonchalantly threw the tennis up to serve. It hung in the air for an eternity. Just when Amy thought Seth missed swinging at the ball, his racquet flew up and whacked the fuzzy yellow object with such ferocity that she wondered how it did not leave a hole in his racquet.

The ball whizzed over the net, skimming above it by only an inch or two before stopping with a thud on the opposite side of the court in Brian's service box. It landed so close to Brian, Amy questioned how he would return the serve, but at the last minute his right arm stretched behind him and a wicked forehand resulted.

The two brothers battled in this manner for several hours. Evenly matched, they simply traded points back and forth. While Brian's forehand and quick footwork bested Seth, Seth maintained a fast serve and his backhand never missed. Amy thought it a shame that they played against one another because they would make an incredible doubles team.

The men played 2 full sets, with Seth having won the first set, while Brian took the second one. In the final set Seth held the lead at match point. It was his turn to serve, and they both appeared exhausted.

Seth wiped thick beads of sweat off his forehead with the back of his right hand, holding the ball. He squinted over the net before tossing the yellow ball high in the air. His racquet rose up and hit the ball with a deafening crack. It was the best serve of the match and Brian hustled to reach the ball, but Seth planted it at the farthest corner of the box just out of his brother's reach.

Brian missed the return and collapsed to his knees. "No!"

Jumping in the air, Seth punched the sky with his racquet, whooping and hollering in victory, "Yeah, yeah! Woohoo!"

His brother punched toward the ground and shook his head. "Awe man, I cannot believe I missed that shot!"

Seth approached the net and reached his hand out to shake Brian's. "Good game, buddy. That was a close one."

Pumping Seth's hand up and down, Brian wore a mischievous smirk. "You know I let you win, right?"

Seth grinned widely. "Yeah. Right. You know the deal. The family record will state that I, Seth Broadstone, am the greatest tennis player in the family."

Amy wiped her own brow filled with sweat from the tense match and the late summer heat. *Brothers.*

Dabbing at the back of her neck with a cotton handkerchief, Nancy turned to Amy. "My, that was a close one. Those boys will give me a heart attack one of these days. Same as when they were kids. They love each other something fierce, but oh my, can they go at it. You'd think grown men would give all this nonsense up. But, no, nothing doing."

Nancy turned to David, who gave a soft snore on the bench next to her. "David." He didn't budge. "David!" Nancy shouted at her sleeping husband, giving him a sharp nudge in the ribs with her elbow.

David rubbed his eyes with his fingers, struggling to wake up. "Huh? What? Have they started yet?"

"Are you kidding me? It's over. You missed the whole thing!" Nancy sent a conspiratorial whisper to Amy, "I think my David could sleep through a tornado on a pig farm." She planted her hands on her hips and shook her head.

Amy giggled to herself after thinking about that mental image for a moment.

Now fully awake, David wore a sheepish grin. "Sorry ladies. I guess I dozed off, huh?"

Nodding her head toward the court, Amy smiled at him. "You missed a good match! It was close but Seth won. I think they're drafting some sort of family declaration right now." She chuckled.

The brothers stood on the court at the net debating who had the better serve, and the discussion became heated.

Nancy cupped her hands to her mouth, "Now boys, hush. That's enough competition for one day. Why don't you boys go change your clothes in the dressing room and meet us at the clubhouse restaurant?" She rose, showing that, as the matriarch of the family, the matter was settled.

Seth and Brian each grabbed their loose tennis balls, picked up their racquets, and placed them back in their covers. They wiped the extra sweat off their faces with their towels and laid their arguing to rest.

"All right mom, you're right. Come on, Brian, I think you've had enough for one day. Let's go grab a burger." Seth winked at his brother.

Brian's mouth formed a thin line. He did not look amused but seemed to accept his fate. "Yeah, ok. But this isn't over. I will demand a rematch soon. I'm sure my near-death experience in the car wreck affected my serve."

Seth rolled his eyes and followed his brother to the club house changing rooms.

Chapter 32

August 11, 2017, Friday

Thirty minutes later, Amy, Seth, Brian, Nancy, and David sat at the premier table at The Point, the main clubhouse restaurant. It was 5:00 p.m., and the upper crust restaurant remained empty at the early hour, making it seem more casual. Their table overlooked the far-reaching green lawn of the main golf course and the view took Amy's breath away.

White linens ensconced the table and black fan shaped cloth napkins perched inside each crystal water glass. A glittering glass chandelier hung overhead casting rays of light throughout the room.

The brother had changed into crisp, white Bermuda shorts. Seth wore a light blue polo shirt, while Brian had on a similar sage green one. Both men looked sharp. Their wet hair glistened from quick showers after the tennis death match, and Seth's recently deepened tan made his smile appear brighter. Every time he sent her a grin butterflies fluttered in her stomach.

She smiled back, and as he settled into his chair, he reached over and gave her hand a tender squeeze. A jolt of electricity shot down her arm at his touch. She caught her breath.

Brian sat down next to his brother, the victor, and ribbed him good naturally about the outcome of the match. "Next time, dude. Next time, I'm coming for you."

Seth grinned at his brother and winked. "Anytime. I'm always ready. Bring it."

Nancy took her seat across the table from Seth and Amy. She placed her napkin in her lap and clasped her hands together on the table before looking up at her two sons. "Now, boys, we have had enough of that nonsense for the day. Let's look at the menu and attempt to appear as if we are southern and still have our manners. Hmm? Thank you." Nancy nodded her head, settling the matter.

Everyone at the table picked up their menus and began perusing the offerings. The prices listed next to each offering shocked Amy. She scanned the entrees listed on the menu and quickly realized the cheapest item was a brined (she did not know what that even meant) chicken, at thirty dollars. With Amy's profession as a doctor, she could afford an expensive meal, but every purchase now reminded her of the hefty price tag due in a few weeks to save her father's house. Plus, she did not love gourmet food. Nope. Give her a burger or, even better, a cup of coffee and a cupcake any day. *Hmm... salad. That should be more reasonable and hopefully larger in size.* She scanned the offerings one final time and settled on the house salad as it was the only one listed containing items she could pronounce. *How could anyone mess up lettuce, tomato, carrots, and dressing?*

A waiter arrived at the table and took everyone's orders. While waiting for their food, the group chatted about everything from the work week to the tennis match. Before Amy knew it, their meals appeared. The waiter, dressed in a long sleeve buttoned down white shirt with a black vest and dark pants, placed Amy's salad in front of her. She almost laughed out loud. On the beautiful white table sat the largest white bone china plate she ever saw and in the middle of the plate a singular green leaf, a sprig of carrot, and a gelatinous red goo with one sliver of onion taunted her. Somewhere at the bottom the small pile resided a microscopic drizzling of dressing she hoped. *Yum.*

Glancing over at Seth, he grinned widely at her with a gleam in his eye. "Careful, Amy, you don't want to get too full."

She tried to keep a straight face, but the humor of the situation got the better of her. "Oh, don't worry. I'll pace myself. This could take a while." She burst into inappropriate, uncontrollable giggles, and before she knew it, Nancy chuckled, too.

They all ate their food fast, and given the size of her salad, Amy finished first. Nancy shared stories about both of her boys in school, and Amy heard the pride in her children in her voice.

David shared tales from Seth and Brian's athletic endeavors and beamed about how well his boys performed over the years in tennis.

By the end of the meal, Amy's stomach remained empty, but her heart was full of happiness. The Broadstone's were extraordinary people. Their wealth did not take away from their kindness, humility, and humor.

As everyone finished their meals, David paid for the dinner, despite Seth and Brian's protests.

Amy thanked everyone for including her in their family time, and Nancy stood up and gathered her in the warmest embrace.

Standing up, Brian grimaced and hunched over to one side.

Amy looked at him and furrowed her brow. "Are you ok?"

He grabbed his flank and rubbed it. "Yeah, I think so. My side hurts."

Seth stepped toward his brother and placed a hand on his shoulder. "Brian, is this the first time your side has hurt recently?"

Turning his head away, Brian avoided meeting Seth's gaze. "Well...it's been hurting off for a week or so. I'm sure it's nothing."

Seth found Amy's eyes, and he frowned.

"Maybe we should take you to the hospital and get it checked out tonight," Amy suggested.

Brian shook his head and waved her concern away with his hand. "Nah, it'll be fine. Maybe I pulled a muscle or something during the match." He stared at the floor below.

Seth squeezed his brother's shoulder and lowered his head, forcing Brian to look at him. "Hey...will you promise me you'll call your doctor next week and make an appointment. Just to make sure everything is ok...you know...with your kidney?"

Brian grinned through the pain and shook his head. "Aw, are you worried about your little brother?"

Seth's brow deepened. "I am worried about you. You have to stay in good shape, so I have a decent tennis rival."

"I don't have to be in that good of shape to beat you," Brian joked.

Nancy moved toward her younger child. She wrapped Brian in a side-hug and kissed him on the cheek. "Honey promise me you'll call Dr. Weinstein on Monday. No excuses, ok? We don't want to take any chances."

"No sweat. It's all good. I'll call the doctor's office first thing Monday morning and get an appointment. Will that make everyone happy?" Brian raised his eyebrows.

Seth's forehead relaxed and he dropped his hand from his brother's shoulder. "Yeah, it would."

David patted Brian on the back. "Son, I want you to take the next week or so off work. You need to rest and get yourself checked out."

Brian protested, "Dad, I can't take off work. There's too much to do."

Shaking his head, David put a hand up. "Nonsense, we can manage. Besides, if I get too swamped, I'm sure your brother could pitch in for a bit." He turned to Seth and raised his eyebrows.

"I'll try my best, Dad. I've got a lot going on at work right now. I'm trying to get the nonprofit funded and I have a few important meetings this week. Is there anyone else that can help you?"

Brian stepped between his father and brother. "Let's not worry about work right now. I'll make the doctor appointment, and I'm sure everything will be fine. Dad, I'll take a few days off from the office and work from home. Seth, if we really need help, I'll let you know, but I'm sure Dad and I can manage."

A long awkward pause followed, so Amy broke the silence by turning to shake hands with David. Instead he gave her a big bear hug. Once he released her, she gathered her purse and cardigan.

Seth took her by the hand and escorted her out of the restaurant to her car.

Nearing the entrance of the club, Seth asked the valet to retrieve Amy's car. He turned to face her while they waited and clasped both her hands in his. "Thank you for coming today. Sorry that my brother and I got intense. Sibling rivalry." Seth shrugged his shoulders. "And I apologize that you had to witness the family debate over Brian's health. We all fret over him and my dad never misses a chance to try to get me to join the family business, even though he really is just channeling his worry for Brian I think."

Amy shook her head and raised her eyes, looking at Seth through her eyelashes. "Hey, no problem. I enjoyed watching you play. You're incredible, and I had a wonderful time chatting with your mom. Dinner was… interesting, but I understand how you all feel about Brian. I'm glad he agreed to go to his doctor soon. Call me if he needs anything over the weekend."

Seth nodded his head and smiled. "Ok, thanks, will do. I'll keep you posted. So, what are you doing for the rest of the evening?"

Amy's stomach growled and she peered down at it. "Well, first thing on the agenda is swinging by a drive-through on the way home to grab a burger. Whoever said their eyes were bigger than their stomach never dined at the Club and ordered a salad. That salad will not cut it."

Seth chuckled.

"Then, I'll head home and crash. I have an early shift tomorrow at the hospital, so I need to rest up for that."

Seth brushed a strand of hair away from Amy's eyes. "Ok, well, will I see you at church on Sunday?"

She gazed up at him again. "For sure. Save me a seat?"

"Of course." Seth leaned in to kiss Amy, but Brian appeared and made kissing noises, like a ten-year-old.

Seth froze and took a step back. He stared stonily at his brother. "Nice. Real mature."

Brian shrugged his shoulders and grinned. "What? Don't let me interrupt."

At that moment, the valet appeared with Amy's car. She took the keys from the driver and thanked him. With the mood disrupted, she walked to the driver side of her car and paused before climbing inside. She turned to face Seth, and he gave her a warm hug. Pulling away, she smiled. "Thanks again for a wonderful day."

Seth held the door open as she slid inside. "I'll see you Sunday." He closed the door and gave her a final wave.

Amy lowered her window and waved back. "See you Sunday." She raised her window, started her car, and headed home. *See you Sunday.* She couldn't wait.

Chapter 33

August 12, 2017, Saturday

Seth walked into his small home office at his house Saturday morning with a steaming cup of black coffee in his hand, determined to conquer the Open Hearts budget problem. He sat down the cream, thick-handled mug on his tidy wooden desk and pulled out his chair. As he sunk into it, he cracked his neck and rolled his shoulders, ready to work.

He raised the lid to his grey laptop and glanced at the time in the upper right-hand corner. Eight am. He gazed at the open spreadsheet on his home screen and the numbers blurred together as his mind wandered to the events of the previous evening. He couldn't help but worry about his brother.

The aroma of the dark roast blend brought him back to the present and Seth shook his head. He needed to get a lot of work done today, but he couldn't get his mind off his brother.

He looked at his cell phone sitting next to his computer taunting him. Seth sighed and picked it up. He punched in the familiar numbers to call Brian and listened to the expectant ringing. While waiting for his brother to answer, he scanned the tiny space encompassing his office and smiled at the fond memories hanging on the walls. Pictures including him and his family from summers, Christmas', and Thanksgivings' past caused a twinge of guilt. He wished he could be in two places at the same time.

"Hello? Hello? Seth, are you there?" Brian's voice interrupted Seth's reflection.

"Hey, buddy. Sorry about that. My mind wandered off while I waited for you to answer."

"Ah, no biggie. Bound to happen in your old age."

Seth rolled his eyes. "Thanks. I'm not that old, you know. Just older than you. Anyway, I didn't call today so you could torture me. I wanted to check on you and see how you're feeling. How's your side?"

"Awe, how sweet. You really do care."

His brother knew how to goad him. Seth frowned. "I'm caring less with each passing minute."

Brian became serious. "No, really, I'm ok. I'm fine. It's still a little sore, but I'm sure it's nothing."

Switching the phone to the other hand, Seth swiveled away from the computer in his chair. "I hope so, but you're still going to see Dr. Weinstein, right? Have you gotten an appointment, yet?"

His brother sighed on the other end of the line. "Dude, it's Saturday. I don't know many doctor's offices open on Saturday. But I promise first thing Monday morning to call and I'm sure they'll get me in soon. Dad called me last night to make sure I stayed home this week. Just a heads up, I think he's plotting to call you today or tomorrow and campaign more for you to come in and help him for the next few weeks."

It was Seth's turn to sigh. He rubbed his forehead with his hand. "I know. He hasn't called yet, but I know Dad. I feel terrible. You know I want to help him, but there's no way I can take time off at the hospital right now. If I don't sell the rest of the Board this week on Open Hearts, then it's over. I can't let all those families it helps down. I'm afraid Open Hearts needs a sizable donation to make it."

Brian cleared his throat. "You always do the right thing. I know you'll make the best choice for everyone. Don't let Dad pressure you into something you can't do. The company will be fine, I'm sure. Besides, Dad has other people there to help him. I think he likes the idea of working with his sons. Don't sweat it."

Seth thought back to when Brian was little and going through surgery and treatments at the hospital. Tears sprang to his eyes. He blinked them back. "Ok, I'll take your word for it. Maybe I'll try to dodge his calls today and perhaps I can help at least one or two evenings next week... I'll see what I can do. But, Brian..."

"Yeah?"

"Please, take care of yourself. Let me know if you need me to call Amy." Seth looked up at one of his favorite pictures of him and his brother at the beach when Seth was ten years old. They each had their arms flung across one another's shoulders and wore wide grins. The sun kissed their hair, lightening it, and their skin turned a golden brown. They looked carefree. He wished he could transport back to that day. They swam, ate crab legs until they nearly popped, and chased one another on the shore.

"I will. I will, big brother. Now, it's Saturday, so I'm going to enjoy my day."

Seth tore his eyes away from the photograph. "What're you going to do today?"

"Probably plant myself on the couch and watch pre-season games all day. It's tough, but someone has to do it."

Seth shook his head again and smiled. "Ok, buddy. Have a good day. I'll call and check on you tomorrow. Love you, Bro."

Brian had turned the television on and was yelling at the announcer on the sports station. "What? Oh, I love you, too, Bro. Talk soon. Bye."

The line went dead and Seth turned off his phone and sat it down on the desk. He believed everything would work out because it must. Hopefully, his brother's visit to the doctor would be uneventful and his father could manage the office without Brian for at least the next week. In the meantime, Seth needed to create room in the budget for the families relying on Open Hearts or find a miracle donor to gift the hospital thousands of dollars. Either way, he had plenty of work ahead.

Seth rubbed his eyes and took a swig of his now tepid brew and began typing. As he worked, his mind drifted off to thoughts of Amy and their upcoming date the next morning at church. He considered calling her to meet him for dinner tonight, but one glance at the spreadsheet again brought him to his senses. No, today he needed to work, but the anticipation of seeing her again spurred him on.

He wanted to kiss her last night. Their lips came close to

meeting one another before his infantile brother broke the mood. Seth tried to focus on data points amid thoughts of Amy's smile and full red lips. He sighed again. *Tomorrow.*

Chapter 34

August 12, 2017, Saturday

Amy walked through the sliding doors at Metropolitan Hospital early Saturday morning, anxious to get a jump on her charting and emails. Her shift started at 7:00 am, but she walked past the central nursing station of the emergency department around 6:00 am. She nodded at two staff nurses dressed in cobalt blue scrubs and sat down at an empty computer station.

As Amy returned patients phone calls regarding X-ray follow-ups, Mark breezed past her desk. He threw her a cocky, flirtatious grin.

She rolled her eyes and tossed her hand in the air as a wave. *Typical Mark.* She hadn't seen him much since the Metropolitan Ball. Lately, they had worked opposite shifts. The one day they did work together had been busy and the only conversation they shared focused on a patient Mark checked out to her before heading off shift for the night. He behaved more serious lately, but it could just be a new schtick. *Who knew with Mark?* She shrugged her shoulders and continued typing at her keyboard.

Her pager intermittently blared, phones rang constantly, and the overhead speaker announced one ambulance arrival after another. Before she knew it, her shift had almost ended. Amy sunk into her desk chair to take a swig of her now-cold coffee when her pager went off for about the one-hundredth time that day. She pushed the display button, and it read Priority Emergency.

Priorities meant the highest level of acuity in the hospital. Things like ATV accidents, car wrecks, gunshot wounds, or even cardiac arrests made up the typical fare. She pushed the button again, urging the pager to reveal a short, detailed message about the emergency. *Adult female, sixty years-old, shock... bradycardia.* Her stomach sank. She loved emergency medicine; the fast pace, the gratification of intervening to make an instant difference. But with Priorities, often the outcome was grim.

The success rate of CPR was only around ten percent. A quick response to a heart attack, stroke, or even a fracture, she could positively impact, but shock with bradycardia (or low heart rate) rarely ended well. Amy wondered what led to this patient's shock. *Hemorrhage?* Perhaps the patient bled out from a ruptured aneurysm. *Hypotensive?* Maybe she took too much of her blood pressure medication? *Sepsis? Most likely.* Maybe from an undiagnosed infection that lingered?

Amy continued running through scenarios in her head, making her differential list and vetting five different plans of treatment while she waited. The overhead speaker announced her patient's ambulance.

Mark appeared beside Amy as she jogged through the hallway until meeting the ambulance at the emergency entrance. The doors parted revealing the patient on a stretcher pushed by one EMT, while the other held a bag mask on her face for ventilation. Two large bore IVs ran normal saline.

Amy glanced at the second EMT. "Tell me about the patient."

He raised his head, continuing to squeeze the ventilation bag. "Patient is a sixty-year-old female, found on the floor of her kitchen by her husband. Her temperature was 101, blood pressure 90/60. Her pulse remained low in the 50s. Her husband didn't witness the fall, so we're uncertain about the possibility of a head injury. The patient takes chemotherapy treatment for lymphoma. Her last treatment dated two days ago. Her husband reported she experienced a low-grade fever this am, but nothing else."

Amy turned to Mark. "I'm thinking neutropenic fever and possible septic shock? Could be dehydrated, too."

The first EMT spoke up, "We started bagging her as soon as we arrived on scene. So far, we haven't lost her pulse, but it's weak. Heart rhythm is normal sinus." The medic took a breath.

Mark slid to one side of the stretcher. "What chemotherapy regimen does she take?"

The first EMT jotted a few words on a clipboard and passed it to Amy before turning to Mark. "She's taking RCHOP."

Amy accepted the clipboard with the patient's vitals and information from the EMT and took over the patient's care. She rattled off verbal orders to one of the nurses, "Ok, let's get her into Bay One. Get me a stat oncology consult and let the intensive care unit know we may send a patient up for strict isolation parameters. Call the lab and get me a stat CBC with diff, metabolic panel, ESR, CRP, blood cultures, and urinalysis. Oh, and please notify x-ray that we need a chest x-ray."

Turning to another of the emergency room nurses on shift who sidled up next to her, Amy continued, "Get an EKG and let's see if there's anything surprising there. Let the CT scanner know we have an unwitnessed fall and need a head CT without contrast right now." She raised her eyebrows and gave her attention to Mark. "Anything you want to add?"

Mark shook his head. "Nope. I think you've got this covered."

Amy nodded. The next hour passed in a blur of activity. Several nurses, residents, and transport staff whisked in and out of Bay One. Anesthesia arrived and determined the patient had a compromised airway, so they proceeded with an elective intubation. With the patient's airway secure and the patient properly sedated, Amy continued her exam.

Amid listening to the patient's heart and lungs, the EKG tech and mobile X-ray unit appeared. Both techs made quick work of taking images and attaching electrodes. Amy turned her attention to a tall, older gentleman, probably in his late 50s, with silver pepper-flecked short hair who stood outside of Bay One.

He wore rumpled clothes and looked like he hadn't shaved in several days. With his furrowed brow of concern, Amy presumed he must be the patient's husband. She wrapped her stethoscope around her neck and glanced into the hallway, catching Mark's eye. Amy nodded her head in the patient's direction and then raised her eyebrows towards the husband.

Mark bobbed his head up and down in understanding. He walked up to the patient's bed and picked up the chart to review the incoming lab results. Amy stepped closer to Mark and lowered her voice." Can you hold down the fort here for a few minutes?"

He set his mouth in a straight line and became serious for once. "No problem, you got it." No wink.

Amy relaxed her shoulders and sent him a slight smile. "Thanks. I'll go chat with her husband."

She sauntered to the concerned gentlemen and held her hand out to greet him. "Hi, Sir. Who are you here with today?"

The grey-haired man looked down. "Uh, oh, I'm here with my wife. I mean, that's my wife in there... in that room..." Before he could finish his thought, he burst into tears. He reminded Amy a little of her father, and she found it unsettling to see him cry. It nearly broke her heart.

"My name is Dr. Harte, and I'm one of the physician's taking care of your wife today. She came in with the ambulance and we got to work on her quickly, but I didn't have a lot of medical history on her. We started a broad workup. It's possible this is from a medication side effect, or she might have contracted a virus or bacterial infection. Can you tell me more about what happened? Has she been sick for long? Does she have any other underlying medical conditions? Oh, and do you know if she hit her head when she collapsed?" Amy finished rattling off her questions and paused to let the patient's husband respond.

The man ran a hand through his hair and took a deep breath. "Well, let's see. She was healthy until a few months ago. Then, out of the blue she got these fevers. Mostly at night. Low grade. Didn't seem like a big deal." The man spoke bullet-style through stuttered sobs.

Amy stepped closer and placed a hand on his shoulder. "You're doing great. Take your time."

The man wiped tears from his eyes with the back of one hand. "At first, we thought she had a cold she couldn't shake. Then, we thought maybe a sinus infection took hold because she got those in the past. The doctors threw antibiotic after antibiotic at her and nothing worked. Finally, an ENT doctor, I think that's what you call them, noticed a large lymph node in her neck. He thought it needed biopsied to make sure it was normal. Well...it wasn't."

Amy peered down the sterile hallway, searching for a box of tissues. She saw one sitting on the wall next to the nurse's station and grabbed it, handing the box to the man. "Sorry, go on."

The husband gladly accepted the tissue and blotted his eyes before crumpling it in his hand. "Seems like that was the last normal day we shared. About a week after the lymph node removal, the doctor called to tell us she had cancer; lymphoma. The day of that phone call they ordered a bunch of tests, x-rays, labs, you name it. Then, they started running that poison into her every few weeks. At first, we felt optimistic that it would work. She stopped having fevers and started feeling more normal. She got nauseous a lot and lost her hair…that was hard, but she said she felt more like herself. She could breathe again and started sleeping through the night."

Amy nodded her head, encouraging him to continue.

"We did three cycles like that, and everything seemed to work well, and then one day we hit a wall. She woke up with a new lump on the opposite side of her neck. Her temperature was up, too. I took her right away to her cancer doctor, and he put her in the hospital. He ordered, what's it called… a PET scan, I think. Cancer was everywhere; in her lungs, her groin, her liver. You name it. Everything lit up."

Amy sighed. "That must've been hard."

The man's eyes filled with more tears. "It was one of the worst days of my life. The doctor talked with us about other options, since the chemo wasn't working anymore. He called it a clinical trial, but to me it sounded like she would be a guinea pig. We didn't have a lot of choices, though. So, we signed her up, stopped the old chemo, and waited a few days to start the new trial medication." He stared with a blank expression for a few seconds.

Amy waited in silence for him to return to his story.

He shook his head and turned to Amy again. "That's what we were doing when she collapsed. Waiting. She was standing in the kitchen, making herself some tea. She loved tea. Then, she turned around, looked me straight in the eyes, and I knew she was going down. All the color drained from her face and her eyes rolled back in her head. Fortunately, I got her in time to catch her. So, no, to answer your question, she did not hit her head. She had a clean bill of health prior to the cancer. I hate it. It's an awful, demonic thing. You a religious woman, Dr. Harte?" The husband raised his eyes to meet Amy's.

He caught her off guard. If he'd asked her that question a few months ago, she may have answered differently. She paused for a moment, considering her response. "Yes. I believe in God. I believe in Jesus. Why do you ask?"

"I just like to know. It makes me feel better to have a fellow believer working on my wife. She's the love of my life. I don't know what I'll do if I lose her." The distressed gentleman clamped his mouth shut. He looked up at Amy with eyes reddened from crying.

"Sir, I promise we're doing everything we can to save your wife. As soon as I have more answers, I'll update you. In the meantime, why don't you sit in the waiting room. I'll have a clerk escort you out there and get you a cup of coffee." She squeezed the kind man's hands with both of hers.

His eyes welled up again. "Okay. Thank you. Please… do everything you can for her."

"I will." Amy watched the man walk toward the waiting room with the clerk and turned back to Bay One. She walked to the patient's bedside to take over for one of her colleagues and help Mark. Grabbing the chart from Mark, she scanned the incoming labs. The white blood cell count was dangerously low at 1.0, the hemoglobin also lingered at a critical level of 7, and the platelets dangled around 100,000. Her other labs looked okay other than a slightly low potassium. The electrocardiogram showed normal sinus rhythm. Her head CT was clear. Amy's eyes skimmed the rest of the page and landed on the patient's chest X-ray results. *Bingo.* It showed bilateral infiltrates with an effusion.

Mark inched closer to Amy. He shook her out of her internal analysis. "So, what do you think?"

Amy glanced one last time at the results and let a sigh slip out before meeting Mark's gaze. "I think she's in trouble. She's probably got a bilateral pneumonia, neutropenic fever, and She's in critical condition and in septic shock. I hate it for her husband." Amy exhaled, rubbing her forehead with her palm.

An alarm sounded indicating an abnormal rhythm on the patient's electrocardiogram. Amy snapped her heads up at the same time as Mark. The monitor presented a flat line, indicating that the woman's heart stopped.

Mark shouted first, "Call a Code! Code blue, Bay One ER,

code blue, Bay One, ER!"

Amy moved closer to the patient, ready to start CPR. "Get a crash cart in here right now!" She worked in tandem with Mark, performing CPR in a way they had done many times before. This time, though, she couldn't help but think about her mother. This woman's case seemed so much like hers. Amy dreaded telling the patient's husband that his wife did not make it. She couldn't let that happen.

Mark continued chest compressions while Amy, filled with new resolve, grabbed medication and paddles from the crash cart. She pushed an ampule of epinephrine and with no response from the patient immediately yelled, "Clear!"

A few seconds later with paddles on the patient Amy called for the charge nurse to give the shock. No response. Mark started compressions again for a full two minutes. They carried on, following the protocol that Amy knew by heart. After forty-five minutes of CPR, multiple shocks, ampules of epinephrine and vasopressin, Mark called the code. Amy blinked back tears.

Peering across the patient at Amy, Mark's eyebrows raised. "Do you want me to talk to the family?"

Amy shook her head. "No, it should be me. I told him I would keep him updated. He trusts me. I'll be back." She took one last look at her patient and turned on her heel, hoping Mark didn't notice the tears building behind her eyes. She stamped them down. Walking with trepidation toward the waiting room door, she rested her hand on it for a minute, willing time to stop. Amy hated knowing the words she had to share with her patient's husband would change his life forever. Her team performed well and did everything possible to save the patient, but she knew the pain of loss and couldn't bear the thought of telling him.

Amy drew in a final deep breath and pulled the door open. The waiting room overflowed with people. Most of them waited on family members and everyone looked up to see if Amy came for them. She searched the room for the patient's husband, and when her gaze fell on him, he looked back at her with hope. She walked over to him and grabbed both of his hands in hers. "Let's go over here to talk."

She guided him to a small private room that resembled an unused coat closet. The hospital had transitioned it into a "conversation room." She gestured for the man to sit down and seated herself across from him. After taking another deep breath, she raised her eyes to meet his. A single tear trailed down Amy's cheek. She never did this. She never cried in front of the patient or the family. She was a professional. "Sir, I'm so sorry... we did absolutely everything we could..."

The man broke down, weeping, and dropped his head in his hands. "Oh, no, please, no, no. Please tell me this is a bad dream. She can't be gone. It can't be true."

Amy wrung her hands. "I wish it weren't," she whispered.

The husband looked up and raised his brow. "Please, tell me, did I do something wrong? Was it her medication? What happened?"

She blinked back more tears of her own. "We don't know for sure, but based on her labs and chest X-ray, I'd say she developed an infection in her lungs because of her suppressed immune system. Between the drain of the cancer and the chemotherapy medications, her body gave out."

The man rubbed the back of his neck and stared into the distance. "What am I going to do now? What am I going to do?" He broke into wracking sobs again and hung his head.

Amy looked around the small room for help and found none. Then, a still, small voice urged her to ask him a question. "Can I pray for you?" She had never prayed for a patient before, but it provided the only answer she knew to his question.

The man paused and his face relaxed a little. "Yeah, that'd be kind of you."

She folded her hands together and bowed her head, unsure of where to begin. "Father, I ask you to be with this sweet man today. Wrap him in your loving arms, and in your peace. Thank you for the wonderful gift of his wife and the time and love with which you blessed them. Guide and strengthen him in the days ahead. Please comfort him in ways that don't seem possible. We know that even though we face trials, you love us. We also know you have a good plan for his life and that you work all things together for the good of those who love you, Lord. In Jesus' name, Amen." Amy held back more tears and squeezed her eyes tight for a few seconds longer before opening them again and raising her head. She met the man's eyes, now filled with puddles of sadness.

The patient's husband sent her a half-smile that did not meet his eyes. "Thank you, Dr. Harte. My heart may be broken, but my faith isn't. I appreciate all you did for my wife. I especially appreciate you praying with me." The man patted Amy on the shoulder and stood up, taking a deep breath. He towered at six feet tall, but the grief painted across his face and the sagging of his shoulders made him look small. He swiped away tears from his eyes with a thumb and headed into the main waiting room, which began to fill with more of his family members. His eyes surveyed the room until landing on someone close to Amy's age.

Amy assumed the young woman must be the deceased patient's daughter.

The husband shook his head at her. The woman crumpled to the floor and wailed, her shoulders shaking with each sob.

Amy stood motionless for a few seconds. Then, shaking herself out of her stupor, she turned and scurried back to the Emergency Department. Blowing through the hallway of the Emergency Department, Amy passed several filled beds with more patients receiving care from other physicians, nurses, and staff. She walked as fast as her legs could move, heading straight for the double doors to the Emergency Department exit. Amy's lungs burned and she worried if she did not get outside of the building immediately, she might suffocate.

The automatic doors separated, and she picked up her pace to a slight jog until she arrived at the opposite side of the parking lot. Turning, she now faced the hospital far enough away to remain out of view of patients and staff. Amy sat down on the curb of the sidewalk and burst into tears. She cried the hardest and longest she had since her mother passed away.

Five to ten minutes passed and gradually her weeping subsided. Her head pounded, and she sighed a shuddering breath. *Stop it, Amy. Take a breath. Inhale. Exhale. Focus on the truth… on the words spoken to that husband.* She hated losing a patient, especially someone who's case reminded her so much of her own's mothers. It broke her heart. Sometimes she questioned how much more of this part of medicine she could endure. It came with the territory, but it didn't make it easier.

She rubbed away her residual tears with the tips of her fingers and glanced at the double doors to the Emergency Department. She thought someone was walking toward her. She rubbed her eyes again. *Oh, great.* Just what she needed right now.

Mark plopped down next to her on the curb and smiled. "Hey, doc. You doing okay?"

Amy wiped her face one last time with the corner of the neck of her green scrub top. She heard a bird singing a pleasant song, ironic given the occasion. "Swell. Just peachy."

Mark placed a hand on her shoulder and Amy stiffened.

"Mark," Amy gave a terse reply with warning in her voice. She was not in the mood for unwanted advances. Sure, in the past they had gone on the one "work outing" to the Metropolitan Ball, but since spending more time with Seth, she realized what a huge mistake that had been.

Mark's brow furrowed, and he became more serious. He didn't move his arm. "Hey, in all seriousness, can't I check in on my friend and colleague? That was a tough case, and I know about your mom. I'm sure this was a tough loss."

Taken aback by his unexpected sensitivity, Amy paused before beginning to wriggle out from underneath his hand and this conversation.

He shifted his gaze downward, appearing uncharacteristically unsure of himself. "Listen, Amy...I hate to bring this up...and I know it's probably not the best time, but, uh, there's something I have to tell you."

She forgot about ploys to avoid his advances and met his eyes for a second. Lines formed between his brow and its furrow deepened. His eyes flitted away, avoiding hers. "What is it Mark?"

Mark cleared his throat before speaking, "Uh, well, the thing is... this morning when I came into work, I ran into Ed Baker. He stopped by the cafeteria between meetings and saw me grabbing a cup of coffee..."

Amy waited for him to finish. "Yeah?"

Mark looked sheepish. "So, I stood in line to check out and he walked up to tell me he had something important to discuss. I thought at first it was about the Metro Ball, honestly. I know I wasn't on my best behavior that night, so I assumed he would tell me to rein it in a little, you know?"

Amy nodded her head to encourage him to keep going.

He swallowed hard. "So, like I said, I thought he would say

'straighten up,' or give me some good-natured ribbing and that would be it. Uh... I don't know how to say this... the thing is, Ed offered me the promotion to Chief of Emergency Medicine." Mark refused to look at her and stared only at the ground.

Her mouth dropped open, and Amy froze. "What? What are you saying? You got the promotion... and the bonus?"

Mark tapped one heel against the pavement, shaking his leg. "Um, yeah, I guess. I'm sorry, Amy. I know you wanted the promotion, too, but I'm sure you and your dad can figure something else out to keep your mom's house. I bet if you went back to the bank and talked with them, they'd understand. Maybe give you an extension or something?" Mark raised his eyebrows.

Amy's hands quivered. She shouted her words through tears in a blind rage, "I cannot believe you. There is no extension. There is no other way. I have no other option to help my dad save that house. This was it. Without this promotion and the bonus, my dad and I lose the house and all of my childhood memories along with the last pieces of my mom." She flung Mark's arm off her shoulder with great force just as she heard someone from the parking lot call her name.

"Amy? Amy, are you okay?" A voice interrupted her speech. She looked up and found Seth standing ten feet away next to his open car door in the hospital parking lot with a confused and pained look on his face. *No! What must he think?* Amy chastised herself for not shrugging Mark's arm away sooner. Even though nothing romantic happened, it looked bad.

Seth rested his arm on his open car door, peering over it. Even though anger clouded his face, he never looked more handsome. He wore a robin-egg blue v-neck t-shirt and khaki shorts with dark brown sandals. His attire appeared relaxed, contrasting further his facial expression.

"Uh," was all Amy could mutter. *Great. Eloquent, really. Good save.* "I mean, um, yes, I'm okay." She heaved a sigh and readied herself to explain further.

Mark flashed Seth a grin and planted a hand on Amy's shoulder nearest him once more. "Don't worry, I've got things under control. Amy and I were in the middle of an important conversation." He gave Amy's shoulder a squeeze.

She wanted to strangle Mark right now.

Seth shook his head and looked down before raising his head again to meet her eyes. "Well, great. Good. Um, I need to go. I totally forgot my brother needed me to come over to his house tonight to help him with something. So, uh, I guess I'll see you around." Seth gave Mark a long stare before sliding back into his car and slamming the door shut. He started the engine, and it roared to life.

Amy jumped to her feet to run after Seth and explain the situation to him, but his car peeled out of the parking lot leaving only a screech in its wake.

Turning to face Mark, Amy placed her hands on her hips. "I cannot believe you said that!"

His eyes widened and he shrugged his shoulders. "What? Can't I comfort my friend?"

"No! You cannot. And moving forward please know that our relationship is strictly professional. I am not your friend. I am your colleague... that's not true. Now you're my boss, and I'm your employee. So, don't touch me ever again."

Amy's entire body shook. Her head bowed and her eyes focused on the ground. She dropped her arms and stood with clenched fists by her side. Before storming off to the Emergency Department, she raised her head and met Mark's gaze one last time. "I just hope you haven't ruined things for me with Seth for good." As she stomped away, Amy apologized to God under her breath for losing her temper and yelling. She also said a quick prayer that He would fix this. What a mess...

Chapter 35

August 12, 2017, Saturday

Beth spoke through muffled chomps into the telephone. "What'd you say? I couldn't hear you between bites of my Cookie Cruncharoos."

Amy sighed. "I said that my life is a fiasco… an absolute wreck right now."

"I'm sure that's not true. Your entire life cannot possibly be a fiasco. Now, your love life might be. That could be true." Beth continued to chew.

Amy yelled into the phone, "Oh, well that's so much better. Thank you for your generous words of encouragement. Great. Glad I called my best friend this morning for some sympathy and advice!"

More chewing on the other end of the line before a muffled response from Beth, "Hey, you said it first. I'm only reiterating the facts as you stated them. Okay, seriously, what happened? I'm sure it can't be that bad."

She blew out a frustrated breath. How could someone eat so much refined sugary children's breakfast cereals and remain a size zero? Life could be so unfair. She heard a phrase in her head her mother used to say to her, "Comparison is the Thief of Joy, Amy." *Yeah, right.* She shook her head, bringing her focus back to the current debacle. She could mull over the unfairness of Beth's metabolic rate later. "I said nothing is wrong... except Seth probably hates me and never wants to see me again... and Mark is a jerk. Oh, and I lost the promotion that could have saved my parent's house. Other than that, life's marvelous."

"Okay, okay, hang on." Beth slurped what Amy assumed was the residual milk in her finished bowl of cereal.

Amy rolled her eyes.

All chewing subsided. "I'm finished eating and you now have my undivided attention. So, start from the beginning. I doubt you did too much damage yesterday. You were at work, right?"

"Right. I went to work. It was a challenging day from the start because Mark shared the same shift with me. So, I had my guard up, but the day was going fine. The emergency department stayed full most of the day. Then, a tough case came in and the patient reminded me of my mom... anyway, I thought we could save her, but then she went into cardiac arrest and didn't make it."

Beth interrupted, her voice full of empathy, "Oh, Amy, I'm sorry. That must've been hard."

Amy nodded to herself. "Losing any patient hurts, but telling her sweet, Christian husband that he lost the love of his life felt like a punch to the gut. I finished talking with him and grief knocked me over like a wave because the situation reminded me of my mom. I couldn't breathe, so, I ran outside to the hospital parking lot and planted myself on the curb for a good cry."

Beth cut in, "Wait, you just left the hospital? Can you do that? Isn't there some doctor code or oath you took to never do that?"

She crossed her arms in front of her chest, but Amy's best friend couldn't see her annoyance through the phone. "Yes, but I didn't 'just' leave. As I ran out, I told my charge nurse I was taking my break, and there were several other physicians around to cover. But thank you, Ms. Goody Two Shoes. I was in crisis mode. I needed a moment to regroup."

Amy imagined Beth sitting at her house and putting her palms up in surrender as she spoke, "Okay, okay. I'm sorry. I misunderstood the situation. Please continue."

She cleared her throat and continued. "Fine. So, I sat on the curb, bawling my eyes out, when who should appear?"

Beth gasped. "Seth? How sweet!"

"Nope. Wrong. Mark. He followed me outside to check on me,

which I'll give him points for doing, but tell me the last time Mark Blakely did anything selfless. He always has an agenda. So, he sat down next to me and flung his arm across my shoulder. In retrospect, I should have shoved him away right then, but in my distress, I let it slide. So, I poured my heart out to him about losing my mom and caring for other patients that remind me of her. For a few minutes he acted like a decent human being other than the arm thing."

"Well, that's good news, right? Seeing an improvement in humanity?"

Frowning, Amy cut her friend off, "Ha! You'd think that, right? Nope. He went on to tell me the glorious news that Mr. Baker gave him the Chief of Emergency Medicine position earlier that morning. He said how he felt bad taking it from me, but not to fret because he knew money would miraculously fall from the sky and save my dad's house some other way. I did not take that news well and threw his unwelcome arm off my shoulder like a shot put at the same time Seth showed up in his car."

Beth drew in a sharp breath. "No! Oh, Amy, you have the worst timing."

"I know. Seth looked upset, bordering on furious. To be fair, I understand it looked suspicious. I was sitting with another guy who I know Seth isn't fond of and the 'other guy' has his arm on my shoulder. Seth assumed something happened between Mark and I, and before I knew it, he tore out of there. See, I told you. Total fiasco." Amy made a bomb going off hand signal to show the disaster level of the situation, even though Beth couldn't see it through the phone.

Beth clucked her tongue. "All right, I get it. So, it's not an ideal scenario, that's for sure. However, you've got to calm down. From what I know about Seth, he is a kind, compassionate, and reasonable person. And he's a Christian, so he should know something about forgiveness and grace. You need to take a deep breath and stop freaking out. Did you try to call him?"

Amy's voice quivered, "I called him on my way home from work last night, but the phone went straight to voicemail. I chickened out and hung up before I could leave a message. What if he never wants to speak to me again?"

"Well, I doubt that's true. He's crazy about you. And the thing with your parent's house... that's tough, Amy. I know you're disappointed about not getting the job and how much you needed that money, but something else will work out. I know it. God will take care of you. You know that, right? Are you going to church tomorrow?"

She wrung her hands together. "Yeah, I guess. I planned on it, but now I'm worried that if I go, I'll see Seth and it'll be weird. Or worse, I'll show up and then he won't go to avoid me. In that case, I won't know if things are okay between us or not. Then, I'll fall down the rabbit hole called 'do I call him or wait for him to call me?' So... win, win."

"Well, at least you haven't lost your positive attitude and faith that everything will work out because God's got this."

Amy rolled her eyes again. "Ha. Ha. You're hilarious. And always super helpful and understanding."

She could almost hear Beth smiling sweetly through the phone as she spoke, "What can I say? I always try to be a blessing."

Both girls erupted in a fit of cackles. That phrase had been a longstanding joke in Amy's family when she was growing up. Amy's grandmother coined it usually after she was, in fact, not being a blessing but doing as she pleased. By the time the laughter subsided, Amy had to wipe tears from her eyes. "Oh, Beth. You're the best. Thanks. I needed that."

"Anytime. But seriously, it will be ok. You love God, God loves you, and you're a good person who tries to do the right thing. The thing with Seth will blow over. All you need to do is see Seth and explain that to him. And then we need to go out to coffee for a post-situation deposition. In that order." Beth started chomping again.

"How in the world is it not only possible that you're still hungry after a massive bowl of cereal, but that you can eat so much food and stay thin. It's really not fair."

Beth chuckled. "What can I say? Being a blessing worked up my appetite."

Both women erupted again in a fit of giggles.

Amy sputtered and tried to catch her breath. "Okay, stop, stop. I can't take anymore today. I'll go to church. I'll see Seth. I'll talk to him and explain everything. It will most likely be fine, but just in case, pray for me tomorrow, all right?"

"You got it, babe. Call me after. I'll meet you at Joe's." Beth hung up the phone.

Amy stared at the silent phone with its blank home screen and shook her head. Beth frustrated Amy sometimes, but she was a good friend, both reliable and honest... and she was usually right. Resolving to talk to Seth, she would pray for God to smooth out the misunderstanding and make everything fine between them again, but for now, Amy only had one thing on her mind... where were her Cookie Cruncharoos?

Chapter 36

August 13, 2017, Sunday

Amy opened her eyes minutes before her phone alarm blared Sunday morning. She stared at a random smudge on the corner of her ceiling, pondering what to say to Seth if she saw him at church today. Her stomach churned. She had prayed last night, asking God to give her the courage to say the words in her heart.

Flinging her legs over the bed, Amy stomped to her closet to find something to wear. She got dressed in a frenzy, caring less for the first time about how she looked when she saw Seth, and more about getting to church early enough to speak to him. Speeding down the road in her car, Amy's mind raced. She fiddled with the knobs on her radio, trying to distract her mind. She pulled into the church parking lot and grabbed one of the closest spots, killed the ignition, and locked the car with a brief press of her key fob.

Amy glanced at her phone and realized she had about twenty minutes before the service began. Seth almost never missed church, and he usually attended the early service. He also hated to be late for anything, so she banked on the fact that he would already be here. She placed her hand on the main door to the church and paused, taking a deep breath. Pulling it open, she continued through the foyer past the coffee station and several familiar faces.

She entered the main auditorium and took tentative steps down the center aisle to her and Seth's usual seats near the front of the stage. Amy froze because what she saw stopped her in her tracks. Dread paralyzed her body and her mouth. Fifteen feet away, near the front of the stage, sitting in her normal seat next to Seth was Samantha—blond, gorgeous, scheming, southern-drawled Samantha.

Something Seth said struck Samantha as funny, because she placed her hand lightly on Seth's forearm and threw her head back, blond curls bouncing, as she cackled. *Perfect.*

Samantha. It figures.

Amy dug her heel in, ready to spin around, when Seth raised his head from the conversation with his breathtakingly beautiful guest and looked behind him. He locked eyes with Amy. Immediately, his smile vanished, and the blood drained from his face leaving it stark white.

Amy debated turning around and running out the back of the auditorium but decided she must at least say hello or risk looking like a complete loser. She drew a deep breath and trudged further down the aisle toward Seth. Her stomach flipped. Amy was falling in love with Seth and if things ended with him today, it would leave her heartbroken.

Samantha's bright blue eyes flashed a challenge. She wore a slim-cut red sundress, heels, and a knowing smile. "Well, look who's here. We can't help but bump into one another everywhere we go." Her excitement sounded forced and Amy could tell Samantha felt as over-joyed to see Amy as Amy was to see her.

Amy swallowed hard. "Samantha… what a surprise to see you here. Down front. And with Seth. What are the chances?" *There, those were honest words. No lies there.* She turned toward Seth and spoke in a soft voice. "Hey, you left so quickly the other day I didn't have time to explain what happened."

Seth cast his eyes downward. "Well… it looked like Mark had things under control… so…"

"No, he definitely did not have everything under control. It wasn't at all like it seemed. I lost a patient, and it was an unexpected and challenging case that reminded me of losing my mom, so it upset me. I went outside to sit alone and have a good cry. Mark was there when the patient coded, so he came out to check on me. He put his hand on my shoulder at the same time you arrived. In fact, I'm angry with him right now. He told me he got the promotion to Chief of Emergency Medicine along with the bonus, so I can't save my dad's house. That's what you saw us discussing, but that's it. Nothing else happened."

Seth opened his mouth to speak, but then closed it again. He frowned.

Searching his face for forgiveness, Amy found none. "I guess if you knew me, you wouldn't have jumped to conclusions. I don't care about Mark. I care about you. A lot. If it was so easy for you to assume that I went behind your back to see Mark, then maybe I misjudged our relationship. I wanted you to know the truth. Seeing you here (Amy looked pointedly at Samantha) with her makes me question if I misunderstood your intentions, too."

She spun around and raced up the aisle to the back of the church, bursting through the doors to the foyer. Amy flung the main front door open. Her lungs burned. She needed air. Turning over the recent events in her mind, she tried to make sense of everything. Amy supposed she and Seth had broken up. The more those words marinated in her mind, the more nauseated she felt.

Amy sprinted to her car, started it up, threw it into gear, and tore out of the parking lot. Amy loved Seth. She didn't want to lose him. She shook her head. The whole situation was unbelievable. For a moment, she hoped to see Seth running after her. Amy imagined him grabbing her, telling her he understood, and everything was fine, and professing his love for her. Contrary to her own wishful thinking, it appeared Seth had stayed put, right next to Samantha. *Ugh.* She rolled her eyes but then promised God she would try to find the good in that girl. Amy couldn't blame Samantha for liking Seth, too, but for the moment, frustration and disappointment reigned. The whole thing was over. All the wonderful dates, the intense conversations, the time with Seth's family. It all ended in a blink. Also, the loss of her parent's house and the precious memories of her mom washed over her.

Out of nowhere a racking sob attacked Amy's body. She cried so hard; she found it difficult to get air. Tears streamed down her cheeks and blurred her eyes to the point she couldn't see the road. Her hands gripped the steering wheel so tightly they turned white. She didn't drive fast, perhaps only twenty or thirty miles per hour.

Raindrops fell from the sky, slow at first, then more steadily. Beads of water trickled down the windshield, thicker and faster with each passing second. Between the rain and the tears pooling in her eyes, Amy struggled to see.

She approached the intersection on Main Street near Joe's coffee shop, when something caught her attention out of the corner of her eye. Turning her head to the left, Amy saw something large and black coming at her. She screamed and tried to turn the wheel away, but heard brakes squealing and the sickening sound of crunching metal. A thought flitted through her mind that she wished she could have hugged Seth and set things right with him, and then everything went black.

Chapter 37

August 13, 2017, Sunday

Metal being pried apart by a large, red, crane-like machine gave a groan. Amy heard of the sound of an ambulance. Then, she faded back out. When she regained conscientiousness, she tried to open her eyes, but they remained blurry. It seemed like someone coated her vision with soap and left it to dry. She laid flat, perceived bright white lights overhead, and sensed the movement of her body along a corridor. Amy recognized voices talking about medical facts. Her eyes shut again. *What happened?*

A booming man's voice interrupted her confused thoughts. "We have a female driver involved in a two-car motor vehicle accident. The other car T-boned her on the driver's side. She appears to have lost consciousness and has been out for most of the trip here. She opened her eyes a few times and pupils are equal, round, and reactive to light, but sluggish, so she might have a concussion."

Amy heard someone above her discussing a case. She wanted to know if the EMT noted any contusions on the patient. *What if the patient had intra-abdominal injuries? Had someone ordered a catscan of the head without contrast to rule out a brain bleed? Were any fractures obvious? What about an abdominal ultrasound to check for internal bleeding? Spleens ruptured easily under much force and, if you didn't think to check for it, the hemorrhaging from them could be fatal.* Amy constructed a differential diagnosis list in her head about the patient in question. *Who was the patient? What about the vitals?*

"The patient's blood pressure is stable, heart rate is 110, but normal sinus rhythm. So, pain might have caused the tachycardia." The EMT informed the physician whose voice sounded eerily like her colleague, Mark.

"Oh, my gosh... no way..." The voice sounded shocked. "Amy, Amy, I can't believe it. How did this happen?"

The EMT responded to the doctor, "Do you know the patient?"

The Mark-sound-alike seemed worried. "Yeah, she's an emergency room physician here... and a... friend of mine. We work together a lot. I can't believe this happened to her."

The EMT voice bellowed into Amy's own ear. "Dr. Harte. Dr. Harte? Can you hear us?"

Realization dawned upon Amy. She was the patient! They were talking about her. She wracked her brain trying to recall what happened. She wondered how she landed on a stretcher in her own Emergency Department... *what had they said? Motor vehicle accident?* Amy pondered for a second... she recalled driving, then it started raining, and she was crying... why was she crying? Her memory blurred.

Ouch! Left rib pain interrupted her thoughts. She prayed they planned to X-ray that to rule out a fracture. Her mind wandered to the events leading up to the wreck. She remembered driving and a large, black something struck her. *Was it a truck? Yes, that might be it.* A large, black truck came up on her left side and struck her perpendicularly. She hadn't seen it until the last minute. Her blurry vision both from rain and tears made it difficult to see... but she couldn't recall the source of her tears.

While the EMT whisked her down the hallway, Amy wanted to reiterate all this information to Mark, who she suspected stood above her at the top of the gurney. She imagined the trip to the CT scanner and expected the workup to come. Her control freak tendencies kicked in and she wanted to tell Mark all the things he needed to order. She couldn't get her mouth to cooperate with her brain and her vision and memory swam in a fog. Amy tried to muster all her remaining strength to tell Mark she could hear his voice, when a searing sharp pain stabbed her left side once more. Pounding in her head distracted her from the rib pain for a minute.

Amy attempted to wiggle her fingers and toes and soon discovered all her extremities still functioned. The effort of her movements didn't translate into the wild gestures she imagined, because Mark didn't notice. At least her abdomen didn't hurt, so hopefully her spleen and liver remained intact. She shifted her shoulders to see if her upper body had suffered any damage, but the strap across her chest holding her to the backboard forbade it. The activity resulted in more discomfort from her left side.

She heard Mark say, "Let's give her two milligrams of morphine. It looks like she's in pain... and tell the scanner tech that we're ready."

That was the last thing Amy heard before the medication kicked in and the world disappeared again in a gradual, but pleasant, fade to black.

Unsure of how long she stayed unconscious, Amy experienced a series of long, strange dreams. During one dream, she strolled through an open wildflower field. Beautiful purple and white flowers stood around her. She felt compelled to reach out and pick a handful of them. As she plucked a flower, a gentle breeze blew and ruffled the hair around her face. She raised her head and her eyes fell upon a well-healed version of her mother. Tears immediately sprang to Amy's eyes, and she yelled, "Mom!" Amy ran and encircled her mother in her arms, holding her tightly. Amy never wanted to let go. She pulled her head back and smiled. "Mom, what are you doing here? How are you here? Or how am I here?"

Amy's mother gave her a peaceful smile. "Amy, my sweet girl. Oh, how I've missed you. I can only stay here with you for a short time. I wanted to tell you I'm fine. Better than fine... and that you're fine, too. I know that you miss me, and you wish I could have gotten better... but I'm healed now. I'm with Jesus, and heaven is wonderful."

Amy's mouth dropped open in shock. "Am I in heaven? Did I die?"

Her mom chuckled. "No, you didn't die. You're unconscious. Think of it like a dream. I need to remind you of a few important things while I'm here with you... things God's probably pressed upon your heart already."

Amy still couldn't decide if this was a vision, hallucination, or a figment of her imagination. She held her breath. "What is it?"

Her mom placed both hands on Amy's shoulders and pushed her back so she could look her daughter in the eyes. "You need to forgive, Amy. You need to forgive yourself for not saving me. You need to forgive the doctors that took care of me. You need to forgive the people in your life that may disappoint you. You need to let go of your anger and embrace the peace that only Jesus supplies. Honey, life is short. You need to trust God's plan for your life and enjoy it. Forgive. Let go. Tell the people you love how you feel every day. Don't be afraid. Live boldly." Amy's mom finished giving her advice.

Amy's throat tightened, and it became difficult to swallow and even harder to breathe. Tears brimmed near the surface of her eyes. "Anything else?" Her mouth hung open now in awe. She couldn't believe her mother stood before her, even if it was a surreal dream.

Pools of liquid filled her mother's kind blue eyes, too. "Just know that I love you... so much. All the good times and memories we shared don't live in our house. They live in your heart. I'm proud to call you my daughter and that God entrusted me as your mom. Know that I'm ok. I'm more than ok. I'm in heaven with Jesus and it's beautiful, Amy. Beyond anything you can imagine. I'm free from pain and hurt, and someday, when it is your time, we will be together again, celebrating Jesus. But it's not time... not yet. You still have life left to live. Your race isn't over." Her mom grinned.

Tears streamed down Amy's cheeks. "But I don't want to leave you. I want to stay here with you, mom. I miss you so much it hurts."

Her mother reached up to her face and brushed the tears away. "I know, baby, I know. I didn't want to leave you, either, but I'm always with you. You carry me with you everywhere you go. A piece of me lives in your heart. You share it with others when you tell them about Jesus, just like I told you about Him when you were four years old. You share it with your patients when you show them compassion. You share it with your Beth when you make her laugh, telling her funny stories about your day over a cup of coffee. You share it with your father when you honor him by calling him every day. All of those things show my love for you pouring out of your heart to others. And we will be together again... but not today." Amy's mom looked softer, almost angelic.

Amy reached forward and hugged her mom with fierceness, still crying.

She could hear her mother saying in her ear, "Amy, you have to wake up."

She shook her head and shouted, "Not yet, mom."

The voice yelled at her louder, "Wake up, Amy! It's time to wake up! Amy, do you hear me? Wake up!"

Amy could hear it clearer now. She felt someone shaking her shoulders. A tightness in her chest persisted, but her breath came somewhat easier now. In fact, it seemed like someone or something was forcing air into her lungs like a huge puff of wind. *What an odd sensation.* The room lightened around her, as if the sun's rays shone brighter. The light soon became so intense that Amy clenched her eyes shut to avoid the painful glare. She wished someone would turn the lights off.

She heard a loud male voice, "Amy! Wake up!"

Amy tried to open her eyes, but they felt glued shut and heavy.

The same male voice finally broke through her reverie and Amy forced her eyes open. "Amy! Hey, that's it, open your eyes. It's time to wake up."

She realized the puff of air came from the oxygen in the nasal cannula attached to her face just below her nose. She reached her right hand up to touch it because she found the situation surreal. When she did so, she noticed an IV inserted into the top of her right hand with tubing taped down holding it in place.

Amy shook her head, still confused. She surveyed the hospital room methodically. To the right a large window with the drapes parted welcomed warm sun beams into the room. A television hung overhead in the right corner of the room, but it stayed silent and black. She looked toward her right shoulder and noted an IV stand holding a normal saline bag. Clear, cool fluid flowed through the tubing leading into her hand.

She noted the oxygen cannula attached to the wall overhead and noticed the dial sat at two liters per minute. There was a monitor attached to the wall as well and it held the familiar pattern of a normal sinus rhythm. Amy realized it must be hers. She palpated her chest through the white hospital blankets lying on top of her with her IV-laden hand and discovered EKG leads in place. Yep, hers. Well, at least her cardiac strip looked good.

She turned her attention to the other monitors. Her blood pressure and heart rate looked stable on the monitor. Her oxygen saturation was normal at ninety-nine percent. Glancing at her left hand, she saw a grey oxygen saturation monitor clamped on her left first finger. At least her vitals looked great. She could not resist her own clinical self-analysis.

Ouch! She rubbed her head. It hurt, and her left side felt sore. She lifted her left hand the source of pain and a sigh of relief escaped when Amy found no chest tube in place. *That's good. No pneumothorax.* She remembered hoping they did x-rays to rule out a rib fracture, although she supposed there wouldn't be much to do about it. *Well, her body seemed intact, so they must have taken good care of her.* Amy rolled her eyes. She needed to settle down. Inhaling to take a calming breath brought the subtle, sweet scent of fresh cut flowers… hydrangeas, maybe?

The low, dull hum of the air conditioner punctuated by the intermittent beeping of her electrocardiogram monitor reassured Amy. It meant she was, at the very least, still alive. Her head throbbed again. She rubbed her eyes with her fingertips. When she opened them, the unwelcome, face of Mark greeted her with a half-smirk.

He sat in a chair to the left side of her hospital bed, his arm draped across the back of the seat.

From the appearance of her room she thought she was in the step-down unit of the intensive care section of the hospital. Only one hospital bed stood in the middle of her room and the glass door and window on the left side of her room allowed the physicians and staff to monitor the patients from the large, central workstation. This part of the hospital remained the most isolated and least trafficked area, but today activity abounded. In the time Amy spent peering out her door, she recognized a few familiar faces in white coats walk past, taking part in their daily clinical rounds. She saw some of her colleagues including the pulmonary and critical care director, the staff orthopedist, and a fellow internist who managed the intensive care unit.

Already five nurses and a handful of medical students wearing shorter white lab coats and terrified expressions of inexperience clustered around the nursing station. Every computer hub held someone charting on a patient or reviewing labs, x-rays, and all the other miscellaneous data to make the best clinical decisions possible.

The hospital carried on its usual hustle and bustle. Stuck in a hospital bed, Amy longed for the normalcy of a routine clinical day. She wished to trade places with a clinician reading charts and visiting patients herself instead of laying here on the other side of the door. She mentally checked out for a few minutes as she gathered her bearings and then realized that Mark still sat beside her in the visitor chair in her room. He hadn't said a word yet.

She met his gaze and his subtle smirk widened. He dropped his arm off the chair-back and placed both forearms on his knees, leaning forward. "Good morning, sleepyhead."

Amy stroked her head again. "Is it morning? What time is it? Better yet, what day is it?"

"It's Monday morning." Mark pulled his phone out of his pocket and peered at the screen. "10:00 a.m. to be exact. The emergency squad brought you in via ambulance yesterday a little after eleven in the morning."

She furrowed her brow. The prior day's details were fuzzy. "How did I get here?"

Mark put his phone away and leaned back in his chair. "Well, do you remember anything at all?"

"Hmm. Let's see... I remember driving my car, I think. Yes, I was driving my car. Then, a dark shadow appeared out of nowhere." Amy gestured to her left. She closed her eyes in concentration. "I heard a thud and a crunching sound. I screamed. Oh, wait, I remember I couldn't see well, either. Was it raining, maybe? Yes, I think it was raining because the windshield wipers were going crazy. I remember crying because something upset me. After the thud and the crunch, everything went black."

"Why were you crying?" Mark asked.

Amy pressed her fingers to her temples. "Uh, let me think. I remember getting ready for church that morning. I wanted to talk to... Seth... that's right. I wanted to talk to him about something..." The memories of the days prior flooded into Amy's mind. She had been on her way to church with the plan to talk to Seth and set the record straight about her relationship with Mark. She planned to tell him how much she cared about him, and how he misunderstood what he witnessed between Mark and her on the curb. Then she remembered the fiasco of her parent's house and Mark's promotion. Her heart ached recalling the disappointments. She remembered walking into the church and seeing Seth with Samantha near the front together.

Amy sat up straighter in her bed. "I was driving home from church, upset because I bungled everything with Seth, and I lost the promotion. I had planned to talk to him about how I felt, but when I saw him at church with Samantha, I freaked out and ran away. That's why I cried. Then, it started raining, and it got hard to see. I think a car turned illegally or maybe it hydroplaned and hit me on the side." Amy grabbed her sore left rib. "That reminds me… did I break any bones?" She turned toward Mark and winced again.

Mark rubbed the back of his neck with one hand. "No broken bones, just a bunch of contusions. Oh, and a concussion, so you have to take it easy the rest of the week or at least for a few days. Do you remember anything else?"

"Well, I remember waking up at some point and thinking I must be in the hospital, and then making a differential list in my head of all my potential problems and hoping you had the wherewithal to order the correct tests." Now it was Amy's turn to smirk.

Mark rolled his eyes.

Amy shrugged her shoulders. "Then, I must have passed out again because I had the strangest dream, or encounter, or something…" Her voice trailed off. She looked around the room and her eyes settled on a gorgeous bouquet. The mixture comprised white hydrangeas, dozens of red roses, and lush greenery. It looked like it cost a small fortune. She glanced back at Mark and raised one eyebrow. She nodded toward the arrangement. "Are those from you?" Amy held her breath.

Mark furrowed his brow and his lips turned downward. He appeared unsure of how to respond. After a long pause, he answered her, "Uh, no. Not exactly. Um… they're from—"

An unexpected figure appeared at the doorway to Amy's room.

Her door opened, and she raised her head, locking eyes with Seth. Amy gasped and a grin spread across her face. *Why was he here? Did he love her, too?* Her gaze shifted between Seth and Mark. Both men eyed one another up but said nothing. *Would Seth misread the fact that Mark sat in her room talking to her?*

"Seth!" She couldn't muster any other words. Her mouth clamped shut. She panicked and tried to search for the right thing to say next. "When did you get here?" She blew her bangs off her forehead. *Well, that sounded lame.*

Seth shifted his weight. "Uh, a while ago... if I'm interrupting anything, I can leave. Maybe I should go, and you can call me when you're feeling better. You know it totaled your car because of the side impact? It's a miracle you're alive. I just wanted to check on you. I couldn't believe it when I heard you had an accident, but I didn't realize you had... company." Seth cast a sideward glance at Mark. Mark shifted in his seat.

Amy's torso flew upright, and she planted her hands on either side of her, ready to fling her legs out of bed. "No, Seth, it's not like that at all. I woke up a few minutes ago and have been trying to regain my bearings. Stay, please."

Seth clenched his jaw tight and stared stonily at Mark. "No, I think it would be better if I left, and we talked later when you aren't busy. Call me when you get home, or when you feel up to it... or I'll see you at church. I'm glad you're ok, Amy... I was really worried about you. The whole church has been praying for you." Seth locked eyes with her and he opened his mouth as if to say more, then closed it just as quickly.

Stirrings in Amy's heart made her yearn to run into Seth's arms, but she still couldn't move fast enough.

"I'd better go. See you later." He paused and gave her a stiff wave before dashing out of her room.

Well, that was a disaster. Amy turned her attention to Mark, and the flowers arranged meticulously on her medical tray. "Mark, did you give me those flowers?"

Mark squirmed in his chair and gave her a sheepish grin. "Uh, well... no. They were from Seth, actually. I got here this morning a few minutes before you woke up. My shift starts at eleven. I was working yesterday when you came in, but when my shift was over,

I went home." He looked away with guilt. "Seth came in after the news got around town about your accident. He stayed here all night in your room until the charge nurse kicked him out because visiting hours ended, so then he slept in the ICU waiting room in a chair." Mark's face flushed beet red with embarrassment as he finished his confession.

Amy's cheeks warmed with anger. "So, let me get this straight. What you're saying to me is that you knew I'd been in a serious car wreck, but you left the hospital as soon as your shift ended, because, hey, I'm just another colleague and I'm stuck here in the ICU, so you might as well head home and catch a few winks. Then, you came to my room today, primarily because you have to work, anyway. So, you showed up here to 'check on me' (Amy air-quoted this phrase with as much force as she could manage) and when I woke up you led me to believe that you'd been sitting vigil at my bedside all night long as a caring friend. Oh, and I almost forgot, you nearly took credit for the floral arrangement, too. Does that just about summarize the course of events?" Amy crossed her arms despite having an oxygen saturation monitor on one hand and an IV running out of the other. She set her eyes in a fierce glare.

Mark coughed and more squirming followed. "Uh, yeah. I guess you could put it that way, but, Amy, what you have to understand—"

Amy put her hand up like a stop sign. "No, what you have to understand is that I am done. I'm done with listening to you gloss over the truth to charm and mislead me. I'm done with you, interjecting yourself between me and someone I care about. And I'm done with letting you manipulate me. I. Am. Done. Now, don't you have actual work to do? Other patients to see? A Chief job to start?"

Mark nodded his head.

"Why don't you go do that while I try to heal up and talk to God about how to forgive you and then pray for revelation on how to fix things with Seth?" Amy finished her speech and collapsed against her pillow, exhausted.

"Uh, ok, Amy. If that's really how you feel." Mark put his hands on his knees and stood upright. He inched toward the door but paused before opening it. He turned to face her one last time.

Amy closed her eyes and nodded her head. "That is really how

I feel. Bye, Mark."

"Bye, Amy. And… I'm sorry."

Amy heard the glass door shut behind her visitor with a click. She whispered to herself, "Goodbye, Mark," and sighed. She'd messed things up this time. Amy couldn't wait to get home to her bed and sleep for a million hours. Then, she would call her best friend and unload the entire saga on her. Beth excelled at combining truth and grace. She would listen with a compassionate ear to Amy's woes and then slam her with truth about letting God make things right. A slow smile formed at the corner of Amy's lips at the thought.

She peered out the window from her bed and her thoughts turned to her father. She couldn't wait to call him. As she had this thought, her phone, perched on the medical tray, rang. A glance at the screen revealed her dad's name. Her grin grew wider, and she picked the phone up with her tethered hand and placed it to her ear with care. "Dad! I can't believe it's you. I sat here getting ready to call you myself. I didn't know if the hospital notified you or not. I don't think I listed an in-case-of-emergency person on my form with human resources at the hospital and my phone automatically locks, so I doubt they knew to contact you. The only people that knew about the wreck were the staff here at the hospital and some people from church, although I don't know how. Since you don't go to my church, it just dawned on me you might not know about the accident."

Her father's voice trembled, "Amy! Oh, thank goodness! Joe had me worried sick. I worked at the house all day yesterday sorting through things, so I hadn't been out. I headed to Joe's this morning for coffee around ten am and someone must've told him, because he asked me how you were doing after the car wreck. I panicked and told him I didn't know what he was talking about and he told me to call you or head to the hospital. So, I did both. I'm on my way there now."

Amy's brow furrowed as she realized what her dad must have been through. On top of the accident, she needed tell him about not getting the promotion, too. She dreaded disappointing him, but hearing his voice calmed her. She missed him terribly. They didn't always talk over the weekend, so it made sense he had been in the dark. Perhaps she might wait until later to unload the news about the promotion and bonus. He sounded concerned enough over the accident. "I'm sorry no one called you, Dad. Please, don't drive all the way over here. I'm fine, really. I don't want to expose you to the germs in the hospital and there's nothing you can do right now. I'm hoping they'll let me go home later today, or at least by tomorrow. I've got my phone, television, food, and a medically mandated vacation. What more could I need or want?"

Her dad let out a long breath. "Are you sure? I don't mind coming to the hospital. I can't wait to see you. When I think I could have lost you, too…"?

Amy's throat tightened and burned her eyes. "I know, Dad. I know, but I'm here. I'm ok. I got a few bumps and bruises and have to rest for a few days, but that's it. All I want to do is find some coffee, eat something delicious, then sleep, in that order. Why don't you come over later this week and we can make dinner together?"

"That sounds great, honey."

She debated for a beat about telling her dad about the Chief job, then decided honesty prevailed. "Dad, there's something else you need to know."

Concern filled his voice again, "What's that? Are you sure you're ok?"

Amy swatted at the air with her hand. "Yes, yes, it's nothing like that. I wanted to let you know… I didn't get the Emergency Medicine Chief promotion… or the bonus money. So… I don't think we'll be able to save the house. I don't see a way to do it. I'm sorry I let you down."

Her father cleared his throat. "Amy, listen to me. This is important. I want you to hear me, ok? I love the house your mom and I raised you in… it has lots of special memories, but… I love you more. You didn't let me down. The fact you wanted to give me money to save it means the world. What matters in life is God and family. I'm just glad you're safe… and who knows? God may surprise us with a way to save the house yet. Keep praying and get some sleep. I'll call you tomorrow and we'll make plans for this week."

A sigh of relief slipped out from Amy's lips. "Thanks, Dad. I'll pray. I love you."

"I love you, too, honey. Talk soon. Bye."

She turned off her phone and sat it on the table next to her. Amy pressed the call button on the side of her hospital bed. Within seconds a seasoned nurse she knew came into her room.

Sally was one of her favorite nurses on staff and Amy guessed her to be in her early sixties. She wore a short, dirty blond pixie cut that flipped out slightly at the bottom like Carol Brady. In front of her eyes sat dark rim glasses that Sally rarely used, but rather let them hang from a metallic chain around her neck. Her kind, yet sharp brown eyes missed nothing. She had on dark blue scrubs like all the other nurses on the unit. White, thick hospital approved tennis shoes completed the ensemble. Sally definitely looked the part. Amy speculated Sally had worked as an intensive care nurse for thirty or more years. She knew her stuff and never hesitated to make it known.

"Yes, oh, Dr. Harte, I didn't realize it was you when you buzzed. I heard from the staff you were up here, but when the call button buzzed, I didn't pay attention to who was in the room. I came straight here." She spoke in a syrupy sweet southern drawl, "What can I do for you?"

"Uh, well, I'm sorry to bother you..." Amy looked down, placing her hands in her lap.

"Oh, it is not a bother at all. Now, come on, what can I do to help one of my favorite doctors?" Sally waited for Amy's reply with her hands placed on her hips.

"Well... I guess you heard about the accident, and I'm a still a little disoriented, or confused. Mark... you know Dr. Blakely, right? Tall, dark-haired physician from the emergency department?" Amy paused.

Sally chuckled and nodded her head. "Oh goodness, yes, I know Dr. Blakely. I think all the nurses here know him." Sally lowered her voice to a whisper, "He has a reputation, you know. I saw him up here earlier checking on you. You two work together, don't you?"

Amy looked up and resisted a grin at the conspiratorial nature of her conversation with Sally. "Yes, he and I cover a lot of shifts together."

Stepping closer, Sally peeked over the rim of her glasses with a piercing stare. "You two aren't an item or anything, are you? Not that it's any of my business. It's just that I imagine the complications of working together and trying to keep everything separated and professional and what not." Sally waited for Amy to spill the juicy details.

Amy shook her head with vigor. "No, we aren't an item. He's a colleague. We went to the Metropolitan Ball together for work, but that's it...but I'm getting off topic here. What I wanted to ask is if you saw another gentleman here? One that came to check on me as well?" She returned the older nurse's gaze, hopeful.

Sally's features softened. Her eyes warmed, and she removed her glasses. "Well, goodness, yes, you're right. There was another gentleman here, probably in his late twenties, maybe early thirties. He had brown hair and a great smile. Handsome young man. Seemed pretty concerned. He stayed here all night I believe. I worked most of yesterday and when I left last night, I overheard one of the other staff nurses telling him he had to leave because visiting hours ended."

Amy's raised her brow. "Is that right?"

"Sure enough. I thought he went home, but when I left through the intensive care main doors, I saw him parked in the waiting room, asleep in a chair. That's where he sat this morning when I came back on shift again. Same waiting room, same chair. I think he stepped down to get a drink or something when Dr. Blakely arrived because he disappeared for a bit. The last time I saw him he had a coffee in his hand. Is he a friend of yours?" Sally crossed her arms in front of her chest.

Dodging the question, Amy looked over at the beautiful bouquet. She noticed a small white card attached to the arrangement. "Sally, do you see those flowers over there?" Amy pointed toward the vase.

"Why, sure, honey, kind of hard to miss those. That might be the largest bunch of flowers I've ever seen. My goodness, those are gorgeous."

"Would you mind reading the card to me if there is anything written on it?"

"Sure, let me see." Sally grabbed her glasses from her chest and placed them with care in front of her eyes, holding them up with one hand while lifting the card in the other hand. "Now, let's see here... it says, 'Dear Amy, thinking of you. Sorry about everything. Hope to talk soon. Love, Seth." Sally took her glasses off again and gave Amy the card. "I take it, this came from our mysterious young man from the waiting room?" Sally grinned.

Amy tried to focus on the words on the card, but tears filled her eyes again. "Yeah, you were right. He is a friend... actually, much more than a friend. I love him and I think he loves me or loved me. We had a silly misunderstanding and then I had that wreck. I guess he came here to set things right and then when he walked in this morning, he saw Mark here. Mark, Dr. Blakely, was part of the problem."

"Yes, I can see how Dr. Blakely might create romantic drama." Sally threw her head back and chuckled.

Now it was Amy's turn to place her hands on her hips. "I hardly see how this is funny. The man I love thinks I have an interest in a man I can hardly stand. And the man I can hardly stand helped save my life, but also contributed to ruining the relationship with the man I love not once, but now twice." Amy paused and blew out a breath. Two seconds later she broke into a deep belly laugh, too. Her love life resembled a tragic comedy. Boy, could she bungle things.

"I guess it is kind of comical." Amy sputtered out the words between laughs.

"Honey, Dr. Harte, forgive me for calling you honey. You remind me of my daughter. Listen, here is what I know to be true. That young man would not have parked his behind in an uncomfortable, small, sweaty chair all night and brought you these beautiful flowers and sweet note if he did not care a lick about you. So, from my perspective, what you've got here is a common, run-of-the-mill, everyday misunderstanding. Happens all the time when you deal with people. All you have to do is heal up and rest. Then, when you get back on your feet, go track down that handsome fellow of yours and tell him exactly how you feel. And quickly. Before Dr. Blakely can pop in again." Sally bellowed again, patting Amy on the arm this time.

"Thank you, Sally. Thanks for listening to me and for helping me laugh and see the humor in the situation. It's been a tough week. You've shown me some good in it. That's great advice, and it's exactly what I'll do. But first, do you have any ice cream... and coffee?"

Chapter 38

August 14, 2017, Monday

Seth took long strides down the hall, walking away from
the intensive care unit holding the hurt and pain of the heartache he
felt. His face warmed and tears stung his eyes. He willed them
back and brushed past the nurse he recognized from the morning
shift. She sent him a half-smile and her kind, knowing eyes bore
empathy for him. He gave her a nod and cast his eyes downward,
staring solely on the white grid-like pattern created by the floor
tiles.

He had to get out of the hospital. He shook his head, angry
with himself. He heard about Amy's car accident the day before
and immediately rushed to the hospital. Regret filled his heart over
their last conversation and all he wanted was to see her again and
set things right. He didn't want to get hurt or risk losing someone
he loved, but he couldn't deny his feelings for her. When he
stumbled upon Amy sitting with Mark at the hospital, jealousy
took over. Once he calmed down, he feared he'd overreacted.

Seth hoped to talk to Amy at church yesterday. When he
arrived at church, Samantha latched on to him like a barnacle. He
understood why Amy fled after seeing him with Samantha, given
their history, and he wanted to kick himself for not chasing after
her. He had called in to work to let them know he was taking the
day off for an emergency and headed straight to Amy's side. *What*

had he been thinking?

No matter now. He slowed his steps for a second, considered turning around and rushing back into Amy's hospital room to kick Mark out. He suspected Mark misled Amy, but he also didn't want to barge in and look like a fool if he was wrong. No, Mark had been there, and Amy hadn't turned him away, so if he didn't want his heart destroyed, he needed to keep walking.

Seth considered swinging by his office to grab some paperwork to do today and use it as a welcome distraction. He'd worry about fixing things with Amy tomorrow. At least he'd laid eyes upon her and knew she was safe. That was the most important thing. It made him cautious about his feelings, which became stronger each time he saw her. He couldn't lie to himself, he loved her. But could he trust her not to hurt him and could he trust himself not to put up walls?

Financial work was much easier. Things happened in black and white. There were enough numbers on the spreadsheet to cover expenses or there weren't, much like with Open Hearts. He submitted his proposal this past week. There still weren't enough funds to get the non-profit into the black. He prayed God would make a way for the Board to give him more time to find new donors and he prayed for a way to make things right with Amy.

Seth found himself at the elevator and wondered how he'd gotten there. Lost in his own thoughts, he pushed the button to head upstairs to his office on the fourth floor. The doors opened and welcomed him like an old friend. He rode alone in silence and when the door opened, he nearly plowed over Ed Baker.

Mr. Baker raised his bushy eyebrows, wearing a look of surprise at the sight of Seth. "Seth! I thought my secretary told me you took the day off. What are you doing up here today?" He shifted his eyes about in a nervous manner.

Running a hand through his hair, Seth sighed. He was eager to get to his office, grab his things, and get home. "Well, sir, I took the day off because a friend had a car accident and I wanted to check on her. She's doing ok, though, so I thought I'd grab a few files and get some work done from home today."

Ed's eyes continued to dart around. He pulled at his shirt collar, buttoned clear to the top. "Oh, I hate to hear that. Glad your friend will make a full recovery, though. Uh, Seth... I don't suppose you heard the news about the Chief of Emergency Medicine position?"

Seth's shoulders sagged. "I did, sir. I understand Dr. Mark Blakely got the job."

Ed smoothed down his burgundy tie that contrasted against his stained white dress shirt. "Yes, it was a tough decision. Lots of good candidates to consider. Ultimately, Mark is experienced and will get the job done. The other thing I wanted to tell you is that the Board will allow a one- week extension for donors to Open Hearts, but that's all we can do. I know it's not a lot of time, and not what you probably wanted to hear, but one more week is something." Ed patted Seth on the shoulder in a consoling way.

Setting his mouth in a firm line, Seth clenched his jaw. "One week, huh?"

Ed nodded his head in reply.

Seth stood up straighter and wriggled out from under the unwelcome reassurance of Ed's arm. "Well, one week is still one week. I'll see what I can do. Don't count Open Hearts out, yet." He took two steps past Ed leaving the elevator open for him. Then, he turned toward his boss again, almost as an afterthought. "I bet Mark's father must be proud of him..." Seth let his final thought linger between himself and Ed, noticing a look of shock on Ed's face before heading down the hall to the safety of his own office. Seth didn't trust Ed, but at least he'd let him know that the fact Mark's father, Ed's close friend, sat on the Board and Mark got the promotion did not go unnoticed by everyone.

Seth flung his door open in frustration and scooped the Open Hearts file, along with some other looming paperwork off his desk. He scanned his office, searching for answers to all of his problems. When the answers did not come, he walked out of the office and slammed the door behind him.

Chapter 39

August 14, 2017, Monday

Seth worked for hours Monday evening, calling every past donor he could think of, trying to scrape together enough funds to keep Open Hearts afloat. He sighed. Maybe he needed to accept the fact that help would not come. He stood from his home office chair and stretched. Tight neck muscles begged him to quit, but he didn't want to give up on the organization without a fight. He rubbed his tired, bloodshot eyes. His stomach growled, reminding him he missed dinner, so he picked up his phone and ambled into the kitchen.

His kitchen remained pristine most of the time as he lived the typical life of a bachelor. Meals consisted mainly of frozen entrees and bagged rice or boiled pasta. The sun set an hour ago, so Seth flicked the light switch casting a bright glow around the room. The black granite counters gleamed, and the gentle hum of the stainless-steel refrigerator beckoned him.

Seth strode to the refrigerator and opened the door, perusing his options. Seeing that he needed to add a grocery store run to his list of activities for the week, he grabbed a soda and a frozen chicken meal and slammed the door shut. He tossed the iceberg of a meal in the microwave and set the timer.

Thoughts of Brian's doctors visit swam through his mind, so Seth decided to check on him. He called his brother's phone, which rang several times before going directly to voicemail. Just as he left a message telling Brian to call him back, another call beeped in.

He glanced at the screen before placing it to his ear, noting his father's name flash across the screen. Seth accepted the call and leaned against the counter, waiting to hear the deep bellow of his dad's voice.

His dad jumped right into the conversation. "Seth! How are you doing?"

Seth ran his hand across the smooth surface of the counter, stalling for time. "Well... not great, Dad, if you want to know the truth. How are you?"

David cleared his throat. "Why, I'm just fine and dandy, but that's not important. What's wrong? Is there something I can do?"

Seth cast his gaze to the ceiling debating how honest to be with his father. His dad was great. He provided for his family, played with his kids when they were younger, encouraged them to work hard, and taught them about Christ's love... but, Seth hated to admit he was struggling with Open Hearts and he feared his father's opinion about it. Also, he didn't want to relive what transpired between him and Amy. He'd made a mess of things and somehow speaking it out loud made it more real.

Between worrying about his brother's health, Open Hearts, and his own heartbreak, he was overwhelmed. "Nothing you can do, Dad. It's been a long day... actually, a long few days. It started with a misunderstanding between Amy and me, then she had a car accident, and I went to the hospital to see her, but I messed things up and I doubt she'll see me again. Then, I ran into my boss and he told me Open Hearts has one week to find new donors or more money from existing donors or it's closed. I've been working all day trying to call anyone and everyone I can think of to help, but so far, I've struck out. To top it all off, I keep thinking about Brian. I tried to call him to see what the doctor said, but he didn't answer. Have you talked to him?"

"Yes, I talked to him. He said he went to his doctor today, and they ordered a slew of bloodwork and a CT scan to check his kidney. He won't know anything more about it for at least a few days. He sounded good, though."

The microwave beeped, indicating Seth's meal was done. He

opened the door and cautiously pulled the black plastic tray out, careful not to burn his fingers. After singeing his first finger, he tossed it on the counter to let it cool. He shook his hand and winced, then spoke through gritted teeth, "That's good news. I'll be praying he gets a good report. I'll try to call him again tomorrow and if you talk to him before then, tell him to keep me in the loop."

His dad paused before answering, as if he weighed his words before saying them. "Will do. He should know something by the end of the week. So, about Open Hearts…"

Seth waved steam away from the top of his meal. A warning tone snuck into his voice, "Dad…"

"What? I wouldn't say anything bad. I know how much you care about it. I only wanted to ask how much you still need to keep it going?"

Seth debated filling his dad in but decided there was no harm in honesty now. "Tens of thousands of dollars… at least."

"Well, now, let's see what we can do. First, try not to worry about your brother. I know how protective you are about him. You've been that way ever since the two of you were little. Remember that time he fell off his bike and skinned his legs?"

Seth gave a half-smile. "Yeah, I forgot about that. He raced down that rocky hillside even though I told him not to do it. He always tried to prove he could keep up with me and my friends even with us being a few years older. He tore off down that hill and flew over the handlebars."

His father chuckled for a second before chiming in again. "You two were a sight when you got back. You had carried him all the way up that hill and down the road to the house. When your mother saw the pair of you, I thought she might faint. He scraped his legs to pieces and both of you had dirt and blood everywhere. Thankfully, neither of you got hurt too badly. So, you see? Everything worked out then and it will work out now. God has a good plan. He'll take care of Brian, so you don't have to do it."

Seth sighed. He knew his father spoke the truth. "You're right. I'll try to remember that." He picked up his cooling tray of food and a glass of water, grabbed a fork out of the silverware drawer, and carried it to his small, four-person table. He pulled out a chair and plopped into the seat, ready to dive into his meal as his dad carried on, doling out fatherly advice.

His father seemed to be just warming up. "Second, I don't know what happened with Amy, but I know that girl has a good heart and a solid head on her shoulders. I trust that the two of you will sort it all out. You may need to give it some time, pray about it, and see what God has for you. The best relationship advice I ever got was from my father the night before my wedding to your mom."

Seth took a bite of still-frozen chicken and choked it down. "Oh, yeah. What was that?"

David cleared his throat again. "He said, 'David, it doesn't matter who is right and who is wrong in a marriage', or in a relationship in your case. 'What matters is love.' Do you love this girl?"

Seth reached for a drink of water and swallowed as his father asked this important question. He sputtered. "Uh... yeah. I mean, yes. I do. At least I think I do."

David laughed. "Well, then. The answer is easy. What you need here is humility. Tell the girl you're a fool and you made a mistake and that you're sorry. Even if part or most of it isn't your fault. Tell her anyway. Then, tell her how you feel. Don't hold back. Life is too short to hold back and family matters most. Marrying your mother and having you boys brought me the most joy in my life. Best thing I ever did."

Seth caught his breath and his throat tightened. "Awe, Dad, thanks. You're embarrassing me, but I hear you. I'll try to do it."

David went on, not yet done. "Last, this problem of funding Open Hearts—"

"I know what you're going to say. It's a fool's errand. I should come back and work for you. You and mom will need help this week and even longer if Brian has to undergo treatment again. Family matters more than anything else. I need to focus on my responsibilities."

Seth's father's voice became sterner, "No! Now listen to me. I had no intention of saying any of that. What I wanted to tell you is I'm proud of you. I know how hard you work at your job and how important that organization is to you. I've seen how hard you've fought for it and I'm cheering for you. Don't lose hope, yet. Sometimes when things seem the bleakest, God gives us the best surprises. I'd love to have you work with me, but that's only because you're a gifted finance guy and I'd love to see you every day. Don't give up on Open Hearts. A donor might come through; maybe an unexpected one."

Seth raised his brow in shock. He'd never heard his dad talk so frankly with him before and he definitely never had his dad tell him to not come running to the family business. "Dad, are you ok? Did you hit your head or something?"

Laughter filled the line for several seconds. "No, I'm fine. Maybe I'm getting sentimental in my old age."

"You aren't old. You're in your prime."

Now his dad guffawed. "Right, my prime. Thanks for the vote of confidence, son. Seriously, though, I'll pray for you about Open Hearts, Brian, and you and Amy. Try not to work too hard. Get some rest and head to bed early tonight. Things look better in the morning after a full night's sleep."

Sleep made Seth's eyelids feel heavy. He turned his attention to his remaining meal and eyed it with suspicion. "Maybe you're right. I'll finish eating my frozen block of chicken." He poked at the hard center of the meat that the microwave dared not touch.

His father laughed.

"Then, I'll turn in, I think. Thanks Dad, for the advice. It helped."

"No problem, son. Anytime. That's what us fathers are here for."

Seth grinned to himself. "I'm sorry I can't help more this week at Tech. I'll try to swing by in the evenings if I can... hopefully Brian will be back at it by next week. Is his side feeling better?"

"I think so. When I talked to him earlier, he sounded more like himself. He joked around with me and I think going to the doctor gave him reassurance. Call him tomorrow. He'll be glad to hear from you. Now, I have a date with the late-night news, and you've had a full day and need some sleep."

Seth gave up on his subpar meal and pushed it toward the center of the table. "You're right, Dad. Ok, I'll talk to you this week and I'll try to catch Brian tomorrow. Tell Mom I said goodnight and I love her. Love you, too. Thanks again for the talk."

Pausing for a beat before responding, his father's voice choked up a bit, "I love you, too, son. Don't worry about things, God will take care of it. If you have time to swing by Tech this week, we'd love to have you, but if not, I understand. Talk to you soon."

Seth heard the line go dead, so he pushed the end button on his phone. He stared at the blank screen for a few seconds, marveling at the conversation he'd just had with his father. They had never spoken so honestly before. He could not believe his dad backed off about him helping out with the family business. Usually, he couldn't wait to jump at the chance to rope Seth into Tech. Hope filled Seth's heart that if he and his father could find a new understanding of one another, then anything was possible.

Seth ran both hands through his hair and sighed. He bowed his head and said a silent prayer for God to heal his brother, provide for his organization, and smooth over things with Amy. He hoped Mark wasn't still in the picture, but if he was, Seth prayed for God to protect his own heart and give him wisdom.

He raised his head from his prayer and uttered the word, "Amen." Seth picked up the cold, black tray containing the residual scraps from his dinner and his empty glass. He carried the glass to the sink and placed it inside and tossed the tray in the trash along with his anxiety from the day. He looked around the kitchen once more and, seeing everything in its place, he flipped the switch and turned off the lights. Maybe his father knew best. Tomorrow was a new day and things might look different in the light.

Chapter 40

August 16, 2017, Wednesday

Amy walked through her front door and had never been so glad to see her comfy sofa. She flopped down on it, grabbed a fluffy pillow, and squeezed it to her chest. *What a week.* She looked around her house and realized it looked like a hurricane blew through it. She rifled in her bag, found her phone, and punched in the familiar number to her best friend. While the phone rang, she sighed, stood up, and tossed the pillow to the side.

She sauntered around the room, carrying dirty dishes to the kitchen and tidying up the clutter, while waiting for Beth's spunky voice on the other end of the line.

Beth started the conversation as if already in the middle of it. "I have so many questions."

Amy placed more cups in the sink. "Hi, it's nice to talk to you, too. Good morning."

"Yes, yes, hi, hello, and all of that. Now, on to the important stuff. It's me, here. Talk to me. What in the world happened to you? I went to see you today at the hospital and they said they had already discharged you. I started to drive straight to your house, but I figured everything wiped you out, so I waited until you called me." In a stream of consciousness, Beth didn't pause for a breath.

Amy shrugged her shoulders. "It's ok. I understand. I want to tell you everything, but I need a real shower and a few minutes to make this place look like it's not a total wreck. And coffee. I need coffee. Real coffee. The stuff they give you in a hospital could barely pass for water with brown food coloring." She stuck her tongue out in disgust. "Can you meet me at Joe's in an hour?"

"An hour? Sure. I'll try to get there a few minutes early to snag our favorite spot. What do you want to drink? I'll order for you. It's the least I can do after my best friend survived a near-fatal car accident." Beth gave a dramatic sigh.

Amy shook her head. "You are ridiculous. I didn't almost die. I felt like it, though." She rubbed her left side, which ached still. "But I didn't. I'll fill you in on all the details, including an interesting exchange between myself and Mark, which Seth interrupted." Amy knew Beth couldn't resist a cliff hanger.

"Ooh. Drama. Ok, I'm there. I'll see you at Joe's. One hour. And, please, try to drive safely. Oh, wait. What are you going to drive? Can you drive? Do you have a car?" Beth sent her questions rapid-fire.

Amy laughed at her best friend. "Yeah, yeah. I can get there. I picked up a rental car today and I'm ok to drive as long as I'm not taking pain medication, which I'm not. So, as long as I go slow, I should be fine. Although, the bus is gaining its appeal."

Beth lowered her voice and sounded uncharacteristically sincere, "Ok, see you there. And remember, be safe. I could've lost you. I honestly don't know what I would've done."

She smiled and her friend's tenderness touched her heart. "Will do. See you in a few. Love ya, babe. Bye."

Hanging up the phone, Amy turned on her favorite Christian radio station to inspire her to finish her cleaning and get moving. She bounced around the room as hastily as her bruised ribs allowed, and within thirty minutes she had scrubbed the kitchen, straightened the living room, tossed a load of dirty clothes in the washer, and picked up her bedroom. She surveyed her home and nodded. *It looked much better.*

She jumped in the shower and smeared on tinted moisturizer and mascara. Amy piled her wet hair on top of her head in a messy topknot bun and swiped some gloss across her lips. She peeked at the time on the clock in her bathroom and noted she beat her personal record for getting ready. With ten minutes to get to the coffee shop, she might still arrive on time to meet Beth.

Amy slid behind the steering wheel of the dark navy rental station wagon and gripped the wheel. Her hands shook. She drew in a deep breath. She underestimated the anxiety of driving after the wreck. She put the key in the ignition and turned on music for reassurance. She had no problem driving from the rental car office to her house, but she had been so focused on getting home that she hadn't given driving much thought. Now, that she took time to absorb the seriousness of the accident and its potential consequences, driving scared her a little. She squeezed the wheel tighter and said a quick prayer to God to help her stay calm and not fear.

Amy checked the rearview mirror and nodded at herself. One of her favorite Christian speakers said to tackle fear head-on and do things even if they were terrifying. So, that was what she would do. She placed the car in drive and pulled out of the driveway, on her way to Joe's Coffee Shop.

Chapter 41

August 16, 2017, Wednesday

By the time Amy arrived at her beloved cafe, Beth had planted herself at the front table by the large bay window. She saw Beth as soon as she parked her car and get out. Amy opened the door to her second home, and Beth sent her an enthusiastic wave with both hands in the air. Amy shook her head and smiled at her long-time, animated friend.

The welcomed ding from the small, golden bell overhead announced Amy's arrival. As she walked in, the waft of her favorite Sumatra blend coffee combined with the smell of the gooey, sugary goodness of Joe's infamous cinnamon rolls greeted her. *Mmm. It felt good to be home.* As soon as she set foot in the cafe, a flurry of people gathered around her. They were regulars at Joe's, people from her church, the hospital, and the local shops and boutiques. She scanned the cafe for Samantha and breathed a sigh of relief in not finding her in attendance.

Joe bounded out from behind the counter and wrapped her in a bear hug, lifting her feet off the ground.

Amy groaned. "Ooh, ouch."

He gently sat her back down and his brow furrowed. "Oh, no! I'm sorry Amy, did I hurt you? I didn't even think about that. I was so excited to see you here, whole, in one piece. What hurts? Can I get you anything?" Joe rattled off multiple questions with his hands still on her shoulders. He finally paused, leaned back to further survey her, and smiled.

Amy laughed and pointed at her side. "It's ok, Joe. I'm fine. I have a bunch of bruises, including these ribs that you may or may not have crushed in that epic hug."

Joe's grin faded. "I'm so sorry. Are you going to be ok?"

She nodded her head and chuckled again, never one to resist an opportunity to tease her beloved barista. "No, I'm fine. And you didn't hurt me... much. Seriously, though, I'll be ok. I'm a little banged up, but otherwise in good shape, considering...and as far as what you can get me, do you even have to ask?" A slow, mischievous smile tugged at her mouth.

"Let me guess. Large black coffee, Sumatra blend, cream, no sugar, because there'll be plenty of that in my world-famous cinnamon rolls. How'd I do?" Joe crossed his arms in front of his chest and raised an eyebrow. He wore his white apron with his brand logo emblazoned on the front.

Amy hugged him again, gentler this time. She hoped that things worked out between him and Beth. Joe was a great guy and they would make a good match. "Perfect. You know me so well." She opened her bag, searching for her wallet. "Here, let me pay you, and do you mind bringing everything over to the table when it's ready? I think if I sit down this instant my best friend will spontaneously combust from impatience." Amy cast a glance at Beth, who resembled a chihuahua hopping in her seat, barely containing her energy. Her wide eyes and waving arms screamed that she needed to know all the details about all the things... right now.

"No problem. And it's on the house." Amy started to open her mouth in protest, but he raised his hand, showing he had no intention of taking her card.

"Joe. You don't have to do that." She placed her wallet back in her purse and smiled at the generosity of her longtime friend and caffeine dealer.

"I insist. Now you better hurry over to your beautiful friend. I don't think she can stand anymore suspense." Joe chuckled and headed back to his counter to pull her coffee.

Amy purposefully dawdled to Beth's table, stressing every step.

Beth sent her a glare.

Bursting into laughter, Amy picked up her pace. "You're too easy to tease." She sat down in the comfortable, oversized grey chair. "So, what did I miss? How's life?" She folded her hands under her chin and stared at her best friend.

"I will never speak to you again, if you don't spill all the details right this instant. Now. Tell me everything." Beth's stern look showed she meant business.

Amy raised her hands in defeat. "Ok, ok. You win. So, I told you about the accident. You already knew that. What you don't know is that I got in the accident after I'd gone to church that morning and left early because I saw Seth sitting in the front row looking cozy with Samantha."

Beth gasped, putting her hand over her mouth. "No! So, what did you do? What did he do? Ooh, that girl. She always seems to stir up trouble."

"Well, I saw them, and I'd planned on telling Seth how I felt about him--"

Beth leaned in closer. "How do you feel about him? Hmm?"

Amy blushed. "Honestly, I think I love him."

Beth grinned at her.

"So, I wanted to tell him that and explain about the Mark thing, and then when I saw them together, I panicked and ran out of the church… I was so upset, I just started driving. I didn't know what to do next. Then, it started raining and I began crying, and it got hard to see."

Beth grabbed Amy's hand and squeezed it.

Amy squeezed back and continued her story. "Out of nowhere, this truck appeared on my side and I didn't see it in time. The next thing I knew, I found myself hooked up to a bunch of wires and machines in the hospital. I had this bizarre dream where I talked to my mom and she told me to forgive myself, live my life without fear, and tell people how I feel."

"So, when I woke up from the dream, imagine my surprise to see Mark sitting in the visitor chair next to me…next to a very large, very impressive bouquet of roses. At first, I was touched. I thought, 'wow, Mark cares. That's nice.' Then, I thought maybe he looked after me all night, because I remembered him being there when I first arrived--"

Beth cut in, "It's hard to imagine Mark sitting vigil at your bedside."

"I know! That's what I thought. When I asked him about it, he got uncomfortable and admitted he went home when his shift ended. So, I sat there, realizing for the final time what a heel Mark can be, when Seth appeared—"

Beth gasped again. "No!"

"Yes. Now, would you quit interrupting me."

Beth gave a slight frown and stuck out her tongue. "I'm sorry I'm expressive. Please continue."

Rolling her eyes at her friend, Amy continued, "He saw Mark sitting next to me in a deep conversation. Honestly, it looked bad. Add that to the whole curbside situation he viewed between Mark and me a few days prior, and he assumed the worst and bolted. I told Mark to leave and quit ruining my love life."

Raising her eyebrows, Beth leaned in further. "Did Seth come back?"

Amy shook her head, wistful. "No…but, a sweet intensive care nurse, Sally, came to my room. I asked her to read me the card attached to the flowers, and it turns out Seth brought them. On the card he signed it, 'Love, Seth.' Sally told me he had been there all evening the day before and stayed overnight in the waiting room. He slept in a chair, Beth. He brought me flowers. He went downstairs find coffee to bring to me when he saw Mark talking with me again."

Beth clucked her tongue. "I've said it before. The worst timing. You have the worst timing."

Amy bobbed her head up and down. "Yep. So, there you have it. Just when you think I cannot possibly make a situation worse; I excel beyond even my own expectations. It's remarkable, really."

Joe sidled up to their table and sat down her much-needed heaping cup of coffee and warm, iced pastry.

Amy turned to him. "Joe, thank you. You're a lifesaver."

He shrugged, then gave Beth a smile and a wink. Joe spun around and ambled back to his bustling counter.

Her mouth dropped open. "Um, I totally saw that. So, now that you know how my romantic life went off the rails, tell me how yours is going." Amy lifted the hot coffee to her lips for a cautious sip, smiling behind her cup.

Beth squirmed in her seat. "Well... what can I say? Joe is a great guy."

Nudging Beth under the table with her foot, Amy spurred her on. "And that's it? Come on. I'm your best friend in the entire world and I demand details." She relished her first bite of Joe's mouth-watering cinnamon roll. *Mmm. So good.* She almost forgot all of her problems with Seth. Almost.

Beth refused to meet her eyes, stalling. "Well, not exactly. Uh... so you knew we planned a date, right?"

"Yes, yes. I knew that. Old news. Now out with it," Amy demanded through a mouthful of icing and bread.

"So... we went. And..." Beth paused.

Amy's eyes widened in frustration.

Beth blushed before continuing, "It was amazing. Spectacular, actually. Best first date of my life. So... we went on a second, and then a third date."

She slapped her hands on the table. "Eek!" Amy bounded out of her seat and grabbed her best friend in a hug.

"Oh, my goodness! Calm down! Joe is here, you know! You're making a scene!"

Amy took her seat again after a few more embarrassing squeezes. "So, are you guys a couple? Are you officially dating? Is he your boyfriend? Has he told you he loves you?"

"Well, I guess you could say we're dating. He hasn't told me loves me, but I think I am his girlfriend. He told me the last time we went out that he didn't want to see anyone else. He said he only wanted to spend time with me." Beth blushed a deeper red.

Tears filled Amy's eyes. "This is such great news! Seriously, I am so happy for you. You deserve it. You deserve it all."

"Well, don't get too ahead of yourself. I still haven't met his family, and he hasn't met mine. We're taking things slow. But... I'm happy. Really, really happy." Beth fell quiet for a second. "So... now that you're up to speed on my dating life, what are we going to do about yours? Come on... you love Seth, right?"

Amy chewed a bite of pastry and answered in a muffled voice, "Well... yes. I love Seth."

Beth took her first sip of her now lukewarm drink. "And he loves you, too. Right?"

She nodded her head and added more sugar to her coffee. "I

think so. I mean if he meant what he said on his card… then, yes."
She stirred her coffee, then froze. "Oh, and you forgot about the problem of how to raise $50,000 in the next week. My dad's house won't save itself."

Beth rested an elbow on the table and plopped her chin in her hand. "So, all we have to do is get you together with Seth and fix this whole misjudgment about Mark. You apologize to Seth; he apologizes to you. You tell him how much you care about him and he professes his love for you, you kiss, and then live happily ever after. Oh, and figure out some way to convince the hospital and Ed Baker to give you a giant raise. Simple, right?" Beth raised her eyebrows.

Amy rolled her eyes. "Yeah, simple."

"It really is, you know. You need to go to church Sunday and march straight up to Seth and let nothing get in your way. Just be honest and tell him how you feel. Oh, and we should probably pray about it, too. Prayer helps everything. It will all be ok, you'll see." Beth gave a nod, settling the matter. "Now, I can tell you'll need my help to finish that cinnamon roll." Beth reached over to Amy's plate with her fork, attempting to swipe a piece of the treasured treat.

"Hey, you may be my best friend, and you may give great advice, but get your own cinnamon roll." Amy deflected Beth's fork with her own and burst into a fit of giggles. Man, it felt good to be home.

Chapter 42

August 18, 2017, Friday

Staring at the front of Metropolitan Hospital, Amy paused. After talking with Beth a few days ago, she made the decision to go for it. She couldn't wait until Sunday to see Seth and she wouldn't give up her parent's house without one last battle. She headed to Seth's house early this morning but must have missed him because he didn't answer the door or his phone. She needed to speak with Ed Baker as well, so, here she stood. Rolling her shoulders back, she drew in a deep breath and exhaled, saying a silent prayer.

Amy stepped through the glass doors feeling out of place in normal attire instead of her scrubs. She told the hospital earlier in the week she wanted to take off a few weeks to recover and help her father. A few colleagues waved and said hi, but she gave a casual flick of the wrist and a quick smile and pressed onward. She was on a mission. Arriving at the bank of elevators in the lobby, Amy reached to press the up button when a rotund man plowed into her. "Oof"

Raising his head to meet her gaze, Ed Baker wore a look of shock with his eyes widened and his mouth hung open. His face reddened with either embarrassment or anger. "Uh, Dr. Harte. What are you doing here today?"

Seeing him unexpectedly caused her to search for her words,

but after another big breath, she prepared her case. "Hello, sir. Actually, I'm glad I bumped into you. I was on my way to speak to you and also see if Seth Broadstone might be in today. I—"

Ed cut her off, sweat beading on his forehead. "I'm going to have to stop you right there. I know you must be upset about the promotion, but there isn't anything else I can do. Now, I'm on my way to an emergency Board meeting and, if he has any sense, that is where Mr. Broadstone will be, too."

Opening her mouth again, she gathered her remaining courage, "But sir, I just wanted to see if it might be possible to consider me for—"

Ed held up a hand as the elevator doors opened. "I've got to go. I heard about your accident...glad you're doing well. "He held the door with his hand, glancing at his watch. "And I hate it for you about the promotion, but those are the breaks. Now, I'm sure you can talk with Mr. Broadstone another time." He let go of the door.

Before Amy could form a rebuttal, the elevator doors closed and took with them Ed Baker and her final hope of saving her childhood home. Her shoulders sagged, but then she remembered her mother's words from the dream. Her mom's memories didn't live in that house; they lived in Amy's heart. Peace washed over her as she spun on her heel and made her way out of Metropolitan Hospital and into a new mindset.

She hadn't given up on Seth, though. She would go home and regroup...maybe help her dad start packing up the house and reformulate a plan to make things right with Seth.

Chapter 43

August 20, 2017, Sunday

Amy woke up early on Sunday morning to help her father finish cleaning out her childhood home. Her hands shook. She recalled the day she took her Emergency Medicine Board Exam and although the three hundred and fifty-question test proved stressful, she felt less anxiety taking it than saying goodbye to precious memories and then later sharing her feelings with the man she loved. She swallowed hard and her throat tightened. *Maybe she could skip church this week and go next Sunday. Yes, that was a fantastic idea.* There was still a lot to do at her dad's house. She would wait until next Sunday to go to church and pour her heart out to Seth then. *Perfect.*

Amy's father left her alone while he headed to the local hardware store to pick up more boxes and tape. She stood in the hallway near the now-empty stairwell. Another open box filled with treasured mementos beckoned her attention. She wiped her dusty palms on her worn, dark denim jeans and wiped the back of her hand across her sweaty brow. Shaking her blouse, Amy tried to create some ventilation. Even with air conditioner running, this time of year in Virginia equaled pervasive heat and humidity, enough to encourage her wavy hair to curl into tight, dark ringlets. She pulled an elastic off her wrist and wound the bulk of her hair into a ponytail.

Scanning the floor for the tape dispenser, Amy found it hiding behind an already-taped box. She knelt down on one knee and paused before closing the open box. Amy saw her parent's wedding photo sitting on top of the pile of memories. She pulled it out and ran her fingers over her mother's face. She recalled her dream and the conversation with her mother.

Amy knew in her heart that God gave her that dream as a gift. To tell her to let go of her pain, fear, regret, and grief, and to trust Him with all of her life; to let Him heal her broken heart. She wanted to open herself to love, to live boldly, and to share God's love with others.

Happy tears filled Amy's eyes and one trailed down her cheek. She wiped it away, thankful to know that even though she couldn't save her parent's home, her mother's memory lived on; in stories she shared with her father, in photos like this one she held in her hand. Her mother's memory extended beyond this house. She sighed.

She helped her father pack for hours the day before and hoped to finish the job today. They still had a few days before the bank deadline expired, but she knew how hard putting away all these memories would be, and she didn't want to feel rushed. The house seemed larger with everything in boxes on the floor. Only large items like the oak dining room table and the couch remained to signify someone still lived here.

Glancing at her phone, Amy realized if she wanted to make it to church on time, she needed to pause on packing. Amy jumped off the floor and rushed to her house to shower and ready herself for church.

Chapter 44

August 20, 2017, Sunday

Amy stepped through the door to her house and rushed
into her bedroom. She peered at her warm, welcoming bed. She
considered climbing into it and avoiding confessing her feelings to
Seth when her phone rang. Amy looked at the caller ID. *Ugh.*

Beth's perky voice boomed, "Good morning, sunshine!"

"Good morning to you, too."

Beth sounded like she was chomping on cereal again. "So...
it's a big day. Are you excited?"

"Uh... well... I was thinking... I've been busy all morning at
dad's house... and there's still so much to do. I'd planned to go to
church, but..." Amy sat on the edge of her bed, picking at an
imaginary piece of fuzz on her bedding.

"Oh, no you don't. Don't you dare tell me you're trying to
chicken out. Nope. No. Negatory. I'm not allowing it. You have to
go to church today for multiple reasons. For starters, you survived
a car crash, so you need to go thank God that you didn't die or get
maimed. Second, you told me yesterday that you'd be honest with
Seth and tell him how you feel. You cannot have lied to me. I
won't allow it. Third, maybe God will give you a revelation at
church about how to get the extra money to save your mom and
dad's house. Finally, and most importantly...You. Cannot. Let.
Seth. Spend. Another. Sunday. With. Samantha."

Hmm. Beth had a point. "Well, if Seth wants to be with Samantha, then I can't stop him, but, you're right. I owe it to him and myself to tell him the truth, and I'm thankful God protected me. So, you win that point, too. Ok, ok. Fine. I'll go." She groaned as she headed to the bathroom to hop in the shower.

Beth persisted. "Are you up? Moving?"

"Yes, yes! I'm moving!" Amy twisted the knob on the shower, filling the background with the roar of water. "I'm getting in the shower now... oh, wait... I can't hear you anymore, water running. Talk to you later, Beth, bye!"

"But—" Beth didn't get to finish as Amy hung up the phone on her. She shook her head. Leave it to her bestie to speak the truth to her. She stood in front of the welcome hot stream of water and closed her eyes, saying a quick prayer for God to give her the strength and words today when she saw Seth. Taking the fastest shower in history, Amy toweled off, wrapped her towel around herself, and wiped the steam off the mirror.

Amy decided on an understated look. She put on a light coat of foundation, some subtle peach blush, one layer of mascara and a swipe of light pink lip gloss. She smacked her lips together and smiled. *Good. Honest. Real.* She blew her hair out using her round brush, and it resulted in loose, effortless waves that framed her face in a flattering manner. She clamored into her bedroom and began the challenge of selecting an outfit for such a momentous day.

Normally, Amy would have fretted and stewed over what to wear, but today the selection came easily. She saw a deep maroon maxi dress with short sleeves that cinched at the waist and fanned out in an A-line skirt. It brushed the floor and made a perfect choice. She layered a dark wash cropped denim jacket and her neutral tan suede wedges. *Perfect.* She looked like herself, but not as if she tried too hard.

Amy glanced at the time on her phone, and although she woke up with more than an hour to spare, she lost minutes stalling and then talking to Beth earlier. With no time for a lengthy breakfast, Amy grabbed a chocolate chip granola bar and poured full strength dark roast coffee into the largest travel mug she could find. Chocolate and coffee—those two things made everything better. She surveyed her kitchen and living room, and it looked like a hurricane ripped through the house again. She shrugged her shoulders. *Oh well, no time to address it now.* If she left at this exact second, she might make it on time to church, but doubted she would have time to speak to Seth before the service started.

She grabbed her bag, locked her door, and hopped in her car. Amy sped down the road, gripping the steering wheel with anxiety and a hint of caution. She drew in a breath and lifted her chin. Today held the promise of a new beginning; the first day of a guilt-free, bold life.

Chapter 45

August 20, 2017, Sunday

Driving to church in his car alone, Seth considered the events of the summer. So much had happened in a short time. His brother had faced a health scare with his kidneys, his father tried to convince him to join him at Tech but then acquiesced, and his non-profit organization came to the brink of dissolution.

Two months ago, he couldn't have imagined opening his heart to someone and falling in love. Now, the thought of Amy's kind smile, bright blue eyes, and quick wit made his pulse race. He ran a hand through his hair and then placed both hands on the wheel, trying to steady them. Seth wanted to get to church as fast as possible to speak to Amy. He swerved into the church lot, parked, and hopped out.

Beth pulled in ahead of him and turned to him and waved. "Hey! Good to see you again!"

Seth returned the wave and smiled. "Good to see you, too, Beth." He paused and scanned the other side of her car. "Did you come by yourself today?"

A knowing grin spread across her face. "Amy's not with me."

Seth's shoulders sagged. "Oh—"

"But, she's on her way. I called her myself this morning and told her I expected to see her here today." Beth gave a firm nod.

Seth exhaled a sigh of relief. "Oh, good. I need to talk to her and set the record straight. Has she said anything about me?" He raised a brow.

Beth paused as if deciding how much information to divulge. She lowered her voice to a conspiratorial whisper, "I shouldn't say anything... but, I know she likes you."

Seth's sent her a broad grin.

Beth giggled. "And I can tell you like her, too. So, tell her." She took a few steps, walking away, but turned to face Seth again. "Oh, and thank you."

"For what?" Seth scrunched his brow, puzzled.

Beth smiled. "For helping my friend find a relationship with God again. It's been nice to see her happy. She carried around a lot of guilt and anger, but lately she's changed. I know you had a part in that... just don't break her heart. Ok?"

He grinned. "Ok. I promise. Thanks, Beth."

She waved goodbye and scurried into the church.

Seth strode forward, but then paused. He raised his eyes to heaven and asked God to help him find the right words and courage to share his heart with Amy. He walked into the church and several friends bombarded him with greetings. He searched for Amy amidst the crowd, and his eyes landed on her talking to Jessie, Jordan, and Matt.

He saw her laugh and his palms began to sweat. He tried to wave to get her attention, but she was in deep conversation. Seth nodded to a few more people and tried to work his way through the sea of attendees like a salmon swimming upstream. The music started playing from within the main auditorium, signaling the start of worship. He exhaled in frustration. He'd have to wait until after service.

Seth accepted his fate and joined the traffic flow carrying him into the service. Please God, give me an opportunity to talk with her later. The band played louder and Seth, now on the opposite site of the auditorium from his friends, planted himself in front of the first empty seat he saw. He shifted his focus to the music and opened his mouth in praise.

Chapter 46

August 20, 2017, Sunday

Amy arrived at church with one minute to spare before the start of the service. It looked like everyone she knew in town came today. She saw one of Seth's friends, Jessie, standing near the auditorium door and waved.

Jessie returned the wave and weaved through the growing crowd to greet Amy. "Amy, it's so good to see you!" Jessie wrapped her arms around Amy in a welcoming embrace. "Everyone's talked about the accident this past week. We were all worried about you! I'm glad you're safe."

Amy squeezed her new friend and then stepped back. "It's good to see you, too. No need to worry, I'm feeling much better. I still have a few bumps and bruises, but I'm thankful. It could've been a lot worse." She took her eyes off Jessie and scanned the foyer.

A slow grin spread across Jessie's face. "Looking for someone?"

Amy fiddled with the lid of her coffee mug before meeting Jessie's gaze. "I thought...no, I hoped Seth would be here today. I need to speak to him." Hopeful, she raised her brow. "You haven't seen him, have you?"

Jessie shook her head. "No, I haven't, but don't worry. I'm sure he'll come—"

"Hey, look who's here in one piece!" Matt bounded over with Jordan following closely behind. Matt gave Amy a side hug.

Amy greeted her new friends, still surveying the room for Seth. "Hey, Matt, Jordan." She nodded to each of them. "I'm happy to see you both... and you're right, I'm not broken." Music swelled from inside, beckoning the churchgoers to file inside. She wanted to look one last time for Seth before the start of service. "Hey guys, I'm going to the coffee stand to grab a refill, then I'll head in." She nodded toward the coffee station.

Jessie turned to Amy and placed a gentle hand on her arm. She sent her a knowing look. "No problem. We'll save you a seat... and don't worry. He'll be here."

With that word of encouragement, Amy watched Jessie, Matt and Jordan meander into the auditorium. She made one last surveillance of the foyer, but Seth wasn't in sight. She did the most sensible thing and filled up her travel mug. She stirred in cream and sugar and the band grew louder. The drums kicked in, signaling the beginning of worship. Amy followed the straggling crowd inside and took an empty seat next to her new friends.

She joined fellow churchgoers, singing thanks to God for his love and protection, especially over the last week. A wave of peace fell over her. She believed even though she lost her childhood home and possibly her relationship with Seth, God's love would sustain her through any storm in life. His love healed her wounds. She hoped Seth and her might mend things, but Amy learned over the last several weeks to put her trust in God and His love alone. Her mother's memories didn't live solely in her parent's home. They lived in her heart. Nothing could take them away. Amy took a deep breath and smiled.

The singing concluded and Amy eased into her seat. She listened to the straightforward, but loving words from the pastor. His words spoke to her heart. He talked about facing fears and living a bold life; a life with no regrets. The sermon wrapped up, and the congregation finished singing a final song with the band. As she belted the words of the closing song, she opened her eyes and found Seth's gaze.

He broke into a slow, broad smile and waved at her with one hand from across the room. An elderly woman came up to him and started a conversation, and the crowd forced Amy into the aisle.

She chatted with a few friends as she headed to the church exit. Looking around, Seth was nowhere in sight. She walked out the main door, and warm sunbeams spread across her face. She would not let missing out on a chance to speak to Seth cloud her mood.

Amy slipped to the side of the church out of the way of those exiting and closed her eyes, enjoying the summer day. The air felt warm, but Amy knew fall was right around the corner. She smiled. She reflected on everything good in her life; her work, her health, her faith, her friends and family, and the chance to start fresh. An exciting season lie ahead... a time to leave behind anger, disappointment, grief, and to move forward with hope toward new beginnings. A tap on the shoulder interrupted her reflection on these things. She turned around and broke into a wide grin. "Seth!" Without thinking, she threw her arms around his neck.

Seth laughed and returned her hug but choked up. "Amy, I'm so happy to see you."

Amy released him and placed a tender hand on his arm. "Seth, are you ok? I have so much to tell you. So much to apologize for."

Seth put a hand up, halting her explanation. "I'm fine, and you don't have to apologize for anything. It was my fault. My misunderstanding. When Beth called and told me you'd been in an accident, I was so scared I might lose you. I realized that none of the stuff with Mark mattered. What mattered was I wanted you to know how I felt. Amy, I love you." Seth stepped closer. He looked down at her and brushed a soft curl off her face.

Amy furrowed her brow. "But Seth, about the stuff with Mark... none of it was true. Nothing appeared how it seemed. Mark really is just a colleague. And he was only checking on me that morning in the hospital. Absolutely nothing happened between us, I promise. I'm so sorry that you thought there was something happening behind your back and I—wait, you love me?" Amy clamped her mouth shut and stared at Seth.

He placed a hand under her chin, tilting her face up to his. "Yes. Amy, I'm in love with you."

Amy's neck warmed, and she grinned. "I love you, too."

Seth's smile broadened. "And I'm sorry I didn't stay that morning and clear things up. I came to the hospital that day to tell you something important. Besides, I love you."

"What did you want to tell me?"

Seth grabbed her hand in his. "I wanted to tell you I received a call from the Board of Directors at the hospital. They found out Ed Baker talked to Mark behind their back about the Chief of Emergency Medicine position. Ed had no intention of considering anyone other than Mark because Mark's father is on the Board. I guess he put pressure on Ed to hire Mark for the job, and also, he and Ed are buddies. One of the other Board members found it suspicious that a fellow Board member's son got the promotion. They held an emergency meeting and voted Ed Baker out as CEO on Friday, and Mark's father is off the Board. Mark won't get the promotion, so..." Seth grinned and raised his eyebrows.

Amy held her breath. "So? What? What is it?"

"So... they plan to offer you the Chief of Emergency Medicine position along with the $60,000 bonus. You got it, Amy! You can save your dad's house!"

Amy's mouth dropped open. "What? Are you serious?" Tears pooled behind her eyes.

"More than serious. And there's more. I got a call Friday afternoon and Brian is doing great. His scans came back clean. He'll be fine."

Amy wrapped her arms around Seth again in a celebratory hug. "That's great news! So, does this mean your dad won't require your services at the family business?"

Seth shook his head. "Brian will return to his post as Chief of Finance with my dad at Tech." He gave her a quick smile.

Amy leaned her head back. "Is there something else?"

Seth took a deep breath. "Yeah, the Board voted to keep Open Hearts funded for another year at Metro."

"Seth, that's unbelievable. I'm so happy for you! But how did you find the money for it?"

"Apparently, a private donor came through with a donation this week. So, I'm staying at Metropolitan Hospital as their Chief Financial Officer and the head of Open Hearts... my dad called me yesterday, and it turns out he made the donation. He said he could tell how much my job and the non-profit meant to me, so he wanted to help Open Hearts continue." Seth sent her a warm smile.

Fresh, happy tears streamed down her cheeks.

"Amy, I was being selfish before, and I guess a little jealous, too. Mark and I will never be best friends, but I trust you, and I believe you. I think you're a beautiful and smart and I'm crazy about you. I want to be with you, and I don't want you to date anyone else. Especially Mark."

Amy chuckled.

Seth placed both hands on Amy's cheeks, cradling her face. "I love you. I've loved you for a long time."

"I love you, too." Amy smiled up at Seth, crying with happiness.

Seth stepped down on one knee and took Amy's hands in his. He looked into her eyes and drew a breath. "Amy, you have healed my heart. You've shown me true love is worth the risk. I was afraid to lose someone else in my life, but now I'm not afraid. I know God brought you into my life and I want to spend the rest of forever, however long it may be, with you. Dr. Amy Harte. Will you marry me?"

Amy's hands shook. "Yes, I'll marry you."

Seth stood and leaned in, and for the first time their lips met in a sweet, tender kiss.

Amy's insecurity melted away. This was the man God had chosen for her. The man who guided her back to a relationship with Him, tearing down her walls. Seth opened her heart to forgiveness, faith, and love. When she stepped back, she glanced at the side of the church and noticed a field filled with purple flowers, the same beautiful flowers she'd seen in her dream; Irises, the symbol of hope.

She smiled and looked up at the clouds. Her mom was with her, and she always would be. She would be ok...more than ok.

"I love you, too." She pressed her lips against Seth's again.

Epilogue

September 20, 2017

Amy sank to the ground, careful to lay her black and white houndstooth skirt in a circle surrounding her. She swept away a few rogue maple leaves from the brass nameplate in front of her with her hand. Letting her fingers linger over the letters for a moment, she smiled. She closed her eyes and inhaled, noting the earthy crisp smell of autumn.

"I have good news, Mom. Great news, actually. I met a man. He's kind and good to me. Oh, and he loves God. You'd approve. I wish you could meet him. He asked me to marry him and I said yes. I still miss you every day, but I think you'd be proud of me. I'm happy. Dad's doing good. We saved the house, so he's thrilled and relieved."

She drew in another breath and exhaled. "I'm not angry anymore and I forgave myself. I needed to tell you that. Oh, and I forgave Mark, too. I love you, Mom. I love you. Talk to you soon." She straightened the vase still containing a few remaining purple irises and pressed her fingers to her lips before touching them to the nameplate.

She arose and dusted off her skirt. The wind rustled, blowing a loose strand of hair across Amy's cheek.

A gentle hand brushed the tendril off her face and tucked it behind her ear. "Are you okay?" Seth joined his other hand with hers.

She looked to the sky and smiled. "I am now." Amy Harte wasn't heartbroken anymore.

The End

About the Author

Jill writes inspirational romantic fiction with a medical theme. Her two debut novels are part of the *A Dose of Love* series. Each story can stand alone, but both feature strong female leads facing challenging life circumstances while finding love along the way. The third book in the series will release in the near future. Jill's debut novel, *Harte Broken*, was inspired by her love of romance and her walk through the grief of losing her mother on the same day of her daughter's birth. It raises the question, "What happens when the best day is also the worst one?"

Jill is a physician and mom, who loves coffee, travel, and anything glittered. She treasures spending time with her husband and children, who are her heart and greatest joy.

Made in the USA
Columbia, SC
23 October 2020